They both had secrets that could drive people apart—or bring them together forever . . .

Keeping his inner demons at bay means Blake Malone has more than enough trouble on his plate. He doesn't need any extra complications. But that's exactly what he gets when, on his way to North Dakota, he leaves his truck unattended—and returns to find a beautiful woman sleeping in the front seat.

Opal Allen seems to have a knack for attracting trouble. Which is why she isn't about to tell her new road trip companion the real reason she needs to hightail it out of town. But Blake has a way of seeing right through her, which is both terrifying and exhilarating. Now her biggest problem is figuring out how to resist their undeniable attraction. Because once this road trip is over, she plans on never seeing Blake again.

But the best adventures don't go according to plan.

The Map to You

A Least Likely Romance

Lindy Zart

USA TODAY Bestselling Author

LYRICAL PRESS
Kensington Publishing Corp.
www.kensingtonbooks.com

Lyrical Press books are published by
Kensington Publishing Corp. 119 West 40th Street New York, NY 10018

All Kensington titles, imprints, and distributed lines are available at special quantity discounts for bulk purchases for sales promotion, premiums, fund-raising, and educational or institutional use.

Special book excerpts or customized printings can also be created to fit specific needs. For details, write or phone the office of the Kensington Special Sales Manager:
Kensington Publishing Corp.
119 West 40th Street
New York, NY 10018
Attn. Special Sales Department. Phone: 1-800-221-2647.

First Electronic Edition: November 2017
eISBN-13: 978-1-5161-0580-9
eISBN-10: 1-5161-0580-X

First Print Edition: November 2017
ISBN-13: 978-1-5161-0582-3
ISBN-10: 1-5161-0582-6

Printed in the United States of America

Grandpa Mueller—

I miss your music. Your jokes and the sound of your laughter. I want you to know I'm okay. I'd like to sit with you one more time, and hug you without it having to be in a dream, or a memory.

Lindy

1

Blake

Last I checked, I was traveling alone.

I walk to my grandfather's truck, a 1987 Ford F-series pickup in blue and white, and blink at the small form curled up on the seat.

Under the darkened dome of the sky, it's hard to discern anything other than the size of the thing inside my truck, and that it has dark hair. It could be a man, a woman—even a kid. I quickly scan the parking lot, searching for any accomplices to a premeditated crime involving yours truly.

It's the end of August, and the days can be wicked humid and hot, but the same can't be said for the nights. I have on a light jacket to help keep the chill off my skin. I glance into the cab of the truck. Small as this person is, they have to be feeling the cold.

The night is still and quiet, only two other vehicles taking up parking spaces of the 24-hour convenience store. It's after midnight on a Wednesday. Most sane people are home and in bed. I focus on the stranger in my truck. Whatever they're up to, it's bound to be nefarious. I like my share of nefarious dealings, as long as I'm the one doing them.

Muttering to myself and craving a cigarette, I carefully set down the plastic bag of chips, beef jerky, and orange juice I purchased to curb the hunger gnawing at my gut. I rub the stubble along my jaw, head cocked, as I come to a decision. It's an easy one—whoever they are, they can't stay in my truck.

Hands out, palms down, I soundlessly skulk around the front of the truck and toward the passenger side. My eyes shift from side to side in pursuit of any possible friends of theirs hoping to make my night especially spectacular with a blunt object to the back of the head. I feel ridiculous, sure I look like the Pink Panther slinking around in the dark.

My boot kicks a piece of gravel and it pings against the side of the truck my mother secretly kept in a storage unit all these years for me. I didn't even know the truck was still around until my brother Graham unknowingly drove it from North Dakota to Wisconsin my last week in the Cheesehead state. I just about cried when I saw it. Just about, but not quite—because crying would be bad for my image. My throat burned from keeping it in, though, and when Kennedy, Graham's girlfriend, commented on the redness of my eyes, I told her it was a reaction to whatever perfume she'd doused herself in.

Smooth, that's me.

I wince, hoping the rock didn't do any damage to the truck. This is one of the last pieces I have of the man who never judged me in all the years he was alive. Good thing for my grandfather's untarnished view of me that my life didn't completely fall to shit until after he died.

A head snaps up, and large, dark eyes slam into mine. I freeze against the unexpected jolt of them. The woman appears youngish, her face pointy and elfin. Her features are interesting, like it couldn't be decided whether to make her look exotic or plain. We study one another for one charged moment, and then whatever had her immobile collapses. Her mouth opens in a piercing scream, and she scrambles to the middle of the cab. I jerk back, her reaction startling me.

"What the hell kind of a person creeps up on someone like that?" she accuses. Her voice is breathless, but there is an undertone of huskiness that brings my nerve endings to attention.

I open my mouth with the intention of apologizing, and then realize what I'm about to do. Scowl taking over my features, I grip the door handle and pull. She scoots across the seat with her back to the driver's side door and, wide-eyed, looks back at me.

"Get out…of my truck," I say slowly, setting my palms on the worn and torn vinyl upholstery to lean forward menacingly.

"You left the doors unlocked. And the windows down," she adds, like that makes it acceptable for anyone to commandeer my vehicle.

I nod. "A clear welcome to all vagrants far and wide."

"I'm not a vagrant," she insists, tightening her arms around herself.

Something in her tone gives me pause, and I sweep my gaze over her. Her hair looks dark brown or black and is styled choppily around her face and jaw. The woman's chin juts forward as our eyes connect, silently rebellious. There are dark splotches beneath her eyes and she's holding herself protectively. Under the cropped jean jacket and jeans, her figure appears slight. She reminds me of a terrier, tiny and fierce with more boldness than common sense.

"Who are you and what are you doing in my truck?"

"I was contemplating hotwiring it and selling it, but then I wondered if it would actually start."

"It starts." Usually.

When she doesn't answer the first question, I lambaste her with my eyes, refusing to be the first to break the stare. Her mouth is small and pursed with annoyance, like I'm bothering *her* by wanting to know what she's doing in my truck. Under the heat of my gaze, she makes a face and looks away, showing me her profile. Her nose is long and slim, her chin sharp and stubborn. It feels like a small victory that she was the one to break eye contact. Something tells me she isn't one to easily give in.

"Conversations generally work best when you talk," I say shortly.

Sighing, the woman regards me as she sits up straighter. "I fell asleep," she mumbles, her mouth twisting at the confession.

I squint my eyes as I straighten, peering over the hood of the truck. We appear to be alone, but that doesn't make me relax any. Appearances are commonly shit and not to be trusted.

My shoulders pop as I rotate them, and I level my gaze once more on the stranger. "I want to make sure I'm understanding this right—you picked a random truck in a gas station parking lot to fall asleep in?"

"No." She picks at the hem of her jacket, a shiver going through her small frame. "I watched you go into the store." Almond-shaped eyes latch onto me. "You seemed harmless enough."

I lock my fingers behind my head and look at the star-strewn sky. This is an insanity I cannot be a part of. An urge to laugh hits me and I repress it, knowing it won't sound in any way normal. I don't need this right now. I have enough problems without this, whatever *this* is.

I stride around the truck and grasp the door handle at the same time she propels herself in the other direction. My blood ignites, and with a stiff jaw, I reach into the truck, grab her tiny wrist, and pull, my eyes refusing to let go of hers. Anger flashes through her eyes and contorts her features. She doesn't look quite as innocent now. She looks vicious, and mighty—for a munchkin. Calling me an assortment of colorful names, she fights to get free of my grip, and I only tighten it, swinging her down from the cab. She lands awkwardly, stumbling into me, and then she savagely kicks my shin with a booted foot. I grunt and twist her around, her back to my front, and barricade her with my arms.

"Let go of me!"

She squirms against my shackled arms, her head barely reaching my chest. Her body is a compact heat source, singeing me where it connects with mine. She's tiny, proportioned more to that of a teenager than a young woman. There's too little of her, and yet her rambunctious attitude seems to make up for it. I put my mouth close to her ear and feel the pulse pick up in her wrist I hold. The pose would be erotic, if not for the hellion in my arms.

"Start talking. Now. Or the police get involved." I am loath to involve law enforcement in anything that pertains to me, but she doesn't know that.

Her body goes limp, tremors having their way with her form. "Please, no. No cops," she beseeches, her small voice twinging my conscience.

Has she been in trouble with the law? Has her past been so twisted with corruption, like mine, that she sees any authority figure as an enemy?

With a frustrated growl, I release her.

She spins around, a triumphant look on her face, and dives to the left. I move with her, blocking her. Her eyes narrow as she calculates her next move. She feints right and goes left again, but I am right there with her. She's fast and sneaky, but I am a professional at games, no matter that I retired from them years ago. There was a time when I spent most of my days either getting in trouble or trying to get out of it.

One word leaves me and it is coated with warning. "Talk."

The woman's shoulders curve inward and the bravado drops from her face, making her look young and scared. "People are after me," she whispers.

Interesting. I cross my arms and widen my stance. "Who?"

"I don't know who." She drops her eyes and resumes her pathetic look, hands clasped before her. "They've been following me for days and... when I saw that your truck was *unlocked*, and *unattended*"—I frown as her voice loses its softness and turns sardonic—"I took cover until they left. But they'll be back. I know they will."

She grabs the front of my jacket and yanks me forward, her eyes enormous and pleading. She is stronger than I would have guessed. "Please, wherever you're going, please take me with you. Before they come back for me. Who knows what they plan on doing with me, but I'm sure it's something bad."

"You've been outwitting and outrunning unknown assailants for days?"

"Yes." She nods vehemently.

"On foot?"

Her hands drop from my jacket and she steps back. "What?"

I gesture around the mostly barren parking lot. "Where's your mode of transportation? How exactly are they following you? How many are there?

What do they look like? And if they're so gung ho on apprehending you, what made them take off?"

"I don't—I don't know. I wasn't paying attention. I've been too busy trying to stay alive." As if knowing I don't believe a word she's saying, her eyebrows lower, and she hides her eyes from mine.

The whole situation is mad, and I'd have to be mad as well to even contemplate having her as a travel mate. And yet…free entertainment. Because if she is nothing else, she is certainly amusing. Something niggles at my brain. Something annoying. Knowing it's my conscience, I could ignore it, or I could face it. There is a reason she is so desperate to leave with me, and I'm pretty sure that at some future time I'll wonder what I was thinking to agree to this, but…

"I'm going to North Dakota," I tell her slowly, never once looking from her.

Hope brightens her eyes. "North Dakota sounds great. Perfect, really. Exactly where I was hoping to go."

I step closer, and she steps back. We do this until her back is flush with the truck box and there is no escape. Her throat bobs as she swallows, and though trepidation runs across her face, she doesn't look away. I set a hand on either side of her, trapping her within my arms as the cool metal of the truck box freezes my palms.

"I have an idea who you are," I say conversationally. I let those words sink in; I watch a million thoughts race across her features.

"Y-you do?" she squeaks.

I focus on her lips. They glisten under the light of the moon, soft and inviting. "How old are you?" I ask absently, my voice a low hum.

"Twenty-three."

Truth.

"How old are you?" she shoots back.

"Twenty-six. What's your name?"

She fidgets, and as if realizing she is, goes still. The pulse at the base of her neck flutters like it wants to fly away. "Piper."

Lie.

But I'll let her have it, for now.

"Piper," I say softly, bringing my face dangerously close to hers. "You…are a liar."

She swallows, her lips parting. The motion is done without thought, a nervous gesture, and yet I fight to straighten from her, to put space between us. To step back. It's either that or kiss her. I can do without knowing what the lips of a con artist taste like.

"Let's go." My tone is rough, strained with unwanted attraction for a duplicitous stranger.

She doesn't move from the side of the truck, and with a hand braced on the door, I turn to her. "Are you coming or not?"

"But you…you said…"

"That you're a liar? Yes. I recall. It wasn't that long ago."

"But…" She hesitantly moves away from the truck.

"You went to great lengths to procure a ride with me." I look her up and down, wondering what secrets she has trapped inside that imaginative brain. "Who am I to deny a damsel in distress?"

Her eyes narrow at my tone as she angles her body toward the passenger's side of the truck. She knows the kind of person she is, but she has no idea who I am. The look she shoots me before she gets in the Ford tells me she's having second thoughts. I wonder if I should tell her to get out while she can. A slow smile, hidden in the dark, claims my face.

* * *

Opal

He's an alternative rock boy. That I am not surprised by. He's got the look—dark unkempt hair, derisive cast to his sharp features. The black bomber jacket with the upturned collar, the straight-legged jeans covering black boots. I bet beneath that jacket he has on a shirt sporting a band name. His vibe screams rebel and bad boy and loner and any other thing most mothers warn their daughters against. My fingernails dig into my palms, wondering if my mom would have done the same.

All he needs is a cigarette dangling from a corner of his mouth and he could be the quintessential man a woman's heart should always avoid. I've met his kind before. I've even dated them. Never for long, and never without wishing I hadn't.

This guy looks and smells like trouble. And his voice—it isn't smooth or all that appealing. In fact, it sounds like broken glass. Grating and sharp. Nothing about him cries "love of my life" material. Which is just as well. I don't need trouble right now.

"Why are you going to North Dakota?" I ask to fill the silence. My eyes want to close and I slide my fingers under the crisp denim fabric of my jacket and pinch the skin near my wrist. Hard. The resulting throb keeps my brain occupied and slumber out of reach.

A good portion of me thinks I will end up regretting my insistence on pairing up with the sullen man with the easily accessible truck. It was a spontaneous decision, brought on by lack of sleep, hunger, and being ditched by my ride when I slapped a roving hand from my thigh. I saw the North Dakota license plates on his ancient truck, and I figured that was a good sign he was heading in that direction. North Dakota is one state over from Montana—my destination.

"What's your real name?" he counters.

"Jackie," I fib, turning my head to look out the passenger window. Shadows and indecipherable shapes meet my eyes.

"We should make it to North Dakota in a day or two, depending on how far I can get before needing sleep," he comments, after a prolonged pause in which he silently called me a liar. Again.

"You never told me your name either," I say, staring at the headlights marking a narrow path on the freeway. Other than us, the road is empty. It's eerie, and makes me think of alternate realities and apocalypses.

"I didn't want you to feel left out with your mysterious persona." He fiddles with the radio, finds repeated static, and then turns it off. "Let's do it this way—you tell me yours, and I'll tell you mine."

"I can't tell you my real name. It's safer for you if you don't know."

The responding snort tells me what he thinks of that.

People usually at least try to believe me before assuming everything that comes out of my mouth is a lie. Which, most of it is. I don't know why I lie, especially now, when I sound like I'm from a cluster of bad action movies that use the same lines. It's habitual, an old form of self-soothing I never outgrew.

I clutch my scuffed and dirt-kissed pink backpack to my chest, my meager belongings inside telling a sad tale of a drifter with no anchors to anything but herself.

"If you know, then they can use that knowledge to hunt me down. They'd torture you, and let's face it, we both know you'd break."

His eyes snap to mine and back to the road.

I'm starting over, reinventing myself. I don't know how, but I am. I figure I'll know who I want to be when I catch a glimpse of her.

"Others have died for knowing it," I continue.

The man shakes his dark head, amusement adding lines to the side of his face I can see. "Really? Do tell."

I uncross my arms and sit up straighter, a spark of excitement entering my voice. "I'm an undercover agent on a top secret mission. That's all you can know."

"Does this mission include pink elephants and machetes?"

"How'd you know?" I swallow back laughter at the look he gives me.

His eyes flicker my way and down. "What's in the bag?"

I protectively pull the bag tighter to my frame. "Machetes and mace. A few stuffed pink elephants. Necessities for my mission."

"What's your mission, to ruin some kid's day by massacring stuffed animals in front of them?"

I freeze, my breaths as immobile as me. *Did I ruin her day, or her week, or maybe a couple months? Did I ruin her life?*

He glances at me, a slice of dark eyes that can shred and rebuild with a single look. "It was a joke."

"Best joke I ever heard," I mutter. I relax against the hard seat, feigning calm that left me with his words.

The man's hands flex on the steering wheel. He expels a loud breath. "You had a shitty childhood."

It isn't a question, and I don't answer. He thinks this is about me, but it isn't.

He swears, loudly and viciously enough that I jump, and I quickly tell him, "Yes, okay? I had a shitty childhood. You don't have to get mad. I mean, it wasn't all bad."

"No—I left the bag at the gas station."

I instinctively look at my backpack on my lap and the black duffel bag on the floor near my feet I was tempted to scavenge through while he was in the store. Lucky for him, I haven't yet added theft to my list of crimes.

I turn to him. "What bag?"

"The bag with food in it. The whole reason I stopped at that store."

"But you picked up something better than food, didn't you?" I chirp.

He scowls. "I need a cigarette."

My stomach constricts and gurgles as if to commiserate with him over the lack of food. When did I last eat? I think back over the many hours since I started this impulsive road trip. This morning—I had a granola bar this morning. Talking and thinking about food reminds me of how hungry I am. I have a total of one apple and three granola bars to last me until I can find a way to come up with more money or let go of the sparse supply I carry.

"Cigarettes are bad for your health."

"So is mentioning that to people who smoke."

That effectively shuts me up.

He uses one hand to roughly rub his face, his aura fraught with agitation. His movements are jerky as he flips on a blinker and takes the next exit.

I brace myself with a hand on the door when the Ford abruptly decelerates and merges sharply to the right. "Where are we going?"

"Hell comes to mind as an eventual destination, but for now, there." He points a finger at a beat-up red sign that has a cartoon chef with a white hat and a wide grin that reads "Chucky's Diner: Open All Hours. Come hungry, leave happy."

"Sounds like sophisticated dining. I feel underdressed."

The truck rolls to a stop at the intersection and the dark-haired man turns to look at me. I can't see his eye color, but that isn't necessary to feel the heat of his gaze as it strips me bare. His eyes feel like they are directly on my skin, burning me, seeing into me, revealing everything I don't want him to see. I don't understand why he is scrutinizing me, or what he thinks he'll find.

The breath I take is shaky, and the sound of it ends whatever spell he has me under. He blinks and faces forward, his motions stiff as the truck accelerates. Silence alive with pinpricks of unnamed sensation travels with us as he drives to the diner. I don't notice my legs are weak until I almost fall as I hop from the truck, gravel spitting under the pressure of my boots as I fight for balance. I shoot upright and pat down my layered waves of hair that take much joy in their constant mutiny. I try to appear nonchalant, even as my pulse dips and sputters and veers in dizzying directions.

He meets me at the front of the old Ford, his head angled to the side as he watches me approach. I think I prefer sound of any kind to his quiet, so I hum to myself as we walk through the partially filled parking lot, the dark building's windows filled with light and people. I hug my backpack to my chest, unwilling to leave it out of sight. A metal sign on top of the roof hangs sideways, swaying and creaking as a cool breeze goes by. I hurry past it, not wanting to be beneath the sign should it decide it wants to come down.

Before we reach the door, the scent of fried food teases my nostrils and I press an arm to my aching stomach as I step inside. I won't be able to order much, and I'll have to eat slowly to trick myself into thinking it is enough, but any food is better than the emptiness I presently feel. I am not a stranger to hunger, but it hasn't ever gotten better just because I got used to feeling it.

The handful of people seated at booths pause in their conversations and shift their attention to me and the man behind me. I inhale and hold it, paranoia telling me to turn around and walk right back out of this place. I scan the faces of the occupants, knowing it's unlikely I'll see anyone I know from my home state but searching all the same.

"I'm all about enjoying the scenery, but we'll get to a table faster if you move your legs," a deep, prickly voice informs me.

I clench my jaw and step forward, heading for a booth straight ahead across the green and white decorated room. With the various fake plants and flowers in pots and on window ledges, it looks like a floral shop threw up in here. Under a ceiling of megawatt-strength light bulbs, I get my first real look at the man I'm traveling with. We slide onto the booth seats, facing one another. His skin is bleached of color, making the blackness of his rumpled hair that much more obvious. The eyebrows are thick and low, giving him a perpetual displeased look. His nose is hawkish and arrogant, and there is a dimple in his chin. He's not handsome, but his eyes are deep, and the character of his features demands notice.

I look into his piercing gray eyes and my stomach spins, and the room spins, and everything but him is spinning. My fingers itch to cast his unsmiling features onto the fibers of a single sheet of paper, but I only have so much paper left, and my charcoal pencils are down to stubs. I can't draw anyone unless it's financially advantageous. His eyes are thunderstorms, lightning, and every natural disaster wrapped up in an iris. The man is unmoving, untouched, as the atmosphere pivots and straightens. Looking at me like he is not all surprised to find me intrigued by his features.

"Like what you see? I don't blame you. Most women do."

I swallow, my mouth dry. "Not especially, but it isn't like I can do anything about it."

His eyebrows shoot up, one corner of his mouth lifting and lowering.

I'm sure I look a fright. Other than sponge bathing from gas station and restaurant sinks, I haven't bathed in days. My hair feels heavy with dirt and the need to be washed, and what I wouldn't give for a proper bath. One I could sink into, with steaming hot water and scented oils and salts. I almost sigh at the thought. I left Illinois in a hurry, and other than the few clothes I tossed in my bag and other necessities, I am without most of my possessions. Possessions are just that, though, and it didn't make sense to take more than me and what I can't live without.

Two clear glasses of water thump to the table and my eyes snap up to the purple-haired waitress with a barbell through each eyebrow. She has a tired smile on her faintly lined face as she hands a laminated menu to me and my acquaintance. "Hi, I'm Vicky. Can I get you two anything to drink?"

"Just water," I say. What I really want to order is an unending supply of sweet, carbonated, caffeinated beverages.

"Coffee, please," he tells her, holding my gaze.

"All right. I'll be right back with that." She takes off, leaving the fragrance of apples in her wake.

He steeples his fingers beneath his dimpled chin and levels soulful eyes on me. "So, Piper-Jackie, did you commit a crime of some kind?"

"Why would you ask that?"

"Me, I like to plan for things." He straightens and shrugs off his jacket. I was wrong about the band name—it's a red Mr. Kool-Aid T-shirt. "If there's a chance I'm going to be viewed as an accomplice, and subsequently arrested, I want to make sure my schedule is free. You know…" he says in a bored tone. "Details."

His coffee is set before him, interrupting the conversation I'd rather not have.

"Are you guys ready to order?"

"No," he says at the same time I say, "Yes."

She divides her gaze between us, a small notepad and pen in hand. "Okay," she replies slowly.

"Toast," I blurt. "I'll take two slices of white toast."

The woman waits, finally asking, "Anything else?"

I chug the glass of water, hoping it will help fill the void in my stomach, and push the empty cup toward her. "More water, please."

Eyeing me, my dining companion orders white toast, two hard-boiled eggs, bacon, and pancakes. My mouth is salivating like crazy by the time he lists the last food item. We hand over our menus to the waitress, and the tension is in full force again. I pick at a loose pink thread on my bag and hope I'll suddenly become invisible and he'll stop examining me like he is. His eyes are like a hot touch as they lay claim to me.

"Is there anything I need to know before we get any further into our little adventure?" he presses.

"No," I respond. Nothing too bad. Nothing it would benefit him to know.

He pauses, turning his head to show me his prominent profile. The sound of his fingertips tapping on the tabletop is the only noise. He stops, looks at me. "You're either running to something, or away from it. I think I know which it is for you."

I don't reply, focusing on the salt and pepper shakers to the left of me. It's a little of both.

Our food is brought, mine small and lacking. I shove a piece of toast in my mouth before putting any butter or jelly on it, and his hand freezes around an egg. I bite off another chunk, swallowing before properly chewing. It's dry and flavorless, but it's sustenance. So much for my plan to take my time eating.

He slowly lowers his hand, and then sets the egg on my plate, his eyes turning to slits when I open my mouth to protest. Next, two pieces of bacon are plopped on the plate. When he moves to add a pancake to the growing pile of food, I snatch the plate away and shake my head. I don't want to be in debt to him.

I tear my gaze from the pancake, in this singular instance really wishing I had less pride, because if I did that pancake would be mine. A slice of bacon teeters on the edge of the plate and I sweep it up and into my mouth before it can fall to the floor and no longer be edible. Although, I'd be tempted to still eat it if it did.

"No more," I command around the crunchy, crispy bits of meat I have yet to swallow.

A barely perceptible nod is the only acknowledgment I get.

I eat everything on my plate before he makes it through his pancakes. I don't care about manners—not that anyone really ever taught me any. Stomach full, I sit back, content and sleepy. My mouth twisting against the words, I thank him.

"I'm not going to be able to last much longer on the road. I'll find the closest hotel and get us a room," he says quietly, adding salt and pepper to his egg before taking a bite.

"I don't need a room." My words are sharp. I don't have money for that. I'll sleep in the truck if he insists on getting one.

Exhaustion slumps his broad shoulders and he trains his tornadic eyes on me. He suddenly looks worn out by life, and it humanizes him, removes a layer of edges from his severe personality. "Where are you trying to get to?"

"Home," I answer immediately, my pulse thrumming at the thought. It is my biggest quest to have a place to call that, for once, finally. When I find it, I'm never letting it go.

"And where is home?"

"I'll know when I see it." I smile, knowing sorrow leaks out through the curve of it.

A frown takes over the space between his eyebrows. Crinkles form around his eyes as he squints at me, and he leans forward, resting his elbows on the table. His dark head tilts, reminding me of a raven as he wordlessly prods and deciphers, looks more into my words than I like.

"Truth," he murmurs, and I don't even ask what he's referencing, because I somehow already know.

2

Blake

"You can't sleep out here," I inform her for the third time, hefting my duffel bag higher on my shoulder as I wait for her to remove herself from my vehicle. I'm beginning to wonder if this is how we'll spend most of our time—with me trying to get her to leave my truck.

Finding a hotel that had vacancies and wasn't exorbitantly priced wasn't as simple as I'd hoped, and we had to drive over another hour and a half to find anything. It is now after three in the morning, and we're at a questionable-looking motel with one letter lit up in its sign. My body is weighted down with the need to sleep, and even standing is getting beyond me. If it was just me, I would have pulled over and slept at a wayside, but this little bit of nothing needs warmth, and from the dingy looks of her, a shower wouldn't hurt. I don't think about why I care.

"I'll be fine." She crosses her arms over her chest as she faces forward.

"You'll freeze." The wind picks up and sends an icy caress over me, as if to emphasize my words.

"I'm sturdier than I look."

"Oh, I have no doubt of that. But you're still not staying out here. There are two beds, if that's what you're worried about."

That snaps her eyes to me, fire dancing in the depths. I now know her eyes to be brown with hints of gold speckled through them, like warm, dark honey. "I didn't ask for—"

"I know," I interrupt shortly. "If you want to keep track of money and pay me back later, fine, but take your pride down a notch, and let's go. I'm cold, and I'm tired, and I don't have the patience for this right now."

She won't pay me back. I don't expect her to. When we part ways in North Dakota, I'll never see her again. Maybe I still won't even know her name. "It's not safe out here," I say in a calmer voice.

The woman turns toward me, hesitating with her body partially leaning forward and her arms hugging her bag. My eyes flicker to the backpack, wondering what's inside it that means so much to her. She hasn't parted ways with it since we've been together. I return my gaze to her, telepathically telling her to get her tiny behind moving. Her eyes get smaller, letting me know she is accurately reading my expression.

She shakes her head and settles back against the seat. "I'm good here. I can protect myself. You go on without me. I'll lock the doors."

She's not my responsibility, and I resent that I feel like she is. I'm not a good person, and I can't forget that.

"I'm sleeping here," she says with firmness.

Briefly closing my eyes, I hold my hands in prayer and nod. "Okay." I look at her and nod again. I'll let her come in when she's ready, and she will, eventually. I can do that. I can wait. "Fine."

That's all I say before turning and striding for the motel room, the key digging into my palm as I think about the pain-in-the-ass sidekick I acquired. My jaw is tight and an ensuing ache forms through my skull. Pebbles crunch under my boots and the moon is my flashlight, trickling over the surrounding trees and hills. The motel is directly off the freeway, the sound of a semi rattling the airwaves as it roars past.

I have met a total of one woman who exasperated me, confounded me, and turned my world on its axis. Kennedy Somers, aka the other half of Grennedy. She happens to be my brother's girlfriend, but that didn't stop me from wanting her at the start of this past summer. They weren't dating then, but it was soon clear that she and my brother Graham were meant to be, and being the chivalrous guy I am, I backed off—for the most part.

This woman, with her no-name and her stories, this woman tops even Kennedy in my estimation of what is considered a difficult person.

The fact that I am unlocking the door with an actual key instead of a card shows the age of the place. And when I open the door and am greeted with a musky smell, faded floral bedding in possibly the ugliest shade of purple I have had the misfortune to witness, and dust-ridden air, I decide that Graham wouldn't step inside this room without a mask, gloves, and a well-stocked supply of cleaning agents in his arms.

The thought produces a smirk, but it soon leaves. I was an asshole to Graham when I first saw him a few months ago. The intention of going to Wisconsin was to bond with my half-brother before taking off for

Australia, and instead, I tried to steal his unofficial girl—and I'm still in the United States. Go figure.

Part of me wanted Graham and me to get along, but then, a larger part blamed him for shit from our childhoods that wasn't his fault. I was antagonistic. Possibly out of line. I smirk. Definitely out of line.

As a child, I wanted someone to protect me from our father, and Graham needed to protect himself. He was my big brother, my idol, and he disappeared. He got to leave; I never did. It was a hard truth to accept, but he was just a kid trying to survive bad circumstances, same as me. He didn't deserve the way I treated him a few months ago, but I like to think I was the catalyst to future good things. Namely, he and Kennedy finally hooking up.

I toss my bag on the closest bed and something thumps to the floor. Frowning, I search the bed and the tan carpet, but don't see anything amiss. The room has a small television on a dresser with a mirror, and the image that looks back from the reflective glass is haggard and bleak. It isn't just lack of sleep that is screwing with me—it's where I'm heading. Literally, maybe spiritually, who the hell knows? I'm driving to somewhere, but I really feel like I'm driving to nowhere. Story of my life.

I viciously rub my eyes and drop my hands, waiting for the woman to allow common sense to enter her thick head. I understand not wanting obligations to another—my motto is to keep my distance from all other human beings in order to stamp out responsibilities of any kind—but this is ridiculous. If she wants to endanger herself on her own time, fine, but it isn't happening while she's with me. Three minutes tick off the clock on the nightstand between the beds, and my patience leaves when it enters the fourth.

It seems I can't wait all that long.

With blood simmering through my veins and eradicating all hints of a good-natured disposition, I stalk to the door and fling it open, not bothering to shut it as I prowl toward the Ford. I swear I can see the sun peeking up from some distant hill, laughing at me for attempting to get rest before it marks a new day. My brain pulses for nicotine, alcohol, anything, really, to dull the emotions. I hate feeling. I hate caring. I hate my addictions. Some days, I hate me. I hate that I crave anything I can never have if I want to have any semblance of control over my life.

Because it's such a perfect one and I'd hate to mess it up.

I grip the door handle, it feeling like sharp ice against my skin, and swing open the truck door. She didn't even lock the doors, a detail that kicks my body temperature up another ten degrees. Senseless, reckless, foolish—I stop there, deciding it is better to not list all her faults if I want to be able to look at her without exploding.

"You," I rumble in a voice I don't recognize, and then words fail me when I actually look at her. The anger slides away, and my chest releases some of its tautness. She looks like a kid. A helpless, vulnerable, lost kid.

She faces me, her hands tucked under her cheek as she sleeps. Lips slightly parted, the tiniest of creases line her wide forehead. Her diminutive form looks cramped, contracted into a sitting-up pose with her knees tucked to her chest. Even in sleep, she hugs her grimy pink backpack. Her eyelashes aren't particularly long, but they're thick and dark. Dainty fans across her sun-bronzed skin. She looks frail in the dark, the moon adding hollows beneath her cheekbones, and softness to her prominent chin.

Beautiful she is not, and yet, there is no denying the charm of her features.

Leaning into the truck, I scoop her and her bag into my arms. She tenses for an instant, and then, as if subconsciously knowing I mean her no harm, she settles against my chest, one arm instinctively moving to my neck as if to anchor herself to me. The other remains glued to her bag. Strands of her hair tickle my face as I partially turn to close the truck door with my elbow, and then I briskly walk. Her hair has a faint coconut smell to it, and in spite of myself, I like it.

"There's a difference between stubbornness, and stupidity," I mutter as I carry her to the motel, finding satisfaction in admonishing her, even if she is asleep during it.

I heft her up higher in my arms and her head rolls toward me, her forehead pressed to the side of my neck. She's a little furnace, and I feel her shallow breaths against my collarbone. Her arm tightens, her fingertips digging into the back of my neck, and a small sigh leaves her. My throat closes and I swallow twice to loosen it. Lust, anger, protectiveness, empathy, insanity—I can't put a name to what I feel right now. I just know I feel more than I should for someone I just met and don't trust.

I close the door behind us and flip the lock, moving to the bed nearest the bathroom. I'm not particularly looking forward to checking out that room just yet. Using my free arm, I quickly tug down the blankets and lay her on the white sheets. I try to take away the bag and she squeezes her arms around it, a frown forming to her mouth. I let it go and pull up the covers to her chin.

I'm not shy about my body. If I wasn't worried about her taking off with my wallet and truck keys sometime during my approaching comatose hours, my jeans would already be off. But I am worried. I'm not saying she is a thief, and I am not saying she isn't. I'd rather not find out. My keys are safely in one front pocket; my wallet is in the other. If she's desperate enough to rove around in my jeans while I sleep, I wish her all the best. A pulse in my groin acknowledges that I might even enjoy it.

I look down and gesture with my hands. "Really? Her?"

Sliding my arms from my jacket, I lay it across the part of the dresser not occupied by the TV. I take off my shirt and do the same with it. Boots and socks come off next. I flip the light switch and with my eyes closed fall onto my bed. Something rumbles and shudders beneath me, and then the top half of the bed slams to the floor.

My eyes fly open.

I could be wrong, but I'm pretty sure it is not natural for my feet to be above my head. That explains the noise I earlier heard—the damn bed was falling apart.

The functioning bed beside me shifts and I feel her eyes on me. A choked laugh fills the silence, overtaking the sound of blood as it pounds through my head. I don't move, a lone muscle jumping in my jaw. I force my eyes closed and my breathing to deepen, and I pretend that I am not about to sleep in a broken bed. I'm on a beach, with warm air and sunshine on my face, and I'm comfortably nestled in a hammock. Yep. That's where I am.

I hear her settle back down, and then there's nothing but quiet and black, and I let myself go.

I wake up to the sound of a revving chainsaw and sunshine on my face, feeling as if I only shut my eyes mere minutes ago. I open my eyes and blink at a misshapen water stain on the ceiling. My head pounds from my sleeping position and my ribcage feels like it's about to meet my throat. The noise stops, then starts, and I slowly turn my head to the left. She's lying on her back, coverless, legs bent, arms flung out wide on either side, and her head is tipped back with her mouth hanging open. She looks absurd, and I fight a grin.

I roll out of the bed and land on my hands and feet, my muscles tight and uncooperative from my sleeping position. The heaviness is there, wanting to take over. I take deep breaths and inwardly fight it. Not today. Today, I decree, is going to be outstanding. I'm not sure I believe that, but maybe I can fool myself.

Standing, I stretch my arms above my head, my joints popping and cracking. I run my fingers through my messy hair and over my face, needing coffee and about another twelve hours of sleep—preferably in a whole, properly functioning bed. A glance at the clock tells me it's just after nine in the morning.

If I push it, I can make it to North Dakota by this afternoon or early evening. My stomach twists, and a tremor takes over my hands, showing how much I'm looking forward to it. I made myself a vow, and if I don't see it through, I'll lose a chunk of what little self-respect I have. There is no getting out of this.

I notice the lack of sound at the same time I feel heat on my back. I look over my shoulder and my eyes collide with hers. She's sitting up, her chin resting on the bag between her arms. Her hair is tousled about her head; her lips are swollen with sleep. Interest shines in the eyes that slowly move along my shoulders and back.

I pretend not to feel the current through my skin. If I'm attracted to her, and I'm not even sure I am, it doesn't mean I can't act as if I'm not.

"You snore," I say in greeting.

Her face scrunches up. "And you break beds. Judge away."

I avert my face, hiding the amusement I feel in the bend of my mouth. I grab my shirt from the dresser and shrug into it. I don't have a lot of money, but selling my Harley a few weeks ago put more money in my checking account than there has ever previously been at one time. I miss my bike. I miss the wind, and the freedom I felt while riding it. The thrill of speed and nothing but air around me. What I don't miss is worrying about money from one day to the next, as I'm sure she is. I have a nice cushion for now, but she seems to have next to nothing. I can afford to pay for her meals for another day.

"I'm going to find us food. You can shower or whatever while I'm gone." I cock an eyebrow as I glance at her and say, "Please shower."

She mutters obscenities as I walk out the door, and I catch a few choice phrases I can't say I've ever heard before. The sun stings my eyes and heats my skin, and I allow my first real, full smile in days to take over my face as I stroll for the truck.

* * *

Opal

The bathroom has cobwebs, chipped green tiles, and the shower water is lukewarm and comes down in a split, thin stream, but it is the equivalent of heaven to my unclean skin and hair. I wash twice with the cheap motel beauty products that smell like Pine-Sol, shifting back and forth under the showerhead to dampen all of me. Shivering as I turn off the water, I grab a bath towel that is more the size of a hand towel and vigorously dry off.

I have four changes of clothes with me, and two need to be washed. I dress in red jeans and a plain black top, run a comb through my thick hair, and go about brushing and flossing my teeth.

Finding a compact blow dryer in a drawer, I attempt to dry my hand-washed undergarments, my thoughts annoyingly shifting to the man who obviously carried me from the truck into the motel room. Generally a light sleeper, it unnerves me to know that I didn't wake up until the bed broke. At the memory, I look up and grin at my reflection in the cracked rectangular mirror, the smile disintegrating as a spark shoots from the front of the blow dryer. I quickly turn it off and unplug it, not wanting to burn down the place.

With my still damp blue bra and purple panties dangling from my hand, I leave the bathroom. I stumble to a stop, unaware until this instant that he was back. The man looks up from the floor where he examines the front part of the bed, his body turning to stone. Hair the color of black ink, thick and disobedient, partially obscures his eyes, but it does nothing to mute the intensity of them as they drift up and down the length of me. I feel their touch like his hands are on me. It's maddening and erotic and makes my throat dry. He acts like it's the first time he's seen a female form. *I* feel like it's the first time a man's ever paid me the slightest amount of interest. My pulse races.

His attention goes to the underclothes in my hand, and my skin burns. I practically dive back into the bathroom, shoving my belongings along with the wet underwear into the bag. When I step into the room again he's gone. I close my eyes and let out a sigh, thankful that he isn't around to comment. I tug on my black boots and arrange my backpack on my shoulder. With a tremor of anticipation I scan the room to make sure I didn't forget anything, and I leave.

The sun is out, quickly warming the top of my head, and the air smells like asphalt and exhaust, a scent that belongs with the nearby highway. There is a bounce to my steps as I think about this impulsive adventure I'm on, and wonder where it will end up taking me. Montana, for sure, but where else? Anywhere has to better from where I started, and as long as I keep moving, it doesn't have to end. I don't want it to end, not until I am exactly where I want to be. And hopefully no one I left behind is looking for me. My mouth starts to tip down and I form it to a straight line.

No one is looking for you. You're safe.

A man about half the size and height of the dark-haired man stands beside his Ford, wildly waving around his hands as he talks to the owner of the truck. My footsteps slow, and the excitement of an unknown future fades. There is no way the older man's appearance has anything to do with me, and yet I feel panic gather inside and cause my stomach to dip. The farther I get from Illinois, the better I'll feel.

What little hair the man has is white and stringy, blowing in sporadic mayhem each time the wind picks up. His shirt is brown and rides up his protruding gut. He seems agitated.

"I understand," the black-haired man says, his backside leaning against the driver's side door of the truck, his arms crossed. Everything about him shows he is calm and relaxed, but his eyes are intense as they flicker to me and back to the man.

"I had no idea that the bed would break again," the older man says in a loud, whiny tone.

I let out a slow, silent exhalation as I stand beside the pair. Once again, I was worried for nothing. And how many times has that bed broken? Something tells me I don't want to know, or why.

"I understand," he repeats, staring at me.

"We're good then? The discount was enough?"

He changed his shirt. This one is charcoal gray and reads "Goonies." I want to ask him if he is stuck in the eighties, but his toned, pale arms have captured my attention. How does one remain as white as he is? Does he never stand in the sun? That can't be right, because he's in the sun now, but it doesn't appear to touch him. My eyes lift to his, and they pulse through me, warming me, confusing me.

"Sir? Mr. Malone?"

As I watch, the stranger's face transforms into blankness as he levels his eyes on the man. The white-haired man looks uneasy, and he backs up, hands lifted. My pulse trips as I take in the change, fascinated by it, wondering where it came from. All the light is gone from him. He's cloaked in nothingness.

"My dad is Mr. Malone," he informs the man in a quiet voice. "I'm Blake."

Blake. My shoulders loosen. I like that name. I silently go over the few details I have of him. His name is Blake Malone and he has issues with his dad. Then again, who doesn't? Most of the people I've met over the years have had some kind of problem with their father. At least he knows his dad.

"Y-yes. Okay. Good. I can go, M—Blake?"

"Yes. The discount was enough." He turns from the stammering man.

"Thank you. Thank you," the guy says, for the first time realizing they aren't alone. His head swivels to me, his mouth open as if to speak. His eyes widen and he backpedals so fast he falls to the ground. I wince at the sound of flesh sliding across gravel. Before I can say anything, he's on his feet and sprinting for the motel, looking over his shoulder once. His hair waves behind him like a straggly flag.

"That was odd," I comment as the office door of the motel slams. "He acted like he was scared of me."

Blake gives me an innocent look that shouts his guilt. "Ready to go?"

My eyes narrow. He did something. I don't know what, but he did. I widen my stance and shake my head. "Nope. Not until you tell me what you did or said to that guy to make him act like that around me."

Shrugging, he hefts himself into the truck. "Have a nice life."

He closes the door, and watching me the whole time, slowly raises a frosted donut to his mouth. Saliva forms inside my mouth in longing. A murmur of satisfaction leaves him as he chews. It's like porn for food, and I am addicted. A curse word flies from my mouth as I stomp to my side of the truck. As soon as I'm inside, the engine sputters and rumbles before finding its unbalanced beat, and Blake navigates us to the highway.

I drop my backpack and grab the small white bag between us, take out two donuts, and with one in each hand, make love to them with my mouth. I should be embarrassed by the sounds that leave me, but I'm too busy enjoying the sugar and carbohydrates to worry about that. One has raspberry jam and cream cheese inside; the other has vanilla pudding with chocolate frosting on top. Have I ever tasted anything so delicious, so fresh? I can't recall, but it doesn't seem possible.

"I wasn't sure what you liked to drink." I feel his eyes on me, but I don't acknowledge it, focusing on finishing off the donuts as fast as I can without choking. "There's a bottle of orange juice and another of water in the plastic bag near your feet."

I lick my fingers and wipe my mouth with the back of my hand. "I'll take both," I tell him, leaning over to procure them. My stomach is uncomfortably full, and bending at the waist makes it hurt. I quickly sit back with the drinks in hand and start on the orange juice. It tastes like liquid bursts of citrus euphoria.

"There are napkins."

I stiffen, turning my voice into a lilt as I reply, "Why waste napkins when you can use your hands?"

He finds a classic rock station and Mötley Crüe fills the cab. Another surprise. His musical taste isn't set to one genre. I want him to be simple. If he's simple, I'm less inclined to be absorbed by all the nuances and ticks that make him up. Not that it matters—we'll be parting ways later today and I'll never see him again. My fingers curl, longing to draw him.

"I take it you grew up in some rich family where everything was proper, right? 'Please' and 'thank you' and 'you're welcome' were part of everyday conversation." I swallow the last drop of orange juice and move on to the water.

"I take it you didn't," is his curt response.

I view the hills and valleys in the distance, their colors and shapes muted. The words come too easily. "My father was born into the mafia, and when he was old enough to make his own decisions, he left. There was a price on his head for doing so. I was an only child, and my mom died when I was three. It was just me and my dad and we spent most of my childhood running from state to state. Manners weren't a priority."

He doesn't say anything for a long time. "You do realize I don't believe a thing you're saying, right?"

One shoulder shrugs. "You don't have to believe it. I know it to be true."

"Is there a reason for the lies, or are you just bored?"

My brain whirs, shift gears, and starts on another route. "I know your name, but you don't know mine. Try to guess it before we reach North Dakota."

Blake pauses. "Or you could just tell me."

"I could." I smile. "But that wouldn't be much fun, would it?"

"I think your idea of fun would probably be considered warped compared to most people."

I settle into my seat, watching a sign for Fargo, North Dakota go by. It's two hundred thirty-four miles away, according to the sign. "I'll let you know the first letter. It's an O."

"What about it being safer for me if I don't know your name?" he taunts, passing a small, red car full of teenagers. The driver waves and I wave back.

"I won't know you for much longer. What can it hurt?" I roll down my window to alleviate the stuffy heat, the wind whipping my hair around my face. For some reason, I want him to know my real name before we part ways. Call it my ego, but I do not want to be entirely forgotten by Blake Malone. Everyone I know has some tainted memory of me. It would be nice if someone could remember me as quirky, yes, but also untroubled. "First, though, tell me why that guy at the motel acted the way he did."

"I told him you had murderous tendencies, and that they were set off by breakable beds in motel rooms."

I turn my head and stare at Blake. I'm shocked, and irritated, and impressed.

He fights a grin, eventually winning as his features smooth into a brood I've seen on his face more times than anything else.

"You're a liar too," I accuse with little ire. How can I be mad at him for something I routinely do?

"I never said I wasn't. I'm just apparently better at it than you." The word that next leaves his mouth stuns me. "Opal." He glances at me, pulling his gaze from me before I am ready.

I blink. "How did you figure that out?"

"It's on the bottom of your bag. I wasn't sure that was your name until you told me it starts with an O. Why all the covertness?"

The memory of a face with chubby cheeks, sparkling blue eyes, and an infectious laugh slams into me, taking my breath and any semblance of joy. A seven-year-old by the name of Paisley Jordan took black permanent marker and wrote my name on my bag without my knowledge. I couldn't be upset with her, not when she later explained to me that she did it to officially brand something as mine after I told her I didn't have anything.

I'd forgotten it was there, and without looking at my pink backpack, my fingers unconsciously brush across the textured fabric. It helps to not think of her. It helps to pretend my life before a few weeks ago never existed.

"Hey. Are you all right?" he asks when I remain silent.

"It's a silly name," I say in a quiet voice. The food I ate turns the fullness in my stomach to sourness and I press an arm to my abdomen, hoping the nausea passes. It's a silly name I like to pretend isn't mine. I like to pretend a lot of things.

"I guess some would say it is a silly name," he agrees, glancing at me to catch the glower I don't try to hide. He turns his eyes back to the road. "It's also unique, like you."

I've been told I'm unique before. It never sounded like a good thing to be, but when Blake says it, it does.

3

Blake

Opal is a terrible singer. Her voice is screechy and off-key, and when she reaches the especially high notes, it causes the skin around my mouth to tighten with discontent. But she bobs her head and taps her foot as she belts out Cyndi Lauper, and her enthusiasm pulls an undesired smile from me. Her lack of self-consciousness is refreshing, even if I want to clamp a muzzle over her mouth to end the torture.

With a sound of triumph, she pulls a candy bar from the front of her backpack and holds it up with sparkling eyes. It's flattened and bent and partially unwrapped. Opal waves it around like it is a hundred-dollar bill. "I didn't know this was in there."

"It looks dead."

Opal gives me a look as she removes the remaining wrapper from the chocolate. She picks off a piece of fuzz and rolls down the window to release it out into the wild. "It was never alive."

"If candy bars could be dead, it would be." I shift my eyes from the road to her and back. "You're really going to eat that? How long has it been in there?"

With a shrug, she bites off half the smashed and crumbling bar in one take, and then offers what's left to me. I shake my head, amazed by how quickly she demolishes the rest of it. She's either starving, or has an unhealthy love for chocolate.

"So good," she murmurs.

So gross, I think.

"Wait." Opal flings out an arm and clips me in the jaw. "Did you see that? Pull over."

"No," I answer, and keep driving. We should reach North Dakota in another hour or two, and then we say goodbye. And I confront my past. Sweat breaks out on my forehead and I swallow down bitter fear at the thought of seeing my father.

"Come on, Blake, I want to take a closer look at something."

"No."

"Please?" Her honey eyes are wide and hopeful. Even as I scowl, I aim the truck to the side of the road.

She jumps from the Ford before I have it in park, and with her backpack in hand, sprints toward a billboard. My eyes slide along the curves and dips of her body as I follow at a slower pace. When Opal came out of the bathroom this morning in her tight pants and shirt, at first I thought I was dreaming the body before me. No way was it the same one I'd come to think of as hers.

Last night her jacket covered her chest and hips, and I was too distracted by circumstances to properly consider her bottom, but I'm not having that problem today. As far as I knew, she was bones without shape. Today, in the formfitting clothing, the woman suddenly has breasts, and hips, and a rounded ass my teeth ache to graze and nip.

Even her body is a lie.

"Isn't it amazing?" she says with awe.

I squint my eyes against the sun, shaking my head at the picture on the monstrous sign Opal stands before with her head tipped back. It's an advertisement for a circus three exits away. The image shows a lion with its mouth open and long, sharp teeth visible, a brown bear standing on its hind paws, and a funny-looking guy with a top hat and gold and red jacket framing his short build. It's called Radley Family Circus and boasts that it's "one of the country's most popular attractions."

I'm doubtful.

"It's a sign," I answer, returning my attention to Opal. Opal—an elegant name for an unrefined woman. Its contradiction is what makes it fit.

Her face scrunches up as she looks at me. "It's not just a sign. It's a symbol of every childhood joy wrapped up in a single photograph."

I snort, the rays of the sun scorching the back of my neck. I went to a circus once, when I was eleven. I wasn't impressed with the clowns or the animals. I wanted destruction and explosions and fire. I guess you could say my issues started at an early age.

"It's a way to earn money at the expense of children," I say. "The animals, along with the parents taking their kids out of a sense of obligation, aren't happy, and the tricks are lame. The only ones who have any kind of fun are the naive kids who don't know any better."

The brown and gold of her eyes clash with emotion, and she looks down, hiding it. Her grip tightens on her backpack and she slings it over her shoulder as her eyes go back to the billboard. She says softly, "I've never been to a circus before."

My teeth grind together and I fist my hands. I turn toward the truck, telling myself not to even respond. I'm sure it's just another one of her lies. The sooner I get to North Dakota, the sooner I can get on with my life. It's taken every drop of courage I have to get this far, and if I don't keep going, I might not make it. Opal is a distraction, a disruption, and just because she *maybe* never experienced the circus scene as a kid, does not mean I am responsible for making sure she experiences it now. She is nothing to me. A stranger who coerced her way into catching a ride. A nuisance. One I'll be glad to be rid of.

Regardless of all that, I find myself turning back to ask, "Have you really never been to a circus before, or is this another one of your lies?"

Her eyes are wide and unblinking. "I thought you had me all figured out. You tell me."

Frustration builds, and a muscle jumps as I flex my jaw. "One hour. You get one hour at the circus and then we go, and if you're not ready to go when that one hour is up, I'm still leaving. With or without you." I feel it is necessary to accentuate that detail.

A gleam enters her eyes, and it's slightly evil. "Two hours."

"One hour," I argue, stalking back to the truck.

Stones crunch under the weight of my boots and I resist the urge to kick them. She is under my skin. I hunch my shoulders like I can physically get her out of my system. It's my own fault for giving in, but damn it, I know what it's like to want things that others take for granted. This circus means nothing to me, but to her, it means a lot.

Unless I just got suckered into another one of her games.

"Two," she tries again.

I whirl around, and not expecting her to be as close as she is, find her directly in front of me. Opal's face bumps into my chest and I grab her arms to steady her, my body exceptionally happy to have her near. She smells like chocolate and caramel. Heat shoots through my body as blood flows to areas I don't entirely want it to. Inches apart, and it feels like there is nothing between us—nothing but blazing attraction. Her skin singes mine, burns my hands where they rest on her biceps.

She stays still, her gaze carefully lifting to mine, as if pulled by forces out of her control. I want to look away, and I can't. She looks like every bad decision I never regretted, and every one I have yet to make. This close, I notice the strands of gold and red in her mop of hair, and the dark ring of brown around her irises. The plump red of her lips tease me, knowing I wonder at the feel of them, and the taste. When they part, and her pupils dilate, I inhale raggedly. I feel my composure slip another notch.

Desire stares back at me, daring me to make a move.

"Don't look at me like that," she whispers.

I blink, wondering how my thoughts came out of her mouth.

"You don't look at me like that," I echo darkly.

Opal's eyes narrow. "Like what?"

"Like…" I gesture to her face. "Like that."

"Because I have a mirror handy and know what you're talking about." She rolls her eyes at me. *Rolls her eyes.*

My features tighten. "If only you could speak without actually saying a word. I'd enjoy our time together so much more."

"How do you suggest that happens?"

"Learn how to mime."

"Whatever." She rolls her eyes again and a tick forms under my eye. "Can you let go of me now?"

I drop my hands and back up, the truck stopping my progress. I didn't realize I was still touching her. My hands are shaking, and I clench them to hide it.

This isn't me. This isn't how I act around women, or ever.

I either take what I want, or I don't want it enough.

I don't second-guess myself. I don't think about things too much. I don't care about anyone more than myself. The last person I opened myself up to slammed me back closed without a second glance, and the thought of having that happen again puts a sour taste in my mouth. There is no way I'm risking looking like a fool again. And *her*—why her? She is a lying, seemingly homeless, most likely criminal woman who aggravates me.

I feel trapped by honey eyes and my inclination to gaze into them.

Opal is the first to break the thick silence, and when she does, her throaty voice glides along my senses. "Two hours, Blake. Just two. I won't ask for anything else. I promise."

Not trusting myself to speak, I turn without a word and get into the truck. Staring straight ahead. Not moving. Hands tight on the steering wheel. Muscles uncomfortably tense. Confused. Two hours. She's asking for two hours. I don't want to give her those two hours, because to me, it seems like I'm giving her a lot more than just one hundred twenty minutes of my time.

I dig in my pocket and find the silver Zippo lighter I always carry. It's a memento, a reminder. A warning. I flip back the lid, and scrape the pad of my thumb along the thumbwheel. The rough edges dig into my skin as a flame, tall and narrow, shoots up. I tilt my head, studying the fire. It's orange and yellow with a hint of blue—a perfect upside-down teardrop. I look at it until my fingers feel the heat, snapping it shut just as Opal climbs into her side of the truck.

She pauses with a good amount of air between her behind and the seat, her eyes locked on me. "What are you doing?"

"Contemplating finding cigarettes." Or drugs. Or alcohol. It's a crutch I can't shake—this need for the things that can make oblivion descend. I'll always want them. I'll always have a decision to make. Every day I'll have a choice. I've resigned myself to this never-ending fight against my own demons.

"Oh." Opal sits down and buckles her seatbelt, setting the backpack on her lap. She turns her head and frowns at me. "Why don't you get some then? Even though they cause cancer and periodontal disease, not to mention make your clothes and breath stink."

"Well, when you put it like that…"

I shove the lighter in the front pocket of my jeans, and with a hand around the key in the ignition, twist my wrist. The engine jerks to life, and checking for oncoming traffic, I pull my most prized possession onto the highway. "I can't get any cigarettes, because as of a few weeks ago, I became the new and improved Blake who doesn't smoke cigarettes. I have to say, he can be a dick at times."

She doesn't reply.

"I guess I was that even before I stopped smoking," I add in an afterthought.

A snort fills the cab. "Why did you decide to quit?"

"I was starting to enjoy life and needed an excuse to be miserable."

"Why, really? And why keep a lighter when you don't smoke?"

"I'm a pyromaniac."

"Sure. Me too."

I clench the steering wheel. "You're asking me to tell you something about myself when you haven't told me anything about you."

Once again, Opal doesn't respond.

To fill the silence, I turn on the radio and find an oldies station.

"Get carrots."

My eyes shoot to her and back to the road. "What?"

Opal twists her body until she is partially facing me. The force of her gaze hollows out a bit of my soul. "Carrots. You need something to keep you busy so you aren't thinking about smoking. Chew on carrots when you want a cigarette. It works. My ex-b—someone I used to know wanted to quit smoking, and they tried that. It helped them. Well, until they didn't want to quit smoking anymore."

Her ex. It's no surprise she has an ex-boyfriend. Who doesn't have an ex from some point in their past? I have my share of exes. What tweaks my attention is that she doesn't want me to know she has an ex-boyfriend. This strikes me as odd and niggles at my brain. Why does it matter to her whether or not I know?

Her arm shoots out, and the next thing I know, we're listening to rap, or some other form of noise, that is supposedly considered music. Glaring, I switch it back to the oldies station. "Don't touch the radio."

Opal scowls and it's back to men singing about welcoming people to their house with champagne and playing too-loud music.

"You like this crap?" I'm offended on the behalf of sensitive ears worldwide.

"It has a good beat. And it's better than the oldies crap you just had on."

I push a button and it's on oldies again.

Her fingers move for the radio and I slap at them. "I'm warning you, Opal."

"Two hours, Blake," she rejoins, her fingers once more outstretched. She catches me watching them and wiggles her fingers menacingly.

Eyes on the road, I take the exit to lead us to the circus mayhem. "You break this radio, and I break whatever is so precious to you inside your backpack." I wouldn't really, but she doesn't know that.

Opal crosses her arms and faces forward, her chin protruding to show her annoyance. "Fine. We'll listen to your music." In a lower voice, she mutters, "Give it enough time and I'm sure every part of this truck will break on its own anyway, along with the radio."

She doesn't want me to know what's inside the bag. Another mystery that is going to bother me until I figure it out.

"This was my grandfather's truck," I tell her, and then I wonder why. It isn't like she cares about an old man who's dead, or his truck.

"I'm sure he's glad you took it off his hands."

"He's dead."

I tried to keep all emotion from my voice as I said it, but even I caught the roughness of the words. I stare straight ahead, missing a man who told me I could do anything, be anyone, I wanted. I just had to believe in myself. I never believed him, so why would I believe in me?

Opal inhales a sharp breath and slowly releases it. "I'm sorry."

I take a left at the stop sign, my chest uncomfortably tight. "So am I—my hair part is naturally on the left side instead of the right. It makes me want to do all kinds of bad things."

She rolls her eyes again, and I can't even get irate about it this time. I deserved that eye roll. I'm a deflector; I deflect from anything that makes me feel anything I don't want, or can't handle. In that sense, Kennedy and I were the perfect, detrimental pair.

* * *

Opal

It's beautiful. There are tents, and music, and animals. People walking, children running and laughing. And the scents! Cotton candy and roasted peanuts and funnel cakes. My nose is in heaven, and my mouth is in hell. I want to taste them all, gorge myself on sweets and salts until I can't walk and Blake has to roll me back to the truck.

I skip alongside Blake, my hands holding the straps of my backpack that rests over my shoulders. The soles of my feet hurt from being trapped within the tight black boots for days, but even that doesn't matter. The sun's rays make my clothes unpleasantly snug to my skin, and I fear my deodorant might decide to give up on me. It doesn't deter me in any way. So I'll stink, and be content in my smelliness. Bonus points if Blake is offended. A smile stretches my lips.

Radley Family Circus is set up in the country, and the ground is green and flat with trees nearby but out of reach. The sky is blue and cloudless. Blake bought the tickets. My thank-you was mumbled, but at least I got it out. We both know I won't pay him back. I can't. Someday, but not today. I glance at him, taking in the thin-lipped and narrowed-eyed expression taking up occupancy on his face. He's not happy about being here. Although, I wonder if he's ever really *happy*.

"I'll meet you by the entrance in two hours," I tell him. I'll have more fun experiencing my first circus without him stomping and scowling next to me. Besides, I need to get some money, and I can't do that with him hovering about.

His eyebrows shoot up as he turns to me. "You're ditching me." He doesn't sound upset about it, merely surprised.

"Yes." I tighten my grip on the backpack straps and nod. "I'm ditching you and your bad attitude."

"You be at the entrance in one hour, not two, or I leave without you," he states.

My head slants to the side as I study his features. I don't believe Blake when he says he'll leave me. He's softer than he wants me to think. He could have said no to me riding with him to North Dakota. He could have watched me eat my paltry meal of toast without practically throwing his food at me. He could have left me to sleep in the truck during the cold night instead of carrying me inside the motel. He even could have taken the functioning bed and told me to sleep in the broken one, or on the floor.

He didn't do any of those things.

"What's one more hour?" I ask.

Blake snaps the distance between us like it's a twig between his fingers. One instant there's space from him to me, and the next, there's heat waving over me from a too-close male body. His face is before mine, and if I leaned forward the slightest bit and lifted my chin, our lips would meet. The realization doesn't repel me like it should.

Silver fire flashes from his eyes. "You get one hour, Opal. That is it. You won't win in this."

My mouth goes dry, and I desperately wish I had water. Either to drink or dump over my head. I admit it—Blake is sexy. He's restrained, hiding most of himself from the world, and me. He has secrets, but then, so do I. His might even be blacker than mine. I was attracted to my ex's unruly side, and in the end, it all blew up around me.

"It isn't a game; I'm not trying to win at anything." I clear my throat. "I just want to spend some time at a circus I'll probably never again have the chance to see."

Blake designated the time limit, and I'm trying to alter it. He doesn't like that. The people who have to be in control are sometimes that way because, at one time, they felt helpless. It's a self-built shield. I've seen it before, in multiple exes. I saw hints of it in my latest ex. He didn't understand that some things are not meant for others to rule over. *He probably doesn't understand your reasoning behind fleeing either.*

I shove the thought, and the apprehension that comes with it, far away—all the way back to Illinois where, hopefully, my most recent ex-boyfriend remains. Logically, there shouldn't be any way for him to come after me. Sometimes, though, I tend to be illogical. And what about the men he ran around with? Where are they?

Blake straightens. "That's all, huh? You're just reliving some childhood fantasy, right?" His tone is skeptical.

My heartbeat slows as he steps back. How is it possible that just from him standing close to me, I forget how to properly breathe and my heart rate goes haywire? This is bad, but the good news is that, after a few more hours, I will never see him again. I should be happy about that.

I think of what a sad child should look like, and I try to imitate that, widening my eyes and sticking out my lips. Innocent, that's me. Through and through and through some more. "That's all."

That isn't all. A circus is a great place to earn some cash. People come to these kinds of places expecting to spend a lot of money. I can help them with that.

"You're so full of it," he mutters, his eyes jumping around the crowd that forms a misshapen, moving wall around us. Blake turns to me and pulls a cell phone from his back pocket, his eyes down. "Give me your phone number. I'll call you in an hour."

I scratch behind my ear, watching a girl in a ruffled dress with a yellow balloon until she disappears around a tent. "Well, I would, but I don't have a cell phone."

Blake stares at me, one eyebrow on the verge of lifting, and instead lowering back to its natural, no less intimidating, form. "I see."

I had a phone, but I left it in Illinois. I was in a hurry, but even if I hadn't been, I wouldn't have brought it. A cellular phone is the last thing I need—if my ex had access to a phone and I had mine on me, Jonesy would never leave me alone. Besides, it's an expense I can't afford, and as I meet Blake's emotionless eyes, I can tell that's where his thoughts are going. He thinks I'm destitute. Not going to lie: I'm pretty much there.

"What if there's an emergency?" is all he asks.

"You almost sound concerned."

Silver molten focuses on me, chars every nerve ending in my body. "Not concerned. Merely curious."

"Right. Curious." I rub my arms as a shiver skips along the skin. I'd like to have a picture of his eyes. They're unusually deep, like everything he's ever been is trapped inside them, waiting to be let out. All his regrets, hopes, dreams, fears. Every mistake. I could draw them all, every last one of them, from looking into his eyes enough times.

Two clowns walk by, one with red hair, the other bald. The bald one wiggles pink painted-on eyebrows at us as he passes. I stare at the pink eyebrows.

Pink.

Pinkie.

I pull my shoulders back and look at Blake. "I don't need a phone in case of emergencies. I have me, and that's all I need. I know how to kill a man with my pinkie."

There's the eyebrow lift, although it's more of a skyrocketing motion. Blake shoves the phone back in a pocket of his jeans and gives me his full attention. "I'd be interested in seeing that."

I frown and take a step back, feigning unease. "You want me to kill someone?"

"What? No." He shakes his head. "You don't know how to kill a man with your pinkie."

I nod, shoving hair from my face. In a somber tone, I say, "Let's hope you never have to find out you're wrong."

He makes a sound like he can't decide whether to be amused or annoyed. He points to the left. "See that tent over there? The big one?"

Squinting against the sun, I focus on a green and white striped tent that is wider and has a higher peak than all the rest. It's where the main attraction is held. This place is magic, the kind of magic that grips hold of a child's imagination, and allows it to spin wonder.

"Yes."

"Meet me outside of there in one hour, and we'll see about staying longer."

Excitement cascades through me, and I beam at the darkly glowering man who won't look at me. I am grateful for his compromise. I know it didn't come easily. When he continues to frown, I lightly shove his shoulder, feeling hard muscle and bone. He doesn't budge. Blake turns his stiff features on me and I instinctively put more space between us.

"Hey." I try to smile. Fail. "Thanks for...you know...the circus and everything," I say hesitantly, suddenly unsure under the intensity of his ire. For the first time, I wonder about his life. Where he's coming from, where he's going. What he does from day to day, and who is a part of that life. I know as much about him as he does me. Close to nothing.

His eyebrows lower, practically obliterating his eyes. "Enjoy the circus. I always do."

That's all the encouragement I need, purposely ignoring the double meaning. He can't mean *my* personal circus; he hasn't been around me long enough to know how crazy things can get in my world. With a wave and a bounce to my step, I head toward the fun-filled melee, calling over my shoulder, "You got it."

As I become part of the mass of people, I glance over my shoulder once. Blake is striding toward the front of the gated-off area and the exit. Even from the back, it's obvious he's agitated and in a hurry. There is a second where I feel fear and wonder if he's leaving right now. It's something I might do—less drama, no responsibility, better for the other person. In fact, isn't that what I did? I blink, the veins inside my neck tight, and then I turn with a deep exhalation. Blake isn't me. He isn't running from something. He won't leave me.

And what if he does? So what? You can fend for yourself. You've been doing it all your life.

I blink again, my confidence fortified, and study my surroundings. The trick is to act like I'm not up to something. I follow a group of kids who, even though they look about a dozen years younger than me, aren't that much shorter. A blonde glances over her shoulder at me and I widen the distance between us. There doesn't appear to be an adult with them, but none of them look old enough to drive, and we're somewhat in the middle of nowhere. They didn't walk here. This makes me think there has to be a money machine—adult—somewhere close by.

I follow them for a while, listening to them chat about clothes and movies, before determining it isn't going to get me anywhere. *Think younger. Less worldly.* One of the guys eyes me, winking when I hold his stare. His face is chubby-cheeked and devoid of facial hair. I'd be surprised if he is past fourteen. I lift an eyebrow, not lowering it until his face goes pink and he faces forward. *Think less hormonal.*

One of the group points to a pen where an elephant is walked in a circle by a harness with a rider on top. With a shout and ensuing laughter, they take off for the elephant rides. I watch them for a moment. I wonder what it's like for them to have stability, to have friends. To know their roots. I wonder if they realize how fortunate they are. I study the elephant, taking in its rough and dry gray skin, the slow gait, and wonder what it thinks about all of this.

Finding an area set apart from the chaos but close enough to be noticed, I tuck hair behind my ears and remove thick drawing paper and the last of my charcoal pencils from my backpack. There are two small green tents behind me—one for a magician and another for "strange and peculiar oddities." They'll do for bringing interest my way. I don't want to use up the last of my precious supply of drawing utensils, but I won't get anywhere if there's no product for people to see. Sighing, I study kids and adults alike, looking for suitable prey.

It doesn't take long to find a target.

It's a young girl around the age of five. Her hair is blonde and styled in silken ringlets. She has on a sky blue top and a cherry red skirt. The girl is beautiful, everything about her face symmetrical and wholesome.

She tugs on her dad's hand and begs for cotton candy as her mom looks on with exasperation on her face. Eyes fixated on her, my hand begins to create. I tune out the scorching sun as it heats my flesh, and sweat forms on my lower back and chest. Sounds fade, and all I see is the girl with the large brown eyes and bowed mouth.

A female voice, sounding distraught and directly behind me, breaks through my concentration. My hand slips as I jump, a line of gray sliding across the page. "I didn't know there was shrimp in it."

"Do you feel okay?" a deep voice replies.

"No. I've been to the toilet twice now. I don't know how I'm going to perform."

"You have to, if you want to get paid."

My hand pauses at the mention of money. I glance up and over my shoulder, noting a tall, bald man standing behind me with a petite blonde. The man is nondescript in appearance; even his outfit of blue jeans and a white T-shirt is plain. The woman has on khaki shorts and a yellow top, along with a grimace. She looks like she's in pain. His hand rests on her elbow, as if helping her to walk, or stand.

"I know." The woman sighs. Her skin is tinged gray and there are bruises beneath her eyes. She slowly turns, cringing as she moves. "Come on, we need to get ready. The show starts soon."

"You can't work like this."

Her lips thin. "Tell that to Radley."

As if my attention to them pulled his notice to me, the man moves closer, his gaze dropping to study the half-finished drawing. "Hey, look at this, Patty."

"Nothing to see here. Be on your merry way." I protectively hunch forward, trying to shield my work from their eyes. They need to go, and I need to finish my drawing before the girl and her parents disappear.

A sheen of sweat covers his bald head, making it shine. He blinks at me, and then turns to Patty, but Patty is racing in the opposite direction, most likely toward a bathroom. He frowns after her, and then focuses on me.

"You draw?" he asks.

"No." *Go away.* My eyes jump to the blond girl, anxiety pumping through my veins in place of blood. This is my chance to make some money, and I don't need this strange man ruining it with his ability to state the obvious.

"Then what's this?" One ginormous finger points to the artwork beneath my arms.

"It's nothing. I found it. You should go after your friend," I urge, speaking fast.

With one final look at the drawing and me, the giant finally turns and leaves.

I heave a sigh of relief and continue on with my work. My eyes flicker down and up, down and up, the charcoal pencil capturing the wrinkle in her brow, the shine in her eyes. A cramp forms in my fingers, protesting the sharp and jerky movements. I ignore it, relishing the act of capturing a living being within the lines of a piece of parchment. When I have enough to hook them, I jump to my feet, toss my supplies back in the bag, and speed-walk to them before I lose the trio.

I have to act like their decision means nothing, when in reality it can be the difference between me having money for food and me going without. It isn't fun, but it is necessary. I stand with my shoulders loose and my knees slightly bent. Inside, my pulse spits and rears and gallops. Outside, my pose is calm and steady. The father, on the verge of giving in to his daughter, looks like the easier conquest of the parents. I stop by him and grin my widest grin.

"Hi," I greet.

"Hello," he replies hesitantly. He has black hair with silver at the temples, a strong jaw, and is dressed in a blue polo shirt and gray shorts. His eyes shift to the woman as if asking her if it was okay for him to acknowledge me.

Reading hostility in her stance, I move my attention to the brunette and give her my most cheerful of looks. Her features would be pretty if not for the glacial look of them. "Are you enjoying the circus?" I ask her.

"I am!" the little girl pipes up, beaming at me. I'd want to draw her even if I didn't need the money.

I crouch to put my gaze level with her happy eyes. Smiling, I tell her, "That's good. Is this your first circus?"

"Uh-huh." She bounces up and down, ready to move.

"Mine too."

Her head tilts. "It is?"

"If you'll excuse us," the woman says, reaching for the girl's hand. Her eyes don't quite meet mine before sliding away. "We would like to go back to enjoying the circus."

This is going to be a hard sale. My skin flushes; my nerves spin in a haphazard dance of anxiety. I lift up the paper and show it to the brunette, praying my smile hasn't turned brittle, and that my eyes do not show the desperation I feel. "I can finish this for you for twenty dollars."

With a derisive lift to her mouth, the woman shakes her head. Her eyes, brown and jaded, don't even look at the paper. She turns to go. "No. We're not interested. Thank you."

"But, Mommy, it's me," the girl protests in a high voice. "Daddy, please?"

She pauses as the man steps closer to better see the drawing. Her tone is strident as she says, "John, come on. We need to find a seat before the show starts."

He ignores her, his eyes locked on the hand drawn image of his daughter. His gaze finds mine, a faint lift to his mouth. I see kindness in the eyes that look me over as thoroughly as they do the drawing. "You did this?"

"Yes," I say, swallowing around a dry throat.

I can't hide the grease stain near the shoulder of my shirt, or how scuffed and dingy my boots are. There is a hole in the right knee of the pants. My hair is wild and unmanageable. I look like a mess; I am a mess. The woman wouldn't look at me, but this man sees all the flaws of my appearance, and he meets my gaze.

"It's good. It's exceptional," he amends.

My shoulders shift back. When I started drawing at the age of ten, I never considered whether my creations would be good or not. I wanted to draw; I needed to draw. It was a bonus that others enjoyed my work as much as I did. I got better with practice, and wherever life took me, I made sure I had my paper and pencils with me.

"John." Her voice is a lash against the sunny day. "The show."

He glances at the woman and holds up his index finger. Looking at me, he asks, "Can you finish it in five minutes?"

"Can you?" the girl repeats hopefully, shaking off her mom's grip and skipping over to her dad. Her eyes are wide as they stare at the portrait.

I nod, my heart racing inside my chest. "You bet." I spin on my heel, find the nearest picnic table, and get to work.

The girl sits opposite me, unusually still as she watches me draw her. John and his wife stand off to the side, speaking in low voices. His silver wedding band winks at me as he runs his fingers through his hair. The sun is higher in the sky, and sweat trickles down the center of my spine. My shoulders hunch as I hear the words "con artist" and "rip off" leave the woman's mouth. Someone needs to hit her with a glitter train, put a little joy in her demeanor. I am not a con artist—well, not when it comes to this. My drawings are the most real thing about me.

"Who taught you how to do that?" the girl's tiny voice questions.

I answer without looking up. "I taught myself."

"Really? How did you get so good?"

"Practice." I wink at her and she grins, revealing a missing lower front tooth. "Lots and lots of practice."

Finishing up the outline, I go about shading and adding final touches. With a flourish, I present the image to her. "For you."

She squeals and claps her hands. "It's beautiful. Daddy, Mommy, look!"

They turn, their conversion abruptly cut off. The woman incinerates me with her eyes, but the man is smiling at his daughter.

I turn to the girl in her blue top and red skirt. "I'll give it to your parents to keep safe for you, all right?"

She nods and clambers down from the picnic table, racing for her parents. "Come see, come on," she urges, holding both their hands as she pulls them over.

As she studies the drawing, the woman's expression microscopically softens, but she doesn't say anything. She takes the drawing and her daughter's hand.

"Twenty dollars, you said?" the man asks.

I swipe a hand across my damp forehead, pushing bangs from my eyes. "You got it."

He moves to block the woman's view of us, and after a brief pause, hands me a fifty-dollar bill. "Thank you."

My mouth waters at the sight of fifty dollars. Fifty dollars is a lot to someone who doesn't have much. Lifting my eyes, I tell him softly, "I don't have change." I really don't.

A small smile claims his mouth, and I think, *That little girl is lucky to have him for a dad.* "I didn't expect change."

I quickly pocket it, holding his gaze. I kick at the ground and blink my eyes against feelings I'd rather not have. "Thanks back. Enjoy the picture, and the circus."

He nods, and taking his daughter's free hand, the family of three walks in the direction of the biggest tent. I slide my fingers in the front pocket of my pants and feel the crisp bill, unable to hide a smile. If I can find a couple more people as generous as that man, I'll be doing pretty good.

The fried bread and sugar scent of the funnel cake stand taunts me as I walk. With the addition of the fifty dollars, I have two hundred dollars to my name, and I can't afford to waste any on treats—but like that matters. I make a beeline for the stand, breathing in the tantalizing goodness that needs to get in my mouth.

I've never claimed to be all that responsible.

At the window, I order a funnel cake with powdered sugar, and a soda. I can already feel the caffeine and sugar zipping through me, making all the bad in my life go away. Junk food is magical that way.

Each hand occupied, I use my mouth to reach my first bite of funnel cake. It's perfectly chewy, warm and texturized, and tastes like the sugar heavens personally blessed it.

At one of the homes I stayed at as a kid, the woman liked to bake. I was only there a few months, but her love for all things sweet apparently rubbed off on me. From cookies to cakes to pies—every day there was a new recipe being tried out. On one such occasion, she made homemade funnel cakes. I thought they were divine, but even they cannot compare to this. I still remember how her skin was naturally flushed and she had a grin that was quick to come. She was short and round and smelled like honey. Her name was Jackie and she gave the best hugs. It was one of my better stops.

"How can you not have diabetes? I feel a diabetic coma coming on just from watching you."

I jump, causing my food to haphazardly teeter on the plastic plate. I whirl around to scowl at Blake. Damn if my eyes don't rejoice at the sight of him. My pulse picks up and I convince myself it's only because he surprised me. "You almost made me drop my funnel cake."

"Heaven forbid." He eyes the food with disdain on his face. "Is sugar a part of every meal for you?"

"It isn't for you?" I move the Styrofoam cup of soda to the crook of my elbow and use my fingers to pull off a chunk of the chewy bread and gnaw on it, purposely talking before I have it fully swallowed. "What are you doing here? I thought we were meeting at the big tent in an hour."

He shrugs. "What can I say? I missed your company."

"I'm surprised you lasted this long." I offer the funnel cake to him, and he immediately recoils. Good. I didn't want to share with him anyway. "You don't know what you're missing."

"A few things come to mind. Like, clogged arteries. Cavities. A heart attack." Blake looks at my face, and smirks.

"What?" I demand.

"Nothing."

My eyes narrow. "What? What is it?"

Although his expression is neutral and his lips are in a flat line, Blake's dark eyes dance. "You would make a great circus clown."

"Why?"

Blake moves toward me and I stiffen. His neck is directly before my eyes and I stare at the thrumming pulse, wondering what sorcery of his makes mine go so much faster from his mere proximity. A lock of ebony hair waves up from his neck, looking like black silk. I shift my eyes to his shoulder, and my stomach flips. My fingers want to caress the shape, feel its heat and strength.

Why must he be attractive? I glower at him like it's his fault. Well, it *is* his fault.

Blake's breath ruffles my hair, tickles the sensitive flesh of my earlobe, and I inhale shakily as the people around us turn into indistinct blurs.

"You have powdered sugar all over your face." He brushes his fingers across my cheek, and then over my mouth. Blake's fingers and eyes linger on my lips before they both leave, taking my breath with them.

My mouth hums with the memory of his touch, and my eyes go on a blinking spree. The air crackles with the promise of passion and regret. He puts enough space between us to be able to look down at me, and as his lightning eyes zap me in my core, yes, I consider kissing him. Heavily.

Blake's eyes darken, his hard mouth relaxes, and I feel myself sway toward him. I want to kiss him. Maybe it will be different with him. Maybe it won't be awkward and clumsy and leave me with a profound sense of disappointment, like all the other guys I've kissed. Even kissing Jonesy felt wrong, and we had close to one year of practicing to get it right.

"Wait." As reality comes back with the reminder of Jonesy, I put out the hand holding the soda to keep him from getting any closer. "I don't—I mean…we can't kiss."

His eyebrows shoot up. "Were we going to kiss?"

"Uh, um, maybe? I don't know. Were we? I don't like kissing guys," I stutter, my face burning at the confession. I really wish I hadn't just said that.

He rears back, studying me as disbelief and doubt gather in his eyes. I count to seventeen before he speaks. "Does that mean you like kissing women?"

"What?" I squawk, feeling my cheeks heat up. "No. I mean…I don't think so. I've never tried it." I chew on the straw as I wait for mortification to incinerate me whole. Why did I say that? That's just asking for problems.

His eyes take on a devilish cast and the corners of his mouth lift ever so slightly.

I release the straw and glare. "Stop thinking whatever you're thinking."

"Why? I particularly enjoy my present thoughts." When I continue to glower, he lifts his hands. "Okay. Tell me why you don't like kissing."

Shrugging, I turn my head and watch as a clown rides by on a unicycle as she juggles three red balls. I stare in fascination before remembering that I'm in the middle of a conversation with Blake. "It's just, um, it never goes well. Kissing never goes well," I specify.

He nods, looking serious. "Why doesn't it go well?"

"Well, sometimes it feels like they're going to suck off my face, and sometimes there's too much spit, or they have not so great breath, and then there's the tongue." I shudder. "I hate having tongues shoved into my mouth."

Blake's lips purse and he cocks his dark head. "Who, or what, have you been kissing?"

"I don't know. I mean, obviously, I know *what*," I add with an eye roll.

Most recently, Jonesy Laxton. Whenever I try to remember what I found appealing about him, I come up blank. I like to think it couldn't have only been the danger element. That quickly sizzled out and changed to recklessness and corruption. As soon as Paisley showed up, it was like an iceberg of accountability slammed into me, and suddenly, things that once didn't matter, did.

I make a square pattern in the grass with the toe of my boot, watching the motion. I don't know why I admit it, and to him of all people, but I hear myself saying, "Maybe it's me. Maybe I'm just a bad kisser."

It only takes him a second to reply, but it feels like ten thousand to my anxious ears. "Maybe you haven't been kissing the right guys."

"Maybe." I finish off the soda and throw it at a nearby wastebasket.

I miss.

Blake gets to the cup before me, tossing it over his shoulder and making it.

"Lucky shot."

"Everything about me is lucky," he informs me, looking wicked and delectable.

His long legs bring him back to me. Blake puts his hands in his pockets and looks me over. A thick lock of hair drops to cover one eye, altering his features from edged intrigue to lethal beauty. Something dark and tumultuous studies me from the center of his eyes.

I gesture to him. "I mean, look at you. You look like the kind of guy who would be able to kiss. But what if you can't? What if you're a really sucky kisser? What if you have garlic breath, and your mouth is full of spit, and you try to eat my face?"

His eyes narrow. "Maybe you should let me kiss you and find out."

My body is all for it, practically pulling me toward him. Men have always been trouble for me, and I intuitively know it would be double that with this one.

But what would one little kiss hurt?

I stare into his dark eyes.

Just one.

"Maybe I'll take you up on that," I whisper, my eyes dropping to his mouth as I take a bite of funnel cake. If my mouth is full of something, chances are we won't kiss. Even though I'm curious about the feel and taste of his lips, I'm not ready for that. The tingling of my lips calls me a liar.

Blake's eyes darken.

"Someday," I add after swallowing.

A horn sounds, splitting my eardrums, and I drop the plate of funnel cake with a loudly executed curse. The moment is over; whatever spell had us trapped is gone. The noise level picks up, and swarms of little bodies, and more reluctantly following larger ones, head for the big tent. I look from the tent to the remnants of my funnel cake, wanting to watch the show and needing to rescue my food. I tilt my head and observe the abused funnel cake. It looks sad, neglected.

It looks like it should be in my mouth.

Maybe it's still okay to eat. I move for it.

"Don't even think about it."

"I was only going to throw it away," I fib, gathering up the dirt and grass-covered fried bread. Dismay fills me at the waste of good food, the weight of it lowering my shoulders. I use my finger to flick off a small pile of dirt from the food.

"Sure you were." Blake tries to take it from me, and I resist, smashing it to my chest. I admit, I didn't think that motion through. Giving me a look, he tugs at the plate. "Opal. Give it up. You can't eat that. You'll get worms or something."

I cast him a dubious look. "Worms?"

"Or something," he emphasizes.

With a sigh, I let it go, allowing Blake to throw it away.

"It could have been salvaged," I grumble, brushing white dust from my chest and stomach before licking the last of powdered sugar from my fingers. Something crunches between my teeth, and it tastes like dirt.

"Some things can't be salvaged," he says all matter-of-factly as he faces me, sounding ridiculous. Something freezes him in place, and he stares. I realize it's me—not trying to be seductive in any way, and yet, somehow pulling it off. His eyes drop to my mouth and his nostrils flare, turning him from brooding mayhem to consuming desire.

I slowly pull my finger from my mouth, nervous under the intensity with which he watches me. A groan, faint and low, sounds from deep in his chest, and my skin prickles. Liquid heat swims through me and makes me ache for him. As our senses collide to examine something new, and discover something wanted, I come to the conclusion that it's too late. I'm already gone.

Doesn't matter. I don't accept it.

The sensible thing for me to do is run—because that's what sensible adults do in tough situations, and I am a sensible adult—so I do. I take off for the tent, not caring how infantile I look. If I don't run away, I'll let Blake kiss me, or worse, I'll kiss him.

I slam into a chest that feels more like a wall, and stumbling back, am halted by strong hands on my arms. I blink and look up, noting a man of huge proportions with a bald head. It's the guy who interrupted my creating process—the one with the blond woman who ate shrimp and got sick.

"We need you," is all he says to me before dragging me behind the tent.

4

Blake

I watch Opal disappear among the throng of children. Nothing snuffs out the spark faster than a runaway damsel. I scratch the side of my head, unable to remember the last time a woman has physically fled from my company. And then I ask myself what the hell I'm thinking, and feeling, and I tell myself to stop. Stop it all.

I'm such an idiot.

Because in spite of knowing better, in spite of knowing this can't go anywhere, and that I have to be a fool to further get involved with Opal, I really, really want to be the guy to get her to enjoy kissing.

Resigned to spend another hour at a circus that makes me want to jump out of my own skin, I aimlessly walk around the grounds for a good ten minutes before heading back to the main tent. Grimacing at the horde of people also heading that way, I slowly make my way toward the multi-colored mass of circus goers lined up outside the tent. The first hour here was spent on my back in the box of the truck, staring up at a sky in hopes of having some kind of life-changing epiphany. All I got was bird poop landing dangerously close to my face. Which fits.

My grandpa John was the one who took me to the circus when I was a kid. First and last time I ever went—until now. I wish I could have appreciated the time spent with him. I wish I could have looked at the experience from adult eyes instead of my kid ones. I was bored, unimpressed. A brat. But I was eleven; what did I know? I thought I had all the time in the world with him. I really only had four more years.

I was angry when he left—at him, at myself, at life.

I jerk my head against the memories, effectively pushing them aside. The line to the tent is steadily moving along, and soon I find myself at the doorway to hell in the form of bright colors, raucous laughter, and creepy-happy music.

I must pause too long; an eager kid behind me pushes at my back, jostling me forward as he exclaims over a pair of white horses with tiny, shiny red hats on their heads. I slowly turn my head to the side and drop my gaze to him. I don't have to do anything but look at him and the boy's eyes go wide and he backs up into his mom. I just have that face—the kind of face that looks angry even when I'm not. Usually, I don't mind. Sometimes, like now, I do.

"He's just excited," the woman explains, her hands protectively moving to the boy's shoulders.

Lately I've been reevaluating my decision to get a degree in child psychology. How am I supposed to help kids when they're all scared of me? I look at them and they practically pee themselves, like this kid. I'm reevaluating everything, including returning to college and going to Australia. But, I have a passport, and I bought a ticket. I'm due to leave in two weeks. It would be stupid to not go. I nod and face forward, my hands clenched at my sides. The stiffness in my hands grows to my arms, and my neck. And visiting my dad—that one I reevaluate from hour to hour.

Pulling back my shoulders and working hard at keeping my expression blank from the turmoil of my mind, I enter the darkened arena. Bleachers, overfilled with chattering kids of all sizes and adults, frame the circular structure. In the middle is a cordoned ring with the man from the billboard standing at the center of it. An unnaturally wide grin lines his tan face, and he nods and waves as people pass.

Everything is meant to appear grand and luxurious, but I notice the tightness of the jacket on the man's stomach when he isn't sucking in his gut, and how his pants could be an inch longer. Slivers of light come in through slits and holes in the tent, and the material looks old and worn. The horses seem gaunt; the caged monkey appears lethargic. And the clown who walks by doesn't look much older than sixteen, his eyes tripping to mine and away. The circus is hurting, and for anyone deigning to take a look, it shows.

"Welcome to the thirty-third year of Radley Family Circus! I am Ringmaster Radley, the owner of Radley Family Circus, and your host for this spectacular event where magic comes to life and unforgettable memories are created!" a voice booms.

A cheer rings out and countless hands applaud, tripling the volume of noise. I don't know if I can take another hour of this. I don't necessarily hate people; I just don't like being around them all that much. I search the crowd for a familiar head of messy reddish-brown hair and a curvy, compact body dressed in black and red with a pink backpack.

How could she have so absolutely vanished? Part of me wants to leave—forget everything about her and our brief association. The other part, the part I wish wasn't there, won't let me.

"We ask that you find a seat at this time, and remain seated throughout the show—unless asked to volunteer. And now, let's begin!" The ringmaster pauses. "First up is Henrietta and Horatio Gonzales, our brother and sister duo who astound thousands each year with their tightrope walking. They've been with Radley Family Circus for ten years now. Please, we ask for your silence during their performance."

I turn in a slow circle, scanning the occupants. "Where the hell are you, Opal?" I mutter.

"Please sit down, sir. The show is starting," a gray-haired and mustached man in black slacks and a sweat-stained white shirt tells me, motioning to an empty spot on the first row of bleachers.

The laminated nametag hung from a cord around his neck states his name as Bill and that he's circus security. I smirk. Circus security. That sounds threatening. I glance down to see if he has a water gun in a holster at his hip.

"*Sir.*" He gives me a pointed look.

"Yeah. Sure. I'm sitting." I lift my hands to show I'm complacent, and move to the nearest unoccupied spot.

The bench is hard, and I know I can expect a sore ass and back in the near future. The lady beside me enthusiastically devours a bag of popcorn in a way that would normally repel me, but because I can envision Opal doing the same, makes me want to smile. I don't. Instead I turn my gaze to the tightrope-walking duo, and prepare to get lost in boredom.

At the sound of applause, I realize the act is done. I straighten, half-heartedly clapping as my eyes dart around in pursuit of Opal. If I don't find her in the next ten minutes, I'm going to lose my shit.

"Next up is Obnoxious Georgie the Clown and Esther the Cartoonist Clown. Watch in amazement and hilarity as Georgie tries to trip up Esther with water balloons as she draws. If you're chosen to be drawn, you can purchase a self-portrait for thirty dollars after the show."

I cross my arms and let my head fall back, searching for tolerance at the peak of the tent.

To the animated cheers of the crowd, an abnormally tall and thin clown gallops to the center of the tent. He's bald, his skin painted white with yellow stars around his eyes, and he's dressed in too-short pants and a purple shirt. He turns in a circle and waves, reaching into a bucket hanging from his arm.

Without looking, his arm shoots out to the side and a red water balloon is airborne, smacking a short clown in a curly blond wig on the side of the head. Only her face is painted, and it's blue with pink hearts. An oversized red dress with a zebra-printed belt is her outfit. She must be Esther the Cartoonist. Laughter erupts from the audience as she slams her hands on her hips and scowls at the giant of a clown.

I straighten, my interest caught by the small being. Something about her seems familiar.

The balloon didn't burst, and with quick movements it's picked up by the short clown and sent flying back at Georgie. It hits his butt and water explodes. He whirls around, the crowd bursting with hilarity as he stomps his feet and waves his arms up and down. Esther takes one look at Georgie and sprints toward the opposite end of the tent, her back facing me as she goes.

Her back with a pink backpack on it.

I shoot to my feet without realizing it, unconsciously walking a few steps toward her before someone yells at me to sit down. I hit the bench hard, staring in bemusement at Opal. What the hell is she doing? Why is she doing it? The questions jumble up in my brain as I watch the spectacle unfold.

She shakes a finger at someone in the crowd, her eyes continually darting to Georgie as he fumbles to retrieve another water balloon. The balloons appear to be slippery; every time he gets one, he drops it. Nodding, Opal-Esther motions to a gangly boy in the bleachers and he steps forward, looking equally worried and eager. She grabs his wrist and pulls him closer, pointing at him as if telling him to not move. He nods, silently agreeing. The female clown pats him on the head and darts toward a desk and chair, jumping over a water balloon as it heads for her legs.

Then she picks it up, and, looking at Georgie, breaks it over her own head. Water cascades down her face as she gives the taller clown a smirk. The kids love that, calling out to her with encouragement and glee. I rest my chin in my hand, hiding a smile behind my fingers.

When she reaches the desk, she sits down on the chair and pulls something from the backpack. I crane my neck and angle my head to the right, catching sight of what looks like paper. Concentration wrinkling her features, her eyes move from the clown to the boy to the paper as she draws, her legs bouncing under the table where she sits.

The tent is hushed with expectant silence, and a tendril of wonder unravels inside me. Opal is doing this. She has over a hundred people captivated. A smile lights up her face and she looks up, giving the bleachers a thumbs-up sign as she stands with the paper in hand.

"Behind you!" someone shouts, and Esther the Cartoonist spins around.

Obnoxious Georgie has a water balloon in each hand, and a wave of boos sound as he ambles closer. Esther shows him the drawing, and his head tilts to the side. She gestures over her shoulder to the boy, and with a resigned nod, Georgie steps back. Esther runs to the chocolate-toned boy and shows him the drawing. Oohs and ahs ripple through the people who can see the drawing. I don't know if I've ever seen a kid look quite that ecstatic at the sight of a picture, and when Opal hands him a blue ticket, the boy hugs it like it is the drawing itself.

Another person—a teenage girl with red hair and crutches—is chosen from the crowd, and similar good-natured fun ensues.

And then Opal finds me, her focus fixated on my face. I couldn't look away if I tried. I realize as she walks toward me that she knew where I was the whole time. Her eyes glitter like gold, and she picks at the loose fabric of the dress, shrugging as our eyes meet. She offers a hand and a smile, and I take both. I know it's impossible, but it feels like tiny shocks tremor up my fingers to my hand and up my arm, ending at my heart. Her skin is hot and damp, and when she gently tugs her hand from mine, I don't want to let it go. I follow her to the desk, and she shakes her head when she notices, pointing to the other side of the ring.

Widening my legs, I cross my arms and stay put. I shake my head back. Chuckles and giggles sound from behind.

Opal steps closer, and when she winks at me with her blue and pink-painted face, my nerves constrict, pulse. Come alive. I take a shallow breath. Using exaggerated force, she pushes at my shoulder, making it look like she's putting all her weight into it. Her cheek is close to my shoulder, and I unconsciously lower my head to breathe her in. Coconuts. Even now she smells like coconuts. Opal goes still for one second that lasts twenty, her breaths caught by mine.

I'm going to kiss her, I determine with absolute certainty. Not now, but soon. Whether or not I think I should, I am.

Swallowing, she jumps back and lifts her arms toward the sky, her vexation plain to see. I have no idea what happened to Georgie, and I don't care—until he shows up behind Opal with a finger lifted to his mouth.

I grab her arm and pull her behind me, and suddenly I'm getting doused with a water balloon. Water splashes down my head and face, into my eyes, and wets the top part of my shirt. The clown's eyes go wide, his hands clapped to his mouth as he drops to his knees before me in silent apology, and the audience loses it. I look up at them, and shrug, eliciting another round of whoops and shouts.

Not one to like attention, it surprises me how much I am *not* bothered by this.

Opal swings me around to face her and pulls out a blank sheet of paper and a drawing pencil from her backpack. I stare back, fighting a smile as I wipe water from my eyes. When she starts drawing, I forget where we are, and what we're doing. Lines become an outline of my face; strokes of black turn into eyebrows, a hard jaw, a fierce nose. Her hand moves fast and strong as she creates hair. It's uncanny how much it looks like me, but better.

As I watch her, I think of my grandpa, and how much he'd enjoy seeing this. How much I wish he was here with me. How much he'd like Opal. And then I think of my dad, and how he would crush her light like it was a bug beneath his polished black shoe.

Opal stands, grinning widely as she produces an image of me that I don't recognize, though it is obviously me. She hands me a ticket and nods for me to go, her hand lingering around mine as she whispers, "I'll meet you out back."

Numb with thoughts and feelings I don't understand, I absently nod and slowly make my way outside the ring. My legs give out and I land on the bleacher, the blue ticket smashed within the palm of my hand. I open my hand and stare at the numbers on it until they blur. Someone pats me on the shoulder, telling me I did great. I nod without checking to see who it is.

An alarm sounds, and Ringmaster Radley jogs out to the center of the ring. He looks out of breath before he reaches it. He speaks into the mouthpiece of a slim microphone. "Obnoxious Georgie the Clown and Esther the Cartoonist have stolen the show, but now it's time to take it back! Can we show some appreciation for the pair, and their fabulous volunteers?"

The noise level turns deafening, and the ringmaster asks that any ticket holders go around to the outside of the tent to pick up their drawings. Obnoxious Georgie takes Opal's hand and the pair bows for the uproarious mob. They hop and skip toward the back of the tent where an opening to outside waits for them. Just before they pass through it, Opal pulls a water balloon out from the top of her dress and smashes it against the clown's head, disappearing through the slit fabric to the sound of laughter.

Not waiting more than a few minutes, I go in search of Opal. The humidity in the air, coupled with the sun at the top of the sky, annihilates any chance of going without a shower later on. Opal stands near a chair with her back to me, Georgie sprawled out on the ground close by. She chugs water from a bottle before quickly tugging off the dress and blonde wig and setting them on a chair, revealing her black top and red pants.

As I approach, Obnoxious Georgie the Clown wipes a brown cloth across his brow and says, "You did great out there—better than the real Esther. But don't tell anyone I said that."

"My lips are sealed." She mimics zipping her lips with an invisible key. "I hope she feels better soon."

I hang back, wanting to see Opal in motion without her being aware. I am not above spying.

"Yeah. I guess she's allergic to shrimp, and she didn't know it was in the lunch we ordered out. We're just glad you agreed to fill in."

"You didn't give me much choice," she mutters, and I frown.

Georgie shrugs. "We were desperate. Sure you aren't looking for a seasonal job?"

"I'm sure." Opal puts her hands in the front pockets of her pants and levels her gaze on Georgie. Her pose is casual, but her voice is strained. He might not catch it, but I do. "I have to get going. How soon until I get paid?"

"Mr. Radley should be around any minute now."

She nods, tapping a foot as she looks around. A good chunk of the people are inside the tent, but there is still a small crowd outside, and more meandering in and out of other smaller tents. I'm about to make my presence known when the boy she first drew appears with a shy smile. He's alone, a hand fisted around crumpled money.

"Hey, you," Opal greets, moving closer.

"H-hi," he answers, looking down and away. He opens his hand. "I o-only have fifteen dollars. Is—is that o-okay?"

Opal looks behind him before refocusing on him. "Where are your parents?"

"My a-aunt brought me, but…she d-doesn't have any extra m-money."

Without responding, Opal turns, noticing me for the first time. Our eyes lock, hers full of secrets, and then she retrieves the drawn portrait. She hands it to the boy. "A gift then."

"R-really?" His brown eyes enlarge as he carefully holds the picture.

"Uh, Rachel," the clown says as he stands.

Rachel. I don't try to hide the smirk I feel coming on.

Opal shushes him with a single look. "It's fine." Turning back to the boy, she shoos him. "Go on. Take your picture before I change my mind."

"Mr. Radley—" the giant begins once the boy has left.

"Can take his percentage out of the money he owes me," she smoothly interjects. "Will you find him, please? My ride and I need to get going."

Georgie's eyes follow the direction of hers, and I wave my fingers at him. His eyes narrow. "You two are together?"

I turn to Opal and tilt my head thoughtfully. "Are we together?"

Her skin flushes and she tries to smile, but it's splintered. She looks at the clown. "Get your boss, please."

"Yeah. Okay. I'll see if he's available." He casts one last look our way before striding around the side of the tent.

"Do you trust them?"

Opal turns to me. "No. But I don't trust anyone."

"Smart," I remark. "I definitely wouldn't trust me."

Smudges of blue paint linger on her cheeks. "Why's that?"

A handful of reasons come to mind, and there all negative characterizations of me—all things my father has called me over the years. He's not the only one. With enough time, his voice somehow morphed into mine. I hear every vile thing I am, or have ever been, with my own voice inside my head.

Killer.

Alcoholic.

Drug addict.

Suicidal.

Depressed.

Worthless.

The red-haired teenager shows up in Georgie's absence, her gait slow and awkward with the crutches. Her appearance saves me from answering. Not that I was going to. A man with receding blond hair and glasses follows with a hand hovering near her elbow. Opal asks her about the crutches, finding out she broke a leg while playing soccer. She tells the girl she's never played soccer before, but that it sounds rough, and the girl smiles.

What the hell kind of a childhood did Opal have? I thought mine was bad. At least I got to experience things. If she's telling the truth, her offhand comments make it seem as if she was locked up and kept hidden away from society. *Not your problem, not your concern.*

Opal does the same for the girl as she did for the boy, and when Mr. Radley shows up with Georgie in tow, she announces what is owed her, minus the royalties from the drawings. I think he's going to argue, his lined and synthetically browned face taking on a calculating edge. I step directly behind Opal and stare death at him.

He blanches, looking from me to Opal with a weak smile. "Thanks for your help in there," he says to her, counting out the money before passing it to her.

I pull money from my pocket and slap it into the man's palm. "That's for mine. Ready...Rachel?"

"You bet!" With the drawing of me in one hand, Opal threads the fingers of her free one through mine and yanks us away from the ringmaster and his clown. Her skin is roughened by calluses and has a sandpaper feel.

"Had enough of Radley Family Circus?" I murmur as she charges in the direction of the exit.

"Mmm-hmm."

I look at her, and then down at our locked fingers, and I disentangle them. I flex my hands, trying to get the tingling feel of hers from them. "What was that all about anyway?"

"What?"

"Esther the Cartoonist," I boom in an exaggerated imitation of the ringmaster.

"The big clown saw me drawing a picture, and his sidekick was sick. He brought me to Radley, who asked me to fill in for her. He said he'd pay me three hundred dollars cash."

"And you were okay with it? How'd you know what to do out there?"

She twists a lock of hair around her finger, a satisfied look on her face. "Yep. The promise of money helped. And I don't know; I just acted how I thought a clown should."

"But you didn't get three hundred dollars, did you?" I ask, already knowing the answer.

Her lips purse and she shakes her head. "No. But it doesn't matter. Those kids will value the pictures more than I will the money I would have gotten for them."

I swallow with difficulty. "What you did for them was nice," I admit.

She shrugs one shoulder, looking uncomfortable. "It isn't like I didn't want to take their money. I did."

"I was waiting for you to use your pinkie-death skills on the ringmaster."

Opal's lips curve. "I thought about it, but then I wouldn't have gotten paid."

We step through the exit, and I breathe easier.

"What do you see when you look around this place?" I ask as we walk to the truck. Directly under the rays of the sun, it doesn't take long for my hair and shirt to dry.

Her eyes shine as she takes a shallow breath. "Magnificent beasts and talented men and women. Dreams. Wonder. History. Delicious foods. Things every kid should experience, at least once."

"You don't see—" My words trail off when she looks at me, and I realize, no, she doesn't see any of the imperfections I do. And I like that about her. Even liking one thing about her is too many, and I'm past that, but there you have it.

"What?" Opal questions.

"Nothing," I tell her. I jiggle the keys in my hand, looking at her as we reach the truck. "I had fun."

She runs fingers through her chaotic hair. "I did too. We'll have to do it again." Her eyes dance mischievously.

Unlocking her door, I shake my head. "No. We won't."

Her laughter follows me around to my side of the truck.

* * *

Opal

With a crack of thunder, rain—violent and vengeful—crashes down upon the earth. I'm not surprised; the skies have been darkening and clouding over for a while now. The outside air turned humid to the point where leaving the windows rolled down wasn't an option. The raindrops are fast and hard, sheets of malleable glass against the windshield. They obscure the road and turn everything around us into murky shapes. Block out the radio. I can smell the scent of cold rain through unseen crevices of the truck, feel the force of the wind as it pushes at the old Ford. Lightning flickers across the black sky in uneven lines of white.

"I'm going to pull over until it lets up some. There's a place I know a few miles from here. We can hang out there until the storm passes," Blake says, squinting at the road with his neck popped out and his shoulders raised. He looks like a sullen turtle.

"A place you know?" I finish recounting my cash and shove it back in the bag. I have over four hundred dollars. This puts flagging optimism back in line.

"Yeah." His eyes flicker to me and back to the road. Blake's fingers are tight on the steering wheel. "A place I know."

"How long until we're to wherever you're going in North Dakota?"

Blake's destination, and the starting point of my next adventure, with a slight detour in Montana first. Funny, but I'm not as excited about it as

I was a day ago. It's the dreary weather messing with my head, that's all. No one can be too happy about anything in the middle of a thunderstorm, right? It has nothing to do with guilt leading me onward, or fear pushing at my back. It's just the weather.

"Depends on when the weather decides to be nice, and it's Bismarck."

"What's in Bismarck?"

I don't think he's going to answer. It's clear he doesn't *want* to answer. Tension fills the cab, swirls around us with suffocating discord, and I think about telling him to get out so I don't have to feel the pressure of his unease anymore—even if it is his truck.

He takes a deep breath, and another. It looks like it's hard for Blake to breathe, and even though I don't know how it's possible, I swear his skin turns paler.

"Never m—"

"My parents," he bites off, eyes riveted to the road.

A couple dozen minutes pass before Blake slows down the truck, taking the next right. I focus my attention elsewhere, giving him the silence, if not the space, he needs. I see a rectangular road sign but can't read it under the shield of rain. Tires collide with gravel and the truck weaves once, straightening out as rocks ping against the underside of the vehicle.

It appears Blake has a strained relationship with his parents. I guess I'm not really surprised. I am surprised, though, that I'm curious as to why. I scowl at the wet scene beyond the truck, writing my name on the fogged-up window. Patches of clarity among the storm show wire fence lining the gravel road, and rolling hills shadowed with gray. The road is narrow, and in the distance, a large white house stands at the end of it. We're on a private driveway, I realize.

"Who owns this place you know?" I ask suspiciously when Blake parks the truck near a white shed bigger than a lot of houses I've seen.

Blake doesn't answer, grabbing his duffel bag and the grocery bag from the store we made a quick stop at after the circus, from the seat. He looks at me with his hand posed on the door handle.

It's another minute before he says, "You coming?"

He doesn't wait for a response, or to see if I'm coming, slamming the door behind him. I watch his tall form make its way to the house, and after a brief pause, up the steps to the wraparound porch. I rub a circle onto the dewy window, pressing my forehead to the cool surface as I watch Blake unlock the door. He doesn't look back to see if I'm following, the door shutting behind him with finality.

I slump back against the seat and chew on a thumbnail. Chances are, no harm will come to me if I go inside that house with him. I mean, it isn't like Blake produced the storm to get me here. And it isn't like we haven't already spent the night together. Of course, that was in a semi-public place, and this house is surrounded by countryside.

He has keys. He knows who lives here. He must know the owners, and trust them well enough. But what if Blake isn't the only one inside the house? Although unlikely, what if something about me leaked to the news, and whoever is inside recognizes my face? What if—

A knock on the window propels my body upright and drags a loud and shrill scream from my lungs. I whip my head to the side and glare at a rain-drenched Blake. "Stop doing that!"

Humor is evident in the tipped up corners of his mouth. "What are you doing?" Blake asks, his voice muffled by rain and window.

"Meditating," I mumble as I shrug my arms through the straps of the backpack.

I meet his gaze through the window and gesture for him to back up. And then I vault from the truck, landing in muddied water that sprays up to coat my legs, and even some of it being brave enough to land on my face. I gasp and shove hair from my eyes. I'm instantly wet, and with panic in my chest, I race for the porch, removing my backpack and flinging it toward the door.

I face Blake. Rivulets of rain trail down his face, and his black hair is plastered to his scalp. It makes his cheekbones sharper, makes the hardness of his face stand out more. Makes my stomach dip and sway. The shirt he has on might as well not be there, images of his bare chest and back from this morning teasing me. Was it only this morning? It seems like a lifetime ago.

"Come on, let's go inside. We're both soaked," he says, jerking his chin toward the house.

With my racing pulse and my tumultuous heartbeat, I shake my head. The rain sounds like a symphony produced by nature, and it's refreshingly cold. Clothes and body soaked, I enjoy it. When did I last stand in the rain? Just stand and take it in, and not worry about being wet? When was the last time I let freedom rule me instead of a person, or a designated role, or myself?

"I'll feed you," he bribes, and I smile. "You're going to get struck by lightning." Blake's voice is impatient.

I tip my face back, close my eyes, and let the rain wash over me. "It isn't lightning right now."

"Opal. What are you doing?" He doesn't sound irritated, but like he's trying to figure me out, like he genuinely wants to know what I'm thinking and feeling. It's rare, and new.

Who cared about me in my former life, really cared about *me*? A girl named Paisley. I spin around and stare at the scene painted in silver and charcoal. I blink my eyes, sure I see a pond beyond the house and to the right. A copse of trees near it sways with the wind, motioning for me to join them. I tried to do right by her, but in the end, I don't know that I really helped Paisley. I blink some more, this time fearing there are tears among the raindrops, and I run.

I throw my arms up, laughing and whooping as I go. The ground is rutted, and it squishes down as my boots meet it. When I get to trees, out of breath and pulsing with exhilaration, I kick off my boots and roll my socks from my feet.

"How deep is the pond?" I call behind me, knowing Blake is nearby. I feel his essence, a flame of life that burns.

"Ten feet, manmade, no fish," he answers quietly.

I look over my shoulder, surprised by the hint of sadness in his tone. "Where are we, Blake?"

He looks to the side. Thunder rolls along the sky. The whiteness of his flesh seems to glow in the overcast afternoon. When he meets my gaze, cynicism glows from his dark eyes. "Where do you want to be?"

I shift my gaze to the darkened house, its exterior blindingly white against the backdrop of a mischievous Mother Nature. "Is anyone else here?"

"No one but us. Does that worry you?" he says faintly, mockingly.

"Do I look worried?"

Before I can change my mind, I tug off my shirt and shimmy out of my pants, leaving them in a sodden pile near my boots. I hear Blake's intake of air, and clad in only a bra and underwear, I look at the rippling water to keep from looking at him. "Where I want to be is in the pond, in the rain."

And that's where I go, barreling through the icy water and dropping down into its dark depths. Eyes closed, I move my limbs just enough to keep myself submerged, and I let my mind go blank. It's peaceful. Quiet. Shivers hold me in their embrace, chilling my skin and chattering my teeth. When I can no longer hold my breath, I shoot up, feeling like a mythical mermaid or some other sea creature. Ariel—I wouldn't mind being Ariel for a day or two. I sputter and laugh as I tread water, the combination an odd sound.

Wiping water from my eyes, I look toward where I last saw Blake, but he's gone. A frown tugs at my mouth. Not that I expected him to watch me frolic in the water, but he could have waited to see whether or not I could swim. I spent one summer—my tenth—with Rachel Hathaway, and during it she gave me the option of helping her clean rooms at the motel she co-managed or to go to the pool one block over. Swimming became one of my favorite hobbies.

A twig cracks, and I turn toward the sound. Blake kneels beside the edge of the pond, his eyes locked on me as he spins a chunk of wood between his fingers. The rain drops onto my skin, warmer than the water I'm surrounded by.

"Are you…just g-going t-to stand there and—and watch…me?" I question around the shaking of my teeth and body. I push water around with my arms, my legs kicking to keep my neck and head above water.

"Nah. I just wanted to make sure you weren't going to drown."

"You do c-care," I tease.

"It's more that I don't want to have to explain the circumstances of your death to anyone. Telling people you decided to take a swim in the middle of a thunderstorm might sound…plausible. Enjoy your swim." He straightens and heads toward the house, looking dry and unruffled, though he is almost as wet as me.

Regardless of the fact that he is far out of reaching distance, I splash water at his retreating form. Thunder starts, low and ominous, gathering volume as it goes. I shiver and look around me, seeing an August afternoon overrun by the elements. It's funny how we humans think we're in control, but a look at our weather says otherwise.

I cock my head at a faint sound, my eyes searching the nearby dark. It sounded like a baby, or a cat. I'm shooting for a cat. My eyes shift over the faint outline of a tree, immediately returning to it as I catch a glow of something. Eyes—yellow eyes. A frown crumples my forehead when my gaze locks with a feline's, and a hiss fills the air.

"Nice kitty," I whisper, even though it doesn't really sound like a nice kitty.

With a low growl, an indistinct, dark shape sprints across the grass, disappearing into the black.

I stare after it for a while, telling myself *I* wasn't what spooked the cat, and that it's most likely harmless. Most likely.

The wind picks up, rustling limbs and leaves. Knowing I don't have much time before the weather escalates once more, I swim the length of the pond and back before turning my attention to the house. It is now lit up from within, and lightning spirals overhead as I watch, as if warning me of its intent.

"Time to go in, Opal," I mutter to myself.

I swim until I can touch the bottom, dropping down my legs as I find the ground with my toes. It's slimy and thick, mud squeezing between my toes as I reach the end of the pond. I pull myself out, slipping in the wet grass as I stand on tired legs. The cool wind attacks my skin, creating paths of goose bumps. I search for my pants and shirt in the gloomy atmosphere, catching a flash of red in the dark.

The wind turns gusting, pushing and pulling at me as I walk. The rain slants, needling my skin with its ferocity. I'm almost to my clothes when the world rips apart, tossing the garments away like they're inconsequential. A sound of disbelief leaves me, a little squeak of surprise, and then I take off after them. The shirt and pants separate, one going to the left toward the pond, the other toward a fence. I curse as I take off after the shirt, hoping to catch it before it lands in the pond. The swear word is slammed back at me, unheard in the roaring wind.

I dive for the shirt as it pauses in its maddening dance and trip over a fallen tree limb. My entire front side, including my face, lands on the soft earth. Mud and water close off my airways, smelling and tasting of worms, muck, and rainwater.

Getting to my feet, I resignedly make a grab for the shirt, coming away with a black top devoured by filth. I find my pants splayed across the fence, mocking me. Muttering to myself, I rip them off the fence, hearing a tear that makes my face burn. With a limp and an armful of destroyed clothing and sodden boots, I slowly make my way to the house.

This storm has literally kicked my ass, and I have to laugh. What else is there to do? Mother Nature unapologetically showed me who is boss.

Blake steps out from the shadows of the porch as I approach, looking caught between amusement and worry. He moves to the edge of the single step that stands between the porch and the grass. The hand holding a towel goes limp, falls to his side. He stares at me for a while, blinks, and then asks in an annoyingly pleasant voice, "What the hell happened to you?"

"The wind took my clothes."

"And did you get the wind back by face planting in the ground?"

"No. I tripped and fell." I reach for the towel and he moves it back toward him. My eyes turn hot with annoyance. I'm sure the dirt in them doesn't help. "What are you doing?"

A calculating mask falls over his features, adding a dangerous spark to his eyes. "I shouldn't look down. Right? A nice guy wouldn't look down."

"You're right." Thunder vibrates the skies, as if agreeing with me. I'm not entirely turned off by the idea of him perusing my body, and anyway, it isn't like he can actually see any of my skin. It's all frosted lumps and bumps of brown goo. "They wouldn't."

With a slow burning smile, he meets my eyes, and then deliberately looks down. "I'm not a nice guy."

An evil smirk takes over my mouth, hiding my reaction to his interest—it is positive to him, negative to common sense. I let my clothes and boots drop from my hands. "I'm not a nice girl either."

His eyes lift to mine, a frown and a tilt of his head stating an unspoken question.

And I throw my arms around his waist and pull. Blake stumbles down the step, his arms instinctively locking around me as we careen toward the ground doing a disjointed dance before straightening. I make a mud pie sandwich with our bodies, smearing my hands in his hair and over his face and head as Blake tries to duck away.

"You look so beautiful, Blake, like a pretty, muddy flower," I say, vigorously rubbing a hand on the top of his head. My fingers tangle in the black silk made cold and brittle with mud.

Blake breaks free, his chest rising and lifting as he glares at me. I grin back, my skin feeling like it's splitting where the mud has dried and turned to dirt. His face is colored in black and brown, making the gray shade of his eyes stand out more. The rain has turned into sprinkles; the wind is calm in the storm of our interaction. Even the thunder is muted, the lightning gone. It is as if Earth is quiet to listen, curious to see how this unfolds.

"Who are you?" he demands roughly.

His hair is standing up, tufts of it wild about his head. It makes my heart pound faster. My mouth opens. Before I can say anything—before I can move or utter a word, he's lunging for me. Blake's hands are on my face and his silver eyes are glowing down at me with nothing short of animalistic seduction. I don't think he even has to try to look sexy. It's just there, naturally. He presses his body to mine, and all I can think is: *Oh, my God. Oh, my God. Oh, my God.* Over and over and over. Any remnant of a chill is gone from my body, scalded from my being with his closeness.

"What I mean is—who am I about to kiss?" His voice is velvet, soft and wicked, and I feel my nerve endings expand and shrink. Underneath the rain and mud is the scent of him, and it's pure male intoxication. Like peppered cloves. Sweet and fiery.

Wait—did he say kiss?

Kiss.

My lips try to form words; nothing happens.

"Piper?" Blake's mouth inches forward.

The "Oh, my God" chant has turned into "Oh, shit." My body is shaking, uncontrollably, wantonly.

A nuzzle of his nose on the side of my neck. "Rachel?"

I go to breathe and out comes a whimper of longing. That's it. No air—just enough noise to announce my undeniable magnetism to him.

"Jackie?" His eyes lock on mine, telling me all the things he wants to do to me.

And they're bad, sinful. Deviant. And I want him to do them all.

My knees go weak, my fingers digging into his forearms to keep me on my feet.

When a whisper is between our lips, he murmurs, "Who am I about to kiss?"

"Opal," I say on an exhale an instant before his mouth descends.

5

Blake

Who in their right mind kisses someone covered in mud? Me. But then, have I ever been in my right mind? Along with the lingering taste of cherry from the sucker she had way too much oral fun with—and tortured me in the process—on the way here, I taste dirt. It isn't enough to dissuade me. Opal's mouth perfectly fits to my lips, her fingers resting on either side of my jaw, her body flush with mine.

We are touching in all the right places, and she is barely clothed.

My heart is thundering, rampant and brutal. Her hair is thick and dirty, and nothing's felt so good to the pads of my fingers. All of me is hard. And hungry. I'm trembling with it, maddened by lust. I want to devour her. Her mouth, her body, maybe even her soul. I could blacken her world and make her love it. It would be wrong. But then, isn't everything about this? Doesn't matter. This feels better than anything I've experienced in a while. A long time.

But Opal is hesitant, shy, holding back. Her lips follow mine, but she won't fully open them. Like she wants to jump, but is scared there won't be anything to jump for. I don't want this kiss to be another disappointment for her. Through the fog inside my head, I tell myself to back off, to go slower. To teach instead of take. She's leery of kissing, and I'm ruling her mouth. I tear my mouth away, instantly regretting it, and try to catch my breath.

When was the last time? I think. When was the last time I felt like this?

I remember, and pressure forms in my chest. It was years ago. A different life, a different me.

"Sorry," I mutter, smoothing hair back from my forehead with a hand that shakes. My hands fist, wanting to reach for her again, and I force myself back a step, my jeans tight and uncomfortable against my erection.

Opal's hands are still raised, her fingers curled, like she either wants to push me away or pull me back. Bemusement looks back at me from a dirty face with wide eyes. Her eyes drop, her throat moving up and down as she swallows. She blinks, and once more brings her gaze to me, looking shocked into muteness. Good or bad, I can't tell.

"I, uh…" I rub at a patch of dirt on my chin. Where is a smartass comment? Where is my confidence, my mockery? Gone. Eradicated by the touch of her soft lips.

"More," is all she whispers, and a shudder runs the length of my spine.

I want to. I want to give her more, give her every part of me I can. Knowing it will be lacking, knowing it won't be enough. Knowing I can't do that to her. Inhaling deeply, I shake my head, backtracking like my feet have the power to wipe away from existence the past few minutes. Still shaking my head, denying the kiss, denying her—most deplorably, denying myself—I spin around and storm for the house.

Who am I? Who is this man?

I feel like a bumbling fool around a woman I barely know.

The door slaps shut, and I force air in and out of my lungs, staring unseeingly at the inside of the house I inherited from my grandfather. I rub my face, and my palms come away brown. The squeak of the door tells me she's behind me. I would have known even if she hadn't made a sound.

"I'll show you where the bathroom is. You can take the first shower," I tell her in a voice I don't recognize. It sounds rough and raw, like I smoked a hundred cigarettes in the span of a minute.

The hardwood floor, original from the time of the house's construction in nineteen sixty-two, creaks as she shifts.

Without looking back to see if she's following, I stride through the open entryway and into the living room. Beyond that is the main bathroom. I open the door and gesture to the room. "Everything you need is in here. You'll smell like a guy, but it's better than smelling like a swamp."

Opal slides past me, closing the door before I have a chance to look at her. I stare at the white door, studying the places where the paint is chipping. I don't generally think about things all that much. I am overthinking *everything* with Opal.

The sound of running water fills the quiet, and I move away from the door. A trail of mud and grass marks our passage through the room, and after removing my mud-logged boots and socks, I set about cleaning it up.

As I sweep, a voice from the past echoes through the room, loud and robust. It brings a partial smile to my face. Being in this house, where I stayed as much as I could as a kid, I feel my grandfather here, like he never left. I hear his laughter. I see his smile that crinkled up his blue eyes. I remember his corny jokes that made him laugh more than anyone else. My smile grows as I remember one in particular that he told every once in a while.

"What do you get when you mix a Pomeranian with a Shih Tzu?"

"A shitty palm!"

I shake my head as I picture him slapping his knee and chortling at his own joke. Tall and wide, my grandpa's presence somehow managed to be larger than him. He stepped into a room and overtook it. John Renner always believed in me. He did too much for me. I wish I was someone he'd be proud of. I wish I could say I've done something to deserve the faith he had in me. Every day I miss him. He was my father more than my real one.

I put away the broom and dustpan in the closet in the kitchen. The windows need to be replaced, the draft stronger in here than the other rooms. There is a long list of things that need to be updated. *And you want to leave it all to fall to disrepair*, a voice reproaches. It sounds uncannily like John Renner's.

I warm up canned soup on the gas stove, Opal stepping into the kitchen not long after I turn on the burner, her hair wet and stringy around her tan face. I turn from the stove to fully face her. A pair of faded jeans caresses her legs and an emerald green T-shirt hugs her upper portion. She has curves that never end, and my mouth goes dry. Other parts of me react as well. Unsurprisingly, that damn pink backpack is in her arms.

Her eyes slide to mine, hold my gaze long enough to quicken my breathing, and move on. "I can watch the food, if you want to shower."

The remembered feel of her body, her lips, has my heart pounding in my eardrums. I need to kiss her again. Not want—*need.* I am alive with her, like I was sleeping for the last how many years, and her entrance into my life awakened me.

"I don't know, I kind of like the mud. It makes for a great facemask." My hair is rigid and posed upright. I feel like a porcupine.

"Worried about fine lines and wrinkles?" Opal moves to the rickety square table near a row of windows that show the backyard and unending scenery presently cloaked in black.

"You can never start too young." When she looks up, I nod toward the counter where bread, cheese slices, and a stick of softened butter are set out. "I was about to make grilled cheese sandwiches."

"You go shower. I can handle a few grilled cheese sandwiches." Her smile is crooked, her eyes hungry as she stares at the food. I'm jealous of the way she's looking at it.

"Help yourself to whatever you need." The floor is cold beneath my bare feet as I walk toward the doorway.

"Blake."

I pause on the opposite side of the room, looking over my shoulder.

"This is your house, isn't it?" Opal takes a wooden spoon from a crock of cooking utensils and stirs the soup, her back to me.

"I saw a picture of you, and who I'm assuming is your family, in the living room," she explains at my silence.

"It's my grandfather's," I answer shortly. "I just occasionally live here."

She glances at me, a single upraised eyebrow her only reaction.

In the living room, I study the framed photograph Opal mentioned. It rests above the faded green couch, taking up more space on the white wall than it should, a monstrosity of disillusionment and lies. The only truth in it is my grandfather, standing between me and my father, as he so often did—figuratively, literally. Dark-haired and bright-eyed, he is grinning broadly in the picture, his arm around my bony eight-year-old shoulder. My eyes burn as I take in his image.

It's the four of us—me, my dad, my mom, and my mom's dad. Grace Renner, my grandma, died when my mom was in her teens, and both of my dad's parents passed when I was a baby. If they were the reason my father is the way he is, I'm glad I don't remember them. In the picture, we're standing in front of this house my grandfather built for his wife. My dad isn't smiling. No shocker there. My mom looks unfocused. Even then she was taking pills to ease her troubled mind, to not see her immediate world.

Vivian Malone has a long list of mental instabilities, and I inherited a few of my own. I used to wonder why some days I felt like everything was wrong, when in reality, everything was the same as it had been the day before. But depression is like that—there isn't a reason to feel bad. I just do. Those who don't have it can't understand it. It's an ever-present darkness that hovers, and with the slightest provocation, it can attack. Debilitate. Destroy. It's always there, in the background. That voice of doubt that tells me to give up, asks me why I bother trying.

I turn from the picture and stalk to the bathroom.

Steam lingers from Opal's shower, turning the air humid and thick. It looks like she tried to hand-wash her clothes; the brown-streaked garments are hanging off the side of the tub and dripping discolored water onto the floor. The washer and dryer located in the cement basement are ancient, but they have to be able to do a better job than her hands. I grab the clothes and, trying not to focus too directly on her undergarments, toss them in the laundry basket.

I strip, tossing my clothes in the laundry basket, and step into the narrow shower stall across the room from the door. I try not to think about Opal's naked body having recently been standing exactly where I am, soaping herself up. Eyes closed, a look of bliss on her face. I can see it clearly, gritting my teeth against the need that pulses through my body. I tighten my hands into fists to keep them off my own body. I take shallow breaths, forcing them to even out. I lower my head under the water and brace my hands to the wall, fighting an attraction I don't entirely understand. I mean, yeah, she's got a great body, and her face doesn't hurt, but lots of women have the same. And she's outrageous more times than sensible.

Maybe that's what it is—her inability to get too serious, to let herself be bothered by life. Then again, if all I did was tell lies, maybe I'd be able to not take things too seriously myself. The water abruptly turns freezing, and I hasten to finish up washing. By the time I step out and wrap a towel around my waist, I have myself convinced that I don't really find her all that attractive.

I step out of the bathroom and sniff. It smells faintly of something burning. Hand clamped around the two corners of the towel to keep them in place, I quickly shuffle for the kitchen as the smoke alarm begins its shrill song. Opal stands in the middle of the room with her back to me, waving her open backpack at the ceiling directly beneath the smoke detector, cursing with each wave of her arms.

My eyes shift to the smoking burner and I sprint for it, turning it off and flinging the pan of blackened bread and cheese in the sink before flipping on the cold water. A searing sound pairs with the piercing alarm, and smoke billows up from the sink. I hear a gasp as I shut off the water, and something falls to the floor.

Spinning around, I take in Opal's gaping mouth and the direction of her eyes, the backpack lying on the floor with its miscellaneous contents spewed over the hardwood floor. The alarm shuts off, the quiet as brutal as the previous aggravating noise. Her face is red, which is saying something with her golden-toned skin. It isn't until I open my mouth to ask what she's gawking at that I feel cold air on my lower extremities, and become aware of my nakedness. Keeping the towel on my body wasn't really a priority as I lunged for the burning food.

"Oh, my God," she whispers without looking up.

Now I know how women feel when guys notice their breasts and nothing else. I feel…objectified. It doesn't bother me, and clearly my manhood likes it, but she is *really looking at it.*

"You're making him feel self-conscious," I say wryly.

Her eyes jerk to mine; her body goes completely still.

"Him?" Opal chokes.

"Bernard." My eyebrows furrow at the spontaneous name. Bernard was the best I could come up with? "What, you don't name your girls?"

"Girls?"

I casually lean down to retrieve the towel and loosely lock it around my hips. Crossing my arms and leaning against the counter ledge, I level my gaze on a flustered Opal. "What happened?"

"I saw Bernard." Opal blinks her eyes, looking to my towel and away.

Laughter is pulled from me, abrupt and rough. I lift an eyebrow. "I meant in here, with the food."

Looking faint, she gestures to the stove. "I don't know," she manages after a time. Opal lifts a trembling hand to her brow, and drops it before it touches her skin. "I just…I went to look at something in my bag, and I must have gotten distracted, and then, smoke, and noise, and you, naked. It's all jumbled up in my head, and it is *so hot* in here."

I walk around, opening a few windows to air the smoke from the room. I am aware of Opal's eyes on me the whole time.

"How soon until we head to Bismarck?" She sounds nervous. Anxious.

As if to mock her, rain pummels the roof and siding.

"Once the storm passes," I tell her, studying the valley miles away as it briefly lights up like it's daytime. "I imagine you want your clothes cleaned first?"

I glance at Opal when she doesn't answer.

She starts, as if only now becoming aware that I spoke. "Um…yes. That would be awesome. And…can you put on clothes?"

I frown.

"I just saw you naked," Opal says in a faint voice.

"Yes. You did," I confirm, glancing at the papers and clothes littering the floor. "The towel seems kind of pointless now, doesn't it?"

Her shallowly indrawn breath is the only reply she gives.

I move for the drawings, taking one and perusing it as I kneel down. The floor is hard and cool against my knees. "Who are these people?" I murmur, looking up.

"Hey. Those are personal," Opal states, scrambling to pick up the drawings before I can reach them.

From what I've seen, Opal likes to draw faces. What's interesting about her work is how she captures the essence of the person. This picture is of an older lady with short hair, wrinkles, and a wide smile. There is toughness in her eyes, like she doesn't take crap from anyone, and I'm in awe that Opal can catch that with a pencil. The bottom of the page reads a single name: Rachel. Looking at this drawing, I can tell that this woman laughed a lot, probably even at herself. I reach for another one. Emily. She is younger, with long, straight hair and heart-shaped lips. She looks shy, but there is a hint of mischief in her smile.

Each time I take a drawing in hand, Opal quickly removes it from my grasp. There are dozens of them, faces upon faces, all named. I note a Jackie as well. She's middle-aged, with wide cheekbones and a full face, her eyes dancing with happiness and kindness. I blink at the image of a dog named Jane. I guess her drawings aren't designated to only humans.

"Blake, I mean it, these are not for your eyes."

"Why?" I ask. We're inches away from one another, on our knees on the floor. I stare into her expressive eyes, seeing her discomfort, her anxiety, and I want to know why it's there. These drawings matter to her. They aren't just something she's good at—they have meaning. This is Opal without shields in place.

"Because they're not yours!" she snaps, gathering them all into her arms as if to protect them from my eyes. She's crumpling some of them, but seems more worried about them being seen than ruined.

"Who are they?"

"People," Opal mumbles, her eyes down, her arms clutching the pictures to her chest. "Just people—and a couple animals."

"Opal," I say softly, the tone of my voice asking her to open up to me. Gently demanding it. I have no right to her thoughts, and still, I want to know them.

She pushes the papers behind her before going for more. She won't look at me, her bottom lip held captive by her upper teeth. "I don't have a mom or a dad, all right? I don't know them; I've never met them. I don't know if they're alive or dead. I just know I don't have them.

"And no one ever adopted me. I spent my childhood in foster care," Opal whispers, a crack clear in her voice, in her heart. "These are the people I grew up around, being shuffled from home to home; these are the people who became my temporary families."

A minor puzzle piece locks into place. She spent her childhood being continually uprooted. Getting comfortable in one home and being moved to another. She must have felt like no one really wanted her. The lies make sense now, but what about the rest of it? The different names, the running?

And she is running.

"You use their names as yours," I realize.

She looks at me, her eyes large and fractured. "I like to pretend I'm someone who meant something to me as a kid. Someone I know is good, someone I cared about, and who cared about me. They didn't have to. They didn't have to be nice to me, but most of them were. I don't use last names; it doesn't hurt anyone. And it keeps my name unknown when I want it to be. I don't have pictures of my foster families, but I have my drawings."

The room falls quiet. I now understand the attachment to the bag, and it puts a funny feeling in my chest. Like an ache. That pink backpack holds all her most precious items. One drawing rests between us, and I slowly pull it my way. Opal doesn't protest, her hands motionless on her knees. It is of a long-haired dog with a narrow snout and large eyes. A name is written at the bottom of the paper. Piper.

With a frown on my mouth, I lift my eyes. "You use the name of a dog for an alias?"

The clouds are instantly erased from her eyes, and she laughs. "I loved Piper more than any of the people I met. Her name is my favorite to use."

We lock eyes just as the sky explodes, the walls shake around us, and the house goes black.

* * *

Opal

"What's going on?" I demand, trying to keep my voice calm. Even so, it is not all that calm.

"The power is out," a disembodied voice answers. "A line close by was probably hit."

"So, what? What do we do?" I slowly stand, my drawings pressed tightly to my chest.

"We wait until it comes back on."

"How long is that going to take?" Panic adds volume to my words, and I swallow it down.

"I don't know," Blake responds, with annoyance clear in his tone. "However long it takes."

"Great. Wonderful. I appreciate how specific that answer was," I mutter.

With one hand before me, I carefully shuffle in the direction of the table and set my drawings on it. The rest of my belongings are still on the floor, out in the open, able to be stepped on and ruined. In the present dark, chances are they will be. I drop to my knees and crawl toward where I think they are, my head bumping into something warm and covered in soft hair. Blake's legs.

My face burns. I saw him naked, and it was glorious. The last, and only, man's anatomy I've seen in such depth was Jonesy's. He's tall and muscular, but he's also covered in hair—Blake is not. His pale skin is like marble, and his muscles aren't bulky like Jonesy's. They're more natural, the kind granted with genetics and manual labor. I could have looked at him for hours; I could have drawn him. I've never coveted that kind of creative intimacy before, but with him, yes, I did.

I do.

"What are you doing?" he asks curiously.

I realize my forehead rests against his shins, and I jerk away. Next thing, I'll be kissing his feet. Worshipping his butt cheeks. I let him kiss me, and I kissed him back. And it felt like perfection. I loved kissing him, or him kissing me, or however it happened. Us kissing. I could kiss him for hours, days, *forever*. Blake is turning me into a sex-crazed hooligan. With his looks, and his lips, and—

"Nothing. Just…trying to get the rest of my stuff." My heartbeat pounds in my ears, and I inhale slowly, letting it out even slower.

I feel him next to me, hear him moving papers as he helps me. The blackness seems erotic, puts a forbidden spin on the scene. Plus, Blake is still in a towel. This is torture. If he reached for me, I would throw myself into his arms. Without hesitation.

"I think that's everything," he says.

I blink, realizing I've been sitting in one place, not moving as I daydreamed about the guy beside me while Blake picked up my stuff. *Get a grip*, I scold myself.

"I'm going to get dressed upstairs, and then I'll try to find us something else to eat."

I hear the sound of his retreating footsteps and jump to my feet, banging my hip against the corner of the table. An immediate sting follows. "Wait! What? You're going upstairs? Don't—don't leave me." I clamp my teeth together at the pathetic words, wishing I could take them back. The large house suddenly seems ominous, especially with the thought of me being alone in the dark, downstairs while he's upstairs.

A rustling sound meets my ears, and then a light is shining in my face. I squint my eyes and turn my head to the side.

"Flashlight," Blake supplies.

"That would have come in handy about five minutes ago."

"Yes, but it would have made the situation so much less interesting." The light moves back and forth, blinding me a time or two. "Here. Take it. It won't take me long to find some clothes and get dressed."

As I take the flashlight, I hesitantly ask, "Can I go with you? I mean, not into the room, but just to wherever you're going."

His head tilts, his silver eyes glowing as the light hits them. "Sure," Blake says quietly, no hint of condescension in his tone. I appreciate that.

He offers his hand, and my heart melts at the gesture. Fingers loosely locked around mine, Blake leads the way to the living room. He opens a door on the opposite side of the wall from the bathroom, and we start up a narrow stairwell. The steps creak as we go, and I aim the flashlight over his shoulder, seeing a wall and not much else. My hand unconsciously drops, the light showcasing his backside, and I hastily lift the light back up. I swear I hear him softly chuckle, and I shake my head.

"You own this house? I know you said it's your grandpa's, but…you said…I mean…he's…" Dead. It feels insulting to say the word, although I am not sure why.

Blake's back stiffens, the motion drawing my eyes to the bare skin. "He left it to me."

"It's a nice place. Lots of land. Seems peaceful." I'm talking to fill the silence, but everything I'm saying is true. This is the kind of place I'd like to have as a home. "You're lucky."

"It needs a lot of modernizing," he says, letting go of my hand as he reaches the top.

"Still, the framework seems sound."

His eyes shift to mine, curiosity in them. "Yeah. It is."

I move away from the stairwell and to the wall opposite it, shining the light around. There is open space to the right of the stairs, a row of windows taking up most of the wall. An antique Singer in black sits on a desk with a chair behind it. The brand name is lettered in gold.

"My grandfather built this house for my grandmother. After she died, he kept a lot of her stuff exactly the way she left it," Blake tells me. "This was where she had her sewing machine set up. She never worked outside the home, but she did a lot of seamstress work and earned a little money that way."

I touch the cool metal, my fingertips coming away dusty. "What did she die from?"

"Cancer."

I drop my eyes.

"My mom had it too," he says.

My eyes lift as I turn to face him, surprised that he told me such a personal thing.

"She's okay," Blake continues, not looking away from me. "It's in remission."

"That's good," I say, because what do you say to that?

"Yeah," he says, directing his attention to the sewing machine.

"I never learned how to sew," I say wistfully as I follow his gaze. I blink my eyes at a memory of me watching a middle-aged woman use a needle and thread to sew up a hole in her grandson's jacket. I smile. "Jackie—one of people I stayed with as a kid—sewed, and she offered to teach me, but we never got around to it before I had to go. She baked too. I blame my love for all sweet things on her."

"It sounds like you never got to do a lot of things," Blake comments, moving to stand beside me. "What *did* you do?"

I shrug, stepping toward a closed door. "I never did a lot of things, but at the same time, I did more than most kids. I got to live a bunch of different lives. Each time I was sent to live with a new family, I learned about new people."

"That's my room," Blake says as I turn the doorknob.

Lifting my eyebrows, I smile mischievously as I step into the room. It has the white walls and hardwood flooring like the majority of the house I've seen. A dresser rests along one wall, what looks to be a king-size bed is in the middle of the room, and there is a bookshelf full of books set between two windows. I aim the flashlight on the spines of the books, noting the majority of authors housed on it are suspense and mystery writers. There's a door that I'm assuming leads to a closet, and an array of pictures on one wall. The other walls are bare.

I walk to the pictures, studying images of Blake at various stages of adolescence. He was rougher looking as a teenager; he was sadder looking as a child. In the few pictures where he's smiling, he is with his grandfather. Still pale, still with those eyes that seem to hold all the problems of the world inside them.

"I used to spend as much time as I could here, and because of that, my grandpa gave me my own room. He told me this was my home too, and that I was always welcome. Weekends, holidays, during the summer—I was here whenever it was allowed. I wanted to live here, but my parents wouldn't let me. I pretended Grandpa John was my dad." His voice is soft, thick with emotion.

I turn to look at Blake, wondering what I'll find in his features, but he crosses the room to the dresser. Hiding his expression. I had an unusual upbringing, but it wasn't all bad. Except for a couple jerks, all the families I stayed with were good to me. The worst part of it all was not knowing who my parents were, or why they chose to give me up. Something in my gut tells me Blake didn't have the greatest childhood, and I already figured out he has issues with his parents. It's his dad, though, who hurt him the most.

With his back to me, he goes through multiple drawers, selecting clothes. His face is blank when he finally faces me. "Unless you're hoping for a second show…"

I spin around, my cheeks heating up. I hastily click off the flashlight, bringing the room to absolute dark. "Go ahead. I won't look." Even though I want to look.

The ceiling lights flicker and stay on just as he tells me he's decent. I smile at the Duran Duran T-shirt he's wearing. I knew he had band T-shirts somewhere. The house comes alive, humming and popping as it does so. Blake takes me on a quick tour of the rest of the upstairs. There are two more bedrooms and a bathroom. One of the bedrooms is set up as an office, and it makes my head spin with possibilities. If this were my house, I would use that room as my art studio. If this were my house—I shake my head, knowing some of my fantasies are best unrealized.

"The storm seems to be slowing down. When your clothes are done drying, we can head into town," Blake tells me in the kitchen as he prepares peanut butter and jelly sandwiches. I told him I could at least handle making those, but the doubtful look in his eyes told me he thought otherwise.

"Great," I say cheerfully.

A lump forms in my throat at my lack of future plans. Do I keep going when I get to Bismarck, or do I see what the city has to offer before moving on to Montana? But if I stay in the area, why? Why would I stay? My eyes shift to Blake. If I stay, will I see him again? Would that be my reason for staying?

I pull off a chunk of the mostly ready sandwich and chew it up and swallow. My mouth and stomach say hello to the taste of sweetened, smooth peanuts with sugary strawberry. "What do you do for a job?"

"As of last spring, I was a college student."

The lump grows. Blake has a life, a career in the making, goals. He seems so much more responsible, and grounded, than me. And I guess he is. I don't even have a home, or a car. Or a job. Or a phone. Or—I shake my head against all the things I don't have.

I focus on Blake. "Oh? For what?"

Blake's motions become jerky as he closes the jar of peanut butter. He hands me the plate with the sandwich I taste-tested, and a glass of water. "Child psychology."

We sit at the table.

"Why child psychology?"

His grin is mocking and fake. "Didn't you know? Women love a guy who's invested in kids. It's good for picking up chicks."

Following Blake's way of calling out an untruth, I say softly, "Lie."

Blake's smile gets twisted, showing me I'm right. "My plan was to take a break from college and go to Australia."

I choke on the drink of water I just took. "Was?"

Blake studies the table as he chews. His gaze touches mine before moving on. "Yeah. Was. Now, I don't know. I don't know about anything." He lowers his eyes, his shoulders stiff. "I already have a passport and ticket. There is no reason for me to not go. It wouldn't make any sense to waste the passport, or ticket. They're not exactly cheap."

"Why Australia?"

He shrugs. "It's warm, and the sun is always out."

I give his colorless skin a pointed look. "Right. Because you obviously love the sun, vampire boy."

Blake looks at me, one half of his mouth lifted.

"How long do you plan on being there?" Unease sharpens my tone. What if he never comes back? What if he stays in Australia, and that's that? Why do I care? I'm never going to see him again anyway. I guess the finality of it bothers me. If he's in the United States, maybe, at some point, I could see him again. If he's in another country, then no, I won't. I don't like the thought of never seeing him again.

"I don't know." Blake studies the tabletop, his eyes tracing a nick in the wood. "For however long I want."

"For forever?" I whisper, dread thickening my voice.

With a frown marring his face, Blake focuses on me.

"I just mean, um, how will I ever pay you back, for—for the food, and stuff, if you're in Australia?" Lame. So lame.

"I guess you won't." His eyes flicker with amusement. "You can always send snail mail."

"For real, why did you choose child psychology?" I ask as I swallow the last of my sandwich and gaze mournfully at his. I'm still hungry.

He notices, tearing off a large chunk and handing it to me. “Tell me why you’re running.”

“Tell me why it’s so important that you see your parents,” I toss back, consuming the food in three quick bites and emptying the glass of water.

“Who are you running from?” Blake returns, his eyes telling mine not to even try to look away.

“You don’t want to know,” I say, honesty reverberating through me. I’m not even sure who is after me, if anyone; I just know there are bad guys out there somewhere, and that there is a good chance they’re looking for me. I can’t tell him that. I can’t tell him anything. The less he knows, the better. *Like Paisley?* my conscience mocks.

He squints. “Interesting.”

I shift in the chair, procuring a sticky hand. I already said too much. “Truce,” I announce, wiggling my fingers near his face. “You don’t ask me questions, and I won’t ask you any.”

Blake stares at me, and then turns his eyes to my hand. His mouth quirks with naughty intent and he leans his head forward, bringing his face near my fingers. I feel his breath on my skin, and goose bumps break out on my arms. My throat tightens like the fingers of desire are wrapped around it.

“You have jelly on your hand,” he says in a voice like silk.

I wonder if he’s going to lick my finger. I kind of want him to lick my finger. That sounds so weird.

Alas, he wipes my finger off with a napkin.

My nerves are shaky, something potent sweeping through me. It feels oddly like disappointment. Maybe yearning. My shoulders slump as I lift my gaze to his and catch the humor in his expression. It’s fleeting, but pure, and it changes his harsh features. Makes them more boyish. Entirely too kissable.

I stand, grabbing the plates and moving to the sink. I hurriedly wash them in the old porcelain sink, setting them in the white strainer to dry. Everything about this house is old, but to me, that only enhances its character. There have been a lot of memories made here, I can tell. A lot of good ones for Blake. I blink at the pinch in my chest and let out the sink water.

“How long until the clothes are dry, do you think?”

Blake’s response is slow in coming. “I’ll go check.”

I wait until I hear his fading footsteps to turn around. Through the windows, I can see that the sun is trying to make an appearance. I look at the blue rooster clock near the door that leads to the backyard. It’s a little after six. Hours have transformed into days while in Blake’s company. Another oddity to add to a list of unusual occurrences since I’ve met Blake.

I dry off my hands on a threadbare blue dishtowel and move for the door. It sticks before opening. Cool air and the scent of rain washes over me as I step outside. With the passing of the storm, the humidity has been cut from the air. The cement is cool on my bare feet as I take in the little stone deck with two lime green metal chairs.

Just as the wind picks up, blowing my hair about my head, I notice the view.

Pushing locks of hair from my eyes and mouth, I drink in the sight of endless hills that look like mountains, and blue skies. There is no separation from earth and sky. It's a picture-perfect scene of country life, and what peace looks like. I wonder if Blake sees it.

I walk around the house and venture farther out. Tree limbs are down, scattered along the grass like a misguided trail. My feet are covered in wet grass, and the hem of my pants is damp. I roll up the pants to my calves and continue toward the pond. It looks tranquil now, not so dark and mysterious as it did under the blanket of the storm.

Without looking, I know when Blake approaches. His eyes are hot on my back, full of questions and thoughts. I face him, holding back wayward strands of hair that want to blind me. He looks at my face, and then his gaze travels down and up. The sexual tension between us is of epic proportions, and so, so dangerous. But I like danger, and I like his mouth, and before our time together ends, I'd like to know more of him. Physically.

"The clothes are just about dry," Blake says, his deep voice breaking the silence.

I nod and turn to look at the pond, dropping my arms to hug myself. Our adventure is just about over. It was a quick one, but so far, my favorite. I ask him a question I've always wondered, and never had someone around I wanted to ask. I think Blake will take my question seriously.

"What do you think happens to people when they die?" I glance at him, taking in his unnaturally straight posture before returning my eyes back to the water. "Do you think they're just gone? It doesn't seem possible. But then, there was a time when they weren't here, right? It isn't like they always existed, even though it feels like they had to."

"Who did you lose?" he asks quietly.

"Who's ever stayed is the right question to ask," I tell him. My chest compresses as I watch the clouds above swirl and float. I don't know if my parents are alive or dead. I was never given any information on them. I've accepted it, for the most part, but once in a while, I wonder. "They all go, Blake. Eventually."

"I don't think they leave," Blake answers in a low voice. "Every life is a soul, and how can those really stop being?"

"That's like saying they've always been. How can that be?"

Blake averts his face. "Maybe none of us really go completely away."

"Seems logical." I purse my lips at the muteness that follows. I'm not saying it isn't possible; I'm just wondering *how*. "So, what, after someone dies, you think they go to Heaven and everything is wonderful? They watch us from above?" Derision adds a rough element of disbelief to my voice.

He runs a hand over the back of his neck. "I don't know. I think they go…somewhere. Sometimes you just have to believe, right? I feel my grandfather. Maybe it's all in my head, but I think he's around, in some way."

"Piper died on my last day with the Hampsons," I admit, my throat closing around the words. I swear she knew I was leaving, because she died that morning, and sometimes during the night, I feel her soft body lying against my side. I'm not telling Blake that. He can confess his insanity all he wants, but I will not be publicly announcing my own.

A furrow appears between his eyebrows. "Piper? Oh. Piper. The dog."

"The first day I showed up, she greeted me with a wagging tail and a friendly bark. And every day I spent there, she was by my side. She loved me, and I loved her. She adopted me." I toe grass from my ankle, my stinging eyes locked on a particularly puffy cloud. "No human being ever did, but Piper the dog did. It sounds dumb, I know."

"It doesn't sound dumb." Blake moves closer, the heat from his body warming my heart along with my side. "How many different homes were you at?"

I shrug, hoping I look more casual than I feel. "I don't know, probably five or six." A dozen. A dozen different homes from the time I was born until I graduated from high school.

"What was it like?"

I take in his dark eyes, his somber expression. "A nonstop adventure." My lips twist. "Honestly, I wasn't the best student, and I never really made a lot of friends. What was the point? I'm not making excuses, but it was hard to constantly have to adapt to new surroundings. I didn't care about a lot of things, because I was never around anything long enough *to* care. I got in trouble a bit, petty stuff, but I could have rebelled more. I wanted to."

"What held you back?"

I inhale, and slowly exhale. "The thought in my head that my parents were watching me, somehow. I deluded myself into thinking they didn't want to leave me. That they were important people in trouble with dangerous criminals and left me to protect me.

"That they'd died—that one I almost hoped for; that they hadn't had a choice in the matter. The stories I used to make up," I say softly. At Blake's snort, I amend, "And still make up, sometimes."

"Have you ever tried to find information on them?"

I smile, feeling the sadness in the bend of it. "No."

"Why?"

"I don't want to be disappointed. At least with my fantasies, they're exactly how I need them to be. And what does it change, knowing how it all went down? Nothing."

Blake's voice is dark and full of regret when he finally says, "I used to be like you, Opal. More dangerous, to be sure, but reckless like you. Never thinking of consequences. Living on impulse and adrenaline. Living in the moment because nothing else meant as much."

My back stiffens. "I'm not reckless. I'm fearless."

He shakes his head. "No. Being fearless means you do things that scare you; being reckless means you take unnecessary risks. It's different."

"I'm not—" I start to protest, but the look on his face erases the words from my mouth.

I guess I can be reckless. I think of my spontaneous trip with little belongings and money to my name. No car, no phone. How I took off without a word to anyone. Okay. So I'm a little reckless.

"What made you stop?" I ask Blake. "Being reckless, or whatever."

Blake levels thunderstorm eyes on me, and I fight not to flinch at the smoldering heat whirling within their depths, like stars and wind dancing. *Don't try to figure me out and I won't try to figure you out*—that's what we both are not saying. I'm not sure what we're agreeing to do, or to not do, but Blake seems okay with it. The warnings are all there.

Don't dig too deep.

Stay back.

Remain unattached.

He crouches, finding a rock. Blake stares down at it as he turns it around and around within his fingers. Squinting at the brightening sky, he chucks it toward the pond. A tiny splash disturbs the calm water.

"Someone died."

6

Blake

The driveway is washed out. Hands on my hips, I stare at the mess that should be a gravel road. I turn and stride back to the truck, slamming the door after me. I sit with my hands tightly gripping the steering wheel. It isn't like there is a deadline on the meeting with my dad, and Opal appears to have no obligations of any kind, other than to her free spirit, but the longer I'm around her, the more my priorities get scrambled. Altered. I have to get to Bismarck, and I have to say goodbye to her.

Before I think up all crazy kinds of things, and maybe act on some of them—more than I already have.

"I take it we're *not* going to Bismarck," Opal says after a time.

"The road is out," I growl.

She shoves something under my nose. "Carrot?"

Without turning my head, I shift my eyes in her direction.

"I bet you're thinking of smoking. Here's a carrot."

"Why did you bring the carrots?"

"I don't know. In case I got hungry."

"You're always hungry."

"See? Good thing I brought them." And she shakes the orange vegetable at my face, bumping my nose with it.

I take the carrot, roll down the window, and chuck it.

Sighing, she asks, "What needs to be done to fix the road?"

"I'll have to call someone."

"So do that."

"I will do that, after I've been angry for an appropriate amount of time," I say around gritted teeth.

Opal laughs, opening the door to the truck. She grabs her bag and hops down, a carrot hanging from the corner of her mouth. "I'll wait on the porch while you do that."

The door slams, and I watch her through the rearview mirror. I wouldn't exactly call her walk ungraceful, but it isn't smooth. It's fast, and there's generally a bounce to it, like she has somewhere to be, and she's happy about it. Opal skips to the porch, doing a spin at the end before she sits down on a step, and a muscle twitches beneath my eye. I think the last time I skipped was in grade school, and it was mandatory for gym class.

I close my eyes and let the back of my head thump against the headrest. I mentioned the death of Billie; my girlfriend I inadvertently killed at the age of nineteen. Because I was stupid and drunk and driving a car. Drunk on love and alcohol and drugs, Billie and I were dynamite, and all we did was race against blowing up. I knew we would, eventually. I just didn't think she'd be the only one destroyed by it.

I left out the particulars, gleamed over what a mess I was at that time of my life, but it isn't hard to figure out. No happy, levelheaded kid would get into the trouble I did. Stealing, fighting, drugs. Skipping out on school. Driving as fast as I could to see if I'd crash. In and out of homes for troubled kids. Drinking. Let's not forget the depression and suicide attempts. Coming home late, not coming home at all. Rehab centers. Anything wild and irresponsible, I went for it.

I did everything I could to get my dad's attention, and when I got it, I didn't want it. It was all so twisted. It still is.

Opal didn't say anything. In fact, she acted like I never spoke. There was *no* reaction. I'm not sure how to feel about that. She looked through me instead of at me. I confessed that I was responsible for the death of someone, and she pretended to not hear me. I suppose, logically, I should be glad. We don't need to bond. We can't.

I turn the key, put the truck in reverse, and aim it back toward the shed.

That done, I get out, reaching into my pocket for my cell phone. My call log shows multiple missed phone calls and unanswered texts. Without checking, I know who they're from. I promised Graham I'd call as soon as I reached North Dakota, and to his way of thinking, I should have been there by now. Vowing to myself to get in contact with him tonight, I make a phone call to one of the local rock quarries.

"Hey, Dan, this is Blake Malone. I have a washed out driveway in need of some gravel. How soon can you get out here?"

"Hey there, Blake," an old, brittle voice greets. "I didn't know you were back."

I look toward the house. Opal lies on her back on the porch, using her backpack as a pillow as she munches on carrots. As I watch, she leisurely dips her hand in the bag of them resting on the step below and procures a handful of baby carrots. It reminds me of a video I saw once of a sloth eating food.

My lips twitch and I turn my attention to the phone call. "Yeah, well, someone forgot to throw me a welcoming home party."

"Assholes."

Laughing, I face the truck. "The world is full of them. Anyway, how's your schedule looking?"

Dan Kline sighs, and I know I'm not going to like what he has to say. "Well, with the storm doing havoc all around the area like it did, we're pretty swamped. Tomorrow, at the earliest, but it's looking more like the day after."

I bite back my inclination to swear.

"Blake?"

"I'm here." I rub a hand against my forehead and gnash my teeth. Shaking my head, I drop my hand. "Yeah. Sure. Put me on the schedule."

"Will do. See you soon."

"See ya."

I look at Opal. Two more days with her. There's running water in the faucets, electricity. I bought a small supply of food on the way here, and there are canned goods galore in the basement, so we're good that way.

I turn my attention to the highway in the distance. It's almost a mile just to get to it, and another fifteen to reach Bismarck. It isn't walkable. I look at the truck, wondering if it could make it over the small pond that's replaced a portion of my driveway. And do I want to take the chance with it? No. I don't. Not with my grandpa's truck.

Kicking at a twig that got pushed this way from the thunderstorm, I amble toward Opal.

"Good news," I chirp as I sit next to her legs. "You get to spend two more days with me."

She propels to a sitting position with lightning fast moves, her boot clipping my ear as she spins her legs around. "That isn't going to work."

"I know—it doesn't seem long enough, does it?" I make eyes at her and she glares back.

"I have places to go," Opal states.

"Where?" I softly demand, rubbing at my stinging ear.

She entangles a hand in her flyaway hair, tugging it and wincing when she finally gets it loose. "I don't know. Places. Places other than here."

"Hmm."

Jumping to her feet and sending the bag that once contained carrots spiraling to the ground, Opal jumps down from the porch and whirls around to face me. Her eyes are glittering; her cheeks are as red as apples. She looks flustered, agitated. Sexy as hell. "What am I supposed to do here for the next two days?"

I stand and walk toward her, stopping when we're face to face. I have to lower my head to meet her eyes; she tips hers back to do the same. "You can work off the expenses you've stacked up," I tell her, making sure my voice is low and suggestive. "I have a long list of jobs for you to perform."

Her throat bobs as she swallows, and I know the direction her thoughts have gone. Mine went there too, briefly. Just long enough to torment me.

"You can start by…" I take a lock of her sunset hair between my fingers and gently tug, staring at the strands. They shine under the glint of the sun. I set my gaze back to her, noting the uneven way her chest moves as she breathes. "Picking up sticks around the yard."

Opal stumbles back a step, blinking at me. When I laugh, her face scrunches up and she gives me a push. It feels like a light tap on my shoulder. "You're not funny, Blake."

"I'm a little funny," I state, grinning.

"Only a little. A very small amount."

And that's what we do for the next two hours—we pick up tree limbs and whatever else the storm blew around. No words are exchanged as we work—only fleeting looks. The sun lowers in the sky, and the atmosphere darkens. It's strange, but I feel like we're a team. Opal and me. The loner and the liar, somewhat reformed and picking up tree debris. One side of my mouth lifts.

"What are you going to do with all the sticks?" Opal asks as we finish up for the night. Daylight is leaving us. Her hands rest on her hips and there's a line of sweat framing the neck of her shirt.

I watch a trail of perspiration travel down the hollow of her neck to get lost within her cleavage. My mouth goes dry. "Build a dam."

She gives me a look before turning her attention to the hills. "There's a lot of land here. Was your grandfather a farmer?"

"No. Other than the garden he put in each year for my grandmother, he wasn't much for working the land."

Opal waits, her eyes on me.

"He liked antiques," I say with a faint smile. "He had his own shop on the highway, a mile outside of Bismarck. He sold it when he started having health problems." And then it was a short seven months later that he had a massive heart attack.

"I didn't notice many antiques in the house." Her eyes haven't left me.

The wind gathers strength, pushing and pulling at my T-shirt, threading through my hair. "That would be because my dad got ahold of them when I was out of commission and sold them. Time to go in." Bitterness fills my mouth, and I stride for the house.

"Out of commission?" she asks, her voice confused.

I fought my dad on it, told him he had no right to take things meant for others, meant for me, but I was in a rehabilitation center at the time—the last one I frequented before cleaning up my act for good—and he had all the power. He always had all the power. The first step to taking it back was to quit wasting my life on drugs, and I did. I'm never going back to that life. The drugs lost. I won.

Drugs are not an escape; they are a prison.

By the time Opal joins me in the kitchen, I've washed up and made egg salad. And calmed down enough that the image of my dad's face doesn't make me want to punch a hole in the wall.

"You're more domestic than me," she observes, stopping beside me. The scent of coconuts dipped in rain and sweat tickles my senses. She grabs the spoon I used to mix the hardboiled eggs and mayonnaise, and scoops up egg salad with it. Opal eats it from the spoon and sets the spoon back in the bowl. "Yum. You can make me egg salad any day. It's good."

"Don't tell anyone. It's bad for my image." I catch her eyes and wink.

She hurriedly turns away and washes her hands at the sink, moving out of my line of vision. The refrigerator door opens. "Do you have anything to drink around here other than water and expired milk? Maybe something with alcohol in it?"

My shoulders tauten and I slap together four egg salad sandwiches. I quickly learned that Opal's size has no bearing on her appetite. "No. Just water."

"Oh. Water it is then." The refrigerator door closes.

I hear the dip in her voice, and I offer her a plate with two sandwiches on it. I don't release it until she meets my eyes, speaking loudly and clearly as I tell her, "I'm an addict. I don't have drugs of any kind around, not even alcohol. I'm no fun at all. Really boring. A guaranteed bad time."

"What happened?" she asks after a brief pause, seeming uninterested in my confession.

I hear myself telling her, "I liked it too much."

"Well." Opal shrugs. "Except for an occasional drink, I don't do any of those things either. We can be boring together."

I can't come up with some smartass comment, like I generally do. She just minimized the whole flawed make-up that is my past. Like whatever happened back then doesn't matter. Like my addictions have no bearing on who I am. I look at her profile, studying the lines of her features. Opal has a natural, even clumsy, elegance to her that should turn me off but doesn't.

"I don't think you're boring," I tell her.

She grabs the plate and sits down, her eyes not meeting mine. Opal takes a hefty bite of her sandwich, chews, swallows, and repeats. She won't look at me, intent on shoving food in her mouth. This goes on for too long; Opal is quiet for too long. It makes my skin twitch. It makes me doubt myself, and my inclination to open up to her like I haven't with anyone else.

"Don't act like that," I say as I sit down, a hint of pleading in my tone. I hate that it was there, that she probably caught it.

Her eyebrows lower as she lifts her gaze. Opal holds up a finger until she swallows. "Like what?"

"Like…I don't know. Like you have to tiptoe around me now."

Eyes softening, Opal says, "Never. I'm just…I'm not sure how to respond. And anyway, it doesn't matter. We all have our messes, right? I mean, look at me. I exaggerate, I'm on the run fr—"

I put a hand on her arm and she stops talking. I gently squeeze and her muscles tighten beneath my palm. I hold her wary gaze. "Exaggerate?"

Her eyes go to slits. "Stretch the truth," she amends.

I lift my eyebrows.

Opal sighs. "Fine. I lie. But only about things that don't matter."

I make a sound of mockery, my palm warming where our skin meets. "Who are you on the run from? I thought it was a 'what,' but it's a 'who,' isn't it?"

She focuses on the table. "I can tell you have a lot of baggage, Blake."

I drop my hand and straighten, feeling like she stabbed me in the heart with her drawing pencil. "I am aware." My voice is iced over.

Opal shrugs. "Well, so do I. I don't want to burden you with it, same as you don't want to burden me with yours. That's why I called a truce. You're breaking our truce," she tells me haughtily.

Both of my eyebrows hike up.

"Maybe we can, I don't know, act like we don't?" Hope lifts her voice.

I frown. "Act like we don't what?"

"Have baggage. You're normal, and I'm normal, and we just met at…a community fundraiser. And we liked each other. And now we're here, at a restaurant, having a gourmet meal." She smiles and chews up the last of her second sandwich.

Her and her fantasies.

I tilt my head. "*Do* you like me?"

Opal eyes my food. "Are you going to eat both of those?"

I wordlessly hand over the plate.

"Do you have any chocolate? I could really go for some chocolate," she says around egg salad sandwich.

"Opal."

Her shoulders slump. "You're okay, I guess."

Chuckling, I grab back one of the sandwiches and get to my feet. "There might be chocolate ice cream in the freezer, but I'm not sure how good it is by now. It's been there a while."

"Good enough."

I take a bite of the sandwich, enjoying the salt and pepper blend with hardboiled eggs and mayonnaise. "You know your name? Opal. It's distinguished, dignified. What if…what if you were named after someone well-loved? Like, a grandmother or something. I think that's pretty cool. And you can choose to think that way, you know? You can believe what you like. You have that right."

Large eyes lock on my face. They don't waver; they don't blink. They stare, and sink into me. I feel them all the way to the pit of my stomach, as if Opal knows my secrets. As if I just unveiled hers. As if she and I have an unexplored connection.

Feeling uncomfortable with the fixated way she watches me, I wave with my sandwich and turn toward the doorway. "Anyway, I'm going to close up the house and call it a night. Did you pick a bedroom?"

"Yes," is her meek response.

"All right. Help yourself to whatever. See you in the morning."

I check all the locks as I eat my sandwich, take a quick shower in the upstairs bathroom, and head for my room. It's funny, but I am no longer worried about Opal taking anything she shouldn't. Even with her somewhat deviant ways, she has a dented form of honor to her. She could have taken those kids' money at the circus, and she didn't.

It doesn't take long for me to fall asleep, and it doesn't take long for me to wake up when I feel the bed shift beside me. I open my eyes in the dark and turn them to the left, where Opal hovers partially above me. Desire streaks through me, unapologetic and undeniable. Her body is pleasing to the eye, but it isn't that that gives me the head rush or ensuing overdose of lust. I can't explain it. It's something about the way she looks at me like she knows me, sins and all, and she doesn't care.

"Blake?" Surrounded by black, her eyes are the only part of her I can see. They're wide and luminous.

"Yeah?"

"Can you…can you kiss me more?"

I take a shuddering breath, my body instantly responding to her request. I'm not really one to have doubts, or second-guess myself. I am definitely attracted to Opal, and if she's sure about this, then so am I.

Moving to my side, I look into her shadowed eyes. "If I kiss you, it won't end at that."

A hand touches my shoulder, light and hesitant. I choke on air as her fingers trail down my arm, becoming bolder, and move to my chest. Her palm stops directly above where my heart pounds, fast and strong. She looks at me with eyes that shimmer with arousal.

"That's what I'm hoping for," she says in her throaty voice that sounds like sex, and I am one hundred percent ready for her.

I have a brief, responsible thought of protection, and sigh with relief when I remember there are some condoms in the nightstand next to the bed.

I drop my gaze to her body, wondering what I'll find. I blink at the sight of one of my older shirts—a bright yellow one with SpongeBob SquarePants's face on it. Not bothering to ask how she came to have it, I remove it, my palms sliding down hot, soft, naked skin. All she had on was my shirt, and now it's gone. A growl emanates from deep inside me. Her hair is damp, and her skin smells like me, like I already claimed her. Already marked her as mine.

On her back, with me keeping my weight from her with my arms braced on either side of her head, I brush my lips across her collarbone and feel her tremble. The boxer briefs I'm wearing are hardly a barrier, and they are uncomfortably tight right now. I told her I wasn't a good guy. I warned her. A decent guy would say no. A decent guy would think of her more than himself. But I'm not that guy. Not in this instant anyway.

"This is all I can give you, Opal," I whisper. "Now. This moment. That's it."

"I'm not asking you to give me anything else."

I nod. "Good." And I let my arms relax.

* * *

Opal

His mouth is my master, and I am the most diligent pupil. Blake's lips move one way, and I mimic the motion. He slants his mouth, and I mold mine to his. When his body moves up, I move down. It's like a dance, erotic and smooth. Sensations pulse through my body, aching for more. I swear my whole body is shaking. And then I take charge, my lips in control. And he follows. I can tell he likes it. His hands are clenched around my hair, tight enough that it stings, and I must be depraved, because I like it too.

"You kiss so good," I rasp, not caring if that sounds tacky. I want to say all kinds of tacky things. Like, his hair is soft. And his mouth is amazing. Blake's body makes mine blaze.

Things are moving fast, but everything about us is that way. If we don't move along with it, we'll get left behind, wondering how we missed one another. I don't want to say goodbye to Blake without having this night. I want him, and he wants me. In this moment, it's right. Because his erection is pressed directly where it should be, and his body is hot and hard against mine, and this feels too good to be wicked. And if it is, well, then everything should feel this bad.

Blake sweeps his tongue across my lips; his teeth nip at my lower lip. It feels like a million tiny pulses of heaven on my mouth, but even so, I lose my rhythm, my confidence. I freeze up. I'm suddenly doubting everything about this, because what if it's terrible? What if we French kiss, and it's the most appalling thing ever? All saliva and rough tongue and gagging? I never should have let Jonesy use his tongue in my mouth. I suppose maybe it was a slight overreaction on my part to refuse to kiss him after that, but it just ruined the whole intimacy thing.

I shudder at the memory, and Blake goes still.

He pulls back and stares down at me with eyes that smolder silver. "If you don't like it, I'll stop," he says breathlessly, the rough timbre of his voice shivering along my skin. "But let me try."

Just like that, I am all for it.

Lightning streaks through my closed eyelids as I relax my mouth and allow him entrance. Because the first thing he does is suck on my lower lip, and then he licks it. I moan, sounding like the debauched heathen I presently am, and then he French kisses the hell out of me. It's sensational, like my mouth is humming with need, and he is providing what I crave. He doesn't demand; he doesn't force. Blake is smooth eroticism. He doesn't just kiss with his mouth. His whole being is involved, and he's really, really into it. Like kissing me is the only thing he wants to do.

God, that's sexy.

I must say it out loud when he moves his mouth to my neck, because he pauses with his face against my skin, and I feel his lips curve up. A faint tremble runs through his shoulders, telling me he's trying not to laugh at me, and it makes me laugh.

"What?" I demand with a grin on my face, pushing at him.

He shakes his head, the inky black of night not able to completely hide his smile. "Nothing. You make me laugh."

What he told me about his past, about the girl who died, and all the things he didn't tell me—I wish I could erase all the fissures of hurt from his bearing. I didn't know what to say, and I knew words wouldn't be enough. His pain was palpable. It resonated through the air and stole my breath. No one but the person experiencing it can heal that kind of anguish. I can only mute it. And now, here he is, laughing. His laughter always sounds abrupt, like he is surprised to find humor in something. I find it sweet, and sad. And his smile—I love seeing his smile, timid and rare as it is. And his stormy eyes, looking at me like I'm something special. Like I took away a little of his sorrow.

And then, what he said about my name, and what it could mean—what Blake said about being named after my grandmother. It sent me to a place I can't explain. A place I know is there, waiting, but one I am not ready to approach. A place of acceptance for who I am, and even who I am not.

"Be careful, Blake, or I'll think you like me too," I whisper just before I slide my fingers down his ridged stomach and hook my thumbs around the fabric of his boxer briefs. I pause like this, knowing the location of my hands to his groin has to be driving him crazy. It's driving me crazy. "It isn't fair, you know."

"What?" he chokes, his breathing unsteady.

"That you still have on clothes, and I have on none."

Blake shudders as I dip my fingers inside the band of the boxers, brushing them over his skin. My heart crashes into a wall and revives itself. Back arched, head back, his chest lifts and lowers as he struggles for air. I go still, staring at the rawness of his pose, and how it affects me. It makes me mad with desire, my fingers twitching to be on more of his skin, to touch what is so close. An inch to the side and he would be mine. Before I can venture past a turning point, Blake springs from the bed, tugging at his boxers with one hand and riffling through a drawer with the other as he hops from foot to foot. It would be comical in daylight.

I go up on my elbows. "What are you doing?"

"I'm about to make history," he says as he turns to me, and I snort.

The humor dies as soon as he joins me in the bed, and his hands are all over me. Testing, touching, memorizing. Fingers on my arms, hands over my thighs. Even his hair is a tool used in my seduction, tickling my flesh wherever it goes. And his lips—his lips join in and then I'm a panting, moaning, embarrassing mess without a shred of dignity or self-consciousness.

Hooded eyes, sensual mouth, magic hands.

Blake.

And to my ever-loving mortification, when Blake finally stops tormenting me with his mouth and decides on another course of pleasurable torture, entering me in one, sure stroke, I shout, "You're my master!"

He goes still, and then he laughs.

I don't care. I have no shame. It feels too good to care.

I willingly bow down to my master.

Blake's still chuckling as his body picks up the momentum, bringing me to the brink of chaos and order and pain and euphoria.

"Yes," he coos. "I am."

* * *

I don't know if it's good or bad that he doesn't bring up the master thing, but I can tell, as we start off the next morning with another round of fornication—our third time—that he's thinking about it. With the light of the sun streaming in through the window and spotlighting the bed and us, he loves me slowly this time. Sweetly. All the while with a secret smile on his face and light dancing in his eyes. He's beautiful. Like a dark, imperfect, savage angel.

"I know you're thinking about it," I say, lifting my hips to better accommodate him.

Blake places his cheek to mine and says into my ear, "Thinking about what?"

He is a great lover. He makes sure I get as much out of it as he does. I've enjoyed this—him, his body, this place, all of it. This is the last time I'll get to have this with him. Even though I'm staying another night, I can't spend it in Blake's bed. The more I'm with him, the harder it'll be to go. It's best to put the barriers in place now. I roll my eyes at how my current thoughts glaringly clash with my present activities.

After this.

After this, the barriers will go up.

"That I called you my master."

I narrow my eyes when he brings his face close to mine. A smile tips his lips, brightens his eyes, and I have a hard time breathing. He looks so sweet it makes my heart hurt. Blake rocks his body just right, and I tense up as pleasure sweeps through me.

"Say it again," he murmurs huskily.

"No…way."

"Say you like kissing me."

When I close my lips to keep the words inside, he goes still.

With his thickness inside me, deep and full, madness digs its claws into my scalp and tightens its grip. Insanity brought on by need pinpricks my skin, escalates my pulse. I buck in an attempt to get him to move, but Blake is solid stone, his hands wrapping around my wrists near my head to further lock me in place.

Gray eyes shot through with desire lock on mine. "Say it, Opal, and we'll continue our lesson."

I chuckle throatily, and his grip slackens. At some point during the night he told me he liked the sound of my voice, and I think he likes the sound of my laughter too. I think he likes quite a few things about me. Blake nuzzles my neck, practically purring with male satisfaction. I shift my hips, and he growls with need. I wiggle, and bump, and he is suddenly out of control. Moving so fast, so wild. Harder. And harder. Sweat clings to me—his, mine. The smell of his skin is like perfumed toxin. I inhale, and I lose my mind, bit by bit.

"Say it," he pants, his breath hot on my ear.

Blake pulls out, fills me. Again, and again, and again.

"Say you like kissing me," is a low whisper along my sensitive shoulder.

"I like kissing you. I *love* kissing you," I confess shrilly as I throb, and build, and descend.

Blake follows close behind, his face strained, his eyes closed. The expression on his face is beastly. Devilish. And then, with his eyes still closed, he smiles. And I melt. All of me melts. Because that smile is happy, and content. And one thousand percent satisfied.

Entwined in one another, we rest, our mingled breaths slowing as one. The side of Blake's face is on my breasts, his arms next to mine, almost hugging me. My heart is pounding, and if someone were to ask me what day of the week it is, I would say monkey. My brain is mush, and my body is limp, and all of me is, I don't know, peaceful. I like this feeling.

He leaves too soon, separating our bodies. I'm instantly cold without the warmth of his body. I watch him walk from the room, and I don't take my eyes from the doorway as I wait for him to return. I refuse to bring words to my feelings. Instead, I let them be, and focus on enjoying the sight of Blake as he reenters the room. Sinewy long limbs, so white I wonder if he's part albino. His black hair looks like a tornado ravaged the thick locks, and when he gets close enough for me to see the stubble on his sharply honed jaw, I shiver at the remembered feel of it scraping along various delicate spots on my body.

Blake leans down, puts a hand on either side of my face, and does that half-smile thing that turns my heart upside-down. "I am the master," he teases, and then he firmly presses his lips to my forehead before straightening.

He grabs clothes from the dresser and pauses in the doorway, his decadent backside at eye level. "Meet me downstairs. I want to show you something."

"It's *my* master, not *the*," I grumble. "It was in the heat of the moment."

I don't bother looking to confirm, because I can literally *feel* his gloating smile.

As soon as I hear the water pipes rumble to wakefulness in the bathroom, I let my head fall back against the pillows and stare at a crack in the white ceiling. Forehead kisses from Blake are more debilitating than full-on lip ones. There was tenderness to it, affection. Things Blake has no right showing me. A funny, sickish feeling swims around in my stomach, and I rapidly blink my eyes until the crack in the ceiling blurs, grows, and fills my eyes.

With his scent wrapped around me and the lingering warmth of his heat captured by the blanket to keep me company, my eyes get heavy, and I relax into the bed. I turn to my side and grab the pillow Blake used last night and cuddle it, snuggling my face to its softness. It smells like a mixture of man and spices. Cloves. Pepper. Satisfaction. A contented sigh leaves me, and I drift off.

"I'm making pancakes," is called up the stairwell, and I soar from the bed.

Spinning around in a crazy circle, I fight to fully open my eyes as I look around my surroundings. I have to remind myself where I am, and what I spent last night doing. A cool draft along my naked skin helps me recollect, as does the ache of my body, and the sated feeling that comes with it. A gloating smile of my own forms to my lips and I charge from the room with exuberance and a hungry stomach.

I wash up in the bathroom with pink walls and cream-colored shelving and dress in jeans and a turquoise T-shirt. Teeth brushed, I turn a critical eye to my hair. It got frisky along with me and Blake, its wanton disposition shown in the disorderly waves. I brush it, which results in added volume it does not need, and then I barrel down the stairs.

Through the multiple windows, the sun streaks the room with light. It smells like strong black coffee and sweetened carbohydrates in the kitchen, and it all feels so natural, so much like a scene from a nauseatingly sappy movie, that my feet trip over a reality I'll most likely never experience. This is pretend, and we're playing. But I like this game.

His shirt is gray, his jeans are low on his narrow hips, and when Blake turns with a plate full of pancakes in one hand, and a spatula in the other, he is the epitome of the perfect man. Sexy, wicked male, offering food. Mmm.

"I could get used to this," I tell him without thinking.

Blake tilts his head.

"The food. You cooking. Food. Food," I repeat firmly. "I like food."

His mouth fights a grin as he walks by and sets the plate on the table. "I have a feeling I know what you like even better than food."

"Oh, yeah? What's that?" Sex with him, kissing him, touching him. Smelling him. Lots of things that involve him.

Blake faces me, and I notice his shirt for the first time. "Oh, my God, I love you," I blurt, staring at the picture of a pony with the words *My Little Pony* above it, all in purple.

He freezes up, the little color that his skin holds draining from him.

"That is to say…I mean…" I stutter, feeling all the color that left him weaves its way into my flesh. "Your shirt. I love your shirt." I reach around him, grab a pancake from the plate, and stuff my mouth with it to keep it from producing words. I can taste vanilla, and yes, I prefer my pancakes doused in butter and syrup, but this isn't bad plain.

"It's cute," comes out garbled.

As if suddenly no longer hypnotized by the spell of words that scare some men, Blake steals the remainder of pancake from my hand and takes a large bite. "I wasn't sure if it was a *My Little Pony* day, or a *Rainbow Brite* one."

"Stop," I moan, putting a hand to my abdomen. I can feel my irrational girl parts falling in love with him. I love cartoons, especially the ones from my childhood.

When I was six, I stayed with an elderly lady who crocheted and didn't do much else. I spent the majority of my summer watching old cartoons as I sat beside her on the couch. Almost every day she made me macaroni and cheese and Jell-O. For a six-year-old, it was pretty amazing, but now I sort of wonder why I wasn't outside on the nice days. Ada wasn't one for conversation, and the television became my friend. In the fall, after a lady came to talk to me, I was shipped off to another home.

Sometimes, I spent a year or so at a home; other times, it was mere months.

"What are you thinking right now?" Blake asks.

I look up and am hit by the full power of his inquisitive gaze. It makes my knees turn noodle-like. I let my body fall into the closest chair, and I commence to avoid the conversation by taking three pancakes and going about making a proper heart attack breakfast. I spread half a stick of butter on the cakes, and drain a good portion of the syrup from the bottle onto them. And then, I eat.

Blake sits down and takes two pancakes for himself. His motions are slow, and his words are careful when he speaks. "You don't have to tell me. You just…you looked sad for a minute."

Peering into the glass near my plate, I see it contains ice cubes and water, and I quickly down it. The coldness turns the inside of my throat into icicles, and I breathe through my nose until it passes.

"I don't get sad; I get awesome." I use my fork to sever a piece of pancake from the pack, and then I pop it in my mouth. Syrup drips from the corner of my mouth and I wipe it away with my hand. If I had to choose a reason to want Blake nearby, I could legitimately and guiltlessly keep him around merely for his pancake-making skills. His other skills are an added bonus.

He shakes his head, his eyes on the black mug he raises to his lips. Blake takes a sip, his lips hugging the rim like they hugged mine. "Get any more awesome and your head might get too heavy to hold up."

"Nonsense." As I chew, I swing my legs and look out the windows—anywhere but directly at Blake. I can feel him, though, like an imprint in the air. And I can clearly visualize last night, and this morning, and his naked body. *Barriers, Opal. Barriers!*

I swallow thickly and stare at the shed. "I don't know a lot about sheds, but aren't they generally windowless?"

Blake twists in his seat, his gaze following mine. "Yeah." He turns back to me with a light in his eyes and a hum of excitement in his frame. "That's what I wanted to show you."

7

Blake

Opal is a being of constant movement, whether it's her hands or her feet; some part of her is always in motion. The only time I've seen her perfectly still was last night while she slept. She looked peaceful in my arms, calm in a way conscious Opal never is. It felt nice, holding her like that. As I unlock the shed door, she shifts and fidgets with restless energy, bumping into me once.

"Are there zombies locked up in there?"

"What?" I ask.

"I saw a zombie once." Opal runs a finger down the length of the white metal siding as she continues. "It was this guy at a hospital I worked at for three days."

I glance at her as I pocket the key. "Why were you only there for three days?"

She shrugs and turns her head to the side. "I decided I didn't like the area. Anyway. I know he was a zombie because he died, and then he came back to life with red eyes and sores all over his face."

I want to ask her if she's ever just stopped moving, just stayed in one place long enough to make it hers. She grew up not having that, and to her, it's normal to be untethered. I always claim to want the same, but I think, under the right circumstances, I'd want something different. With the right person, I'd want more. Some kind of permanence in a world without much of it.

Opal says, "I asked him his name and he said, 'Brain.'"

"Are you sure he didn't say, 'Brian?'"

"Pretty sure. Do you think there might be some in there?"

I give her a sidelong look. "Not that I am aware of."

Opal grins, her eyes twinkling. "So there's a chance?"

"There's also a chance you'll stop telling outrageous stories, but I find it unlikely."

Her husky laughter slides down my back like nails dipped in lust.

I grab hold of the door and pull. It groans, shudders, and finally gives in, swinging open to show darkness and dust. The air is thick and hot from being trapped inside the sturdy walls for too long. I don't even know the last time I was in here. Every time I was, I saw my grandpa's unrealized dream. Like the pond out back, this too is a reality he never got to witness in its completion. I finished the pond; I couldn't bear to do the same for this.

"My grandpa had a lot of ideas," I explain as I step into the large space. I look behind me, thinking Opal is there, but she isn't. "No zombies," I confirm with a touch of exasperation.

She pops inside, immediately going still. And then she's walking, turning this way and that, drinking up everything she can see. Soaking it up with her animated, imaginative brain.

"Wow." Awe resonates through that single word.

Moving to the wall, I flip on the lights. They're fluorescent, and it takes them a minute to heat up from where they rest along the high, vaulted ceiling. They flicker on, one at a time, bringing the interior of the large building into better sight. The walls are done but bare of paint, and the floor is cement. Somehow, it smells fresh to me, like this place was just constructed, even though it hasn't been new for over a dozen years. Everything is covered in a thick layer of dust, but I know, like the worn appearance of the circus and its occupants, Opal doesn't see that. She sees the unfinished kitchen as it should be, bright-colored and functioning, and the partially furnished rec room is alive with activities. She sees the second floor with a wraparound hallway, and she sees them in color, in life.

"This is amazing," she says.

Through her eyes, looking at the room like she does, I see the possibilities as well. I see what my grandfather intended, and a spark flickers inside me. Opal sees what this space can be, and it makes me want to finish what my grandfather started. I know that's why he willed the land to me. He saw the direction my life was heading, and he wanted me to know it didn't have to go that way.

"I could live here! I mean, lots of people could live here. There are so many rooms! What is this place?" Opal calls from across the room.

"My grandpa had a lot of ideas," I begin again, looking around. I stood by him in this building as it was being worked on. He wanted to know my thoughts, and he listened as I gave them. I blink my eyes against stinging and slowly walk the first floor's length. My boots echo as I move.

"He, uh, he wanted to help troubled kids. This was supposed to be a kind of retreat, a safe place for kids who were in trouble at home, school, with the law, wherever, to stay. There were supposed to be supervised activities, counseling, games, and personal goals—just about anything you can think of."

Opal clambers up the wooden stairwell and starts opening and closing doors. "These are all bedrooms?"

"Yeah, and activity areas."

She grips the railing and peers down at me. "Come up here. Show me what this place was meant to look like. Tell me everything."

I slowly ascend the stairs, the wood creaking in two spots as I step. I didn't really think about why I decided I wanted to share this with Opal, but I now know why. Everywhere she goes, she adds her light to the darkness of her surroundings. Just showing her this, seeing her enthusiasm and wonder, it lights me up as well. I needed to see her response to this to get my head on straight.

Opal meets me at the top of the stairs, grinning widely. Her eyes sparkle, and there is a smudge of dust on her cheek. I look at her for a moment, seeing the beauty in her features I couldn't before, wondering how I could have been blind to them. She practically glows, the meaning of life personified through her. I take a breath, and it catches as I exhale.

"I get it now. I understand why you're going to school for child psychology. You want to work with kids because you saw what your grandfather hoped to do, and you want to do that for him. It isn't all for the chicks."

My nod is slow, and I can't decide if I want to smile or frown. I do neither. "That's not the only reason, but yeah, that had a lot to do with it."

"You could do so much with this place. Are you going to?" Opal tilts her head as she waits for me to answer.

I look around the second floor, knowing what I want to say. Knowing what I should say.

I take too long to reply, and Opal moves on—literally, conversationally. She stops near a door. "By the way, your grandpa sounds like the best person ever."

My throat tightens as I step into the first room. "He was."

"I would have loved to have met him," she says reflectively, moving ahead of me. Opal looks around the room with bare walls and flooring, and walks to the window. The sun locks on her hair, turns it a deep shade of burnished fire.

"He would have liked you." I step closer, stopping when I'm directly behind her.

"Of course he would have." Opal turns and aims a smile at me, and I move without thought.

I cup her face and bring my lips to hers, fireworks exploding behind my eyeballs at the feel and taste of her. So sweet, so warm. So eager. I press my lower half to hers, and she moans low in her throat. She did that last night, and it made me crazy. My nerve endings are hardwired to respond to each sound she makes. And she makes a lot—all erotic, all coveted. I move forward, my legs tangled in hers, and she moves back, until she is against the wall and can't go any farther.

My fingers move down, to the back of her neck, to her throat, to her shoulders. Down her breasts, up her back. I mold my hands to her bottom and bring her even closer to me; the only thing between us is our regrettable clothing. Opal twists her fingers around my hair and tugs, and my legs shake with need. My whole body hurts, all from wanting her.

She tears her mouth away and gasps, "Barriers."

A rough laugh is the most I can initially produce. "You say the oddest things when you're turned on."

"No. You. Me. Barriers." Opal pulls her shirt back into place and moves away from me. "We can't, you know, fool around anymore."

I blink at her, sure I misheard her. We spent the night having sex, and now we're just supposed to turn that off? Act like it didn't happen, multiple times? "Did we have an expiration date?"

Opal runs trembling fingers through her hair, mussing it up more. She turns her face to the side. "Yes. I guess. I'm leaving tomorrow. I'll never see you again. We shouldn't make it harder when it's time to say goodbye by complicating the situation with more sex. I mean, last night was amazing, completely amazing. But it was one night, and even you said it was all you could give me. And that was fine. I'm leaving tomorrow," she says again, finally looking at me.

My heart jumps, races, and slows at the thought of never seeing her again. It's almost like I don't want her to go. What freaked me out more than hearing Opal say she loved me this morning, even if it was in jest, was the fact that hearing her say that didn't repel me. It stunned me, yeah, but it wasn't all bad. It was kind of nice to hear, unintentional or not. My grandpa made sure I knew I was loved, but anyone else? Not so much.

I feel *giddy* when I think of Opal, when I look at her. I don't get giddy. I don't even get happy all that often. And right now, I am. I feel like I could spend a lot of nights with Opal, and I wouldn't mind. Days sound even better. It's a hazardous way of thinking, and it's probably best that this is our last day together. Opal, I fear, has the power to change my way of viewing the world. My world is optimal the way it is, flaws and all.

She's right. It would be smartest to keep our distance. It would make tomorrow easier. Easier is good.

"You're right. We should keep our distance," I say conversationally.

"Definitely. It's the best idea."

I nod. "Yeah. We don't need to complicate things."

"Yeah," Opal echoes, her eyes down.

"You like kissing me too much. We keep doing that, and that next thing you know, you'll never want to kiss anyone else ever again. Not that I can blame you," I continue, resting my back to the wall and crossing my arms as I study her.

"Right. We can't, um, we can't have that," she says with false cheerfulness.

"And everyone knows kissing leads to sex. Generally. We can't have that either. Right?"

"We should probably just not even be around one another," she commiserates.

"That would be best. Or…" I drop my arms and straighten from the wall. "We *can* be around one another. See what happens."

"You know what will happen." A hint of accusation rings out from her words.

"Yes." I take a step closer to her. "And so do you."

Opal's eyes shoot to my lips, a blush crawling up her neck. We lock gazes, my chest on fire, my body tight with need, and Opal lunges for me at the same time I go for her. We hit hard enough that our teeth knock together, and I feel a pinch and taste blood. Needing to touch her, to look at her, I grab her shirt and tug it over her head. I efficiently remove her bra, a strap snapping her skin as I do so. She hisses at the sting. I set my mouth on the red mark and gently suck, her head dropping back against my chest as her hands rove up my thighs.

"I just want to have sex with you to hear what you'll cry out next," I whisper as I slide my hands up her stomach and mold them to her full breasts. She's hot, and soft, and for the moment, mine. It makes my head spin.

"That's it, huh?" Opal whirls around, her eyes burning. "You're just using me for a laugh?"

"Never," I swear, brushing sweaty hair from her face. I give her a lopsided smile. "But it is a nice addition."

Opal laughs, and I shudder, wondering how even that can turn me on. I don't think about it too much, though, because her fingers are on the button of my jeans, and then the zipper, and all I can think about is feeling her around me. *Need it, want it, need it, want it.* Her hand slips down, wraps around me, and I jerk, instinctively moving against it. The friction is maddening, the touch blissful.

"Wait. Wait," I mutter, setting her away from me. I can barely stand. I can barely think. My head is bowed, my forehead resting against hers. Our breaths are loud and fast. "I don't have any condoms on me."

Her response is instantaneous, and makes me painfully hard.

"I guess we'll have to get creative," she announces, and drops to her knees.

I close my eyes as she tugs down my jeans and boxers, and I fight to not completely lose it before it's really begun. Then I go to my knees, taking off my shirt in the process. I put it on the hard floor, and I lower Opal's head to it.

I take off the rest of my clothes.

I take off hers.

I stare at her quivering body, desire pounding through me.

"I get to be creative first," is all I say before I lower my mouth.

* * *

Opal

"Want to go for a ride?" Blake wiggles his eyebrows.

My body, recently satisfied, is languid and limp, and I am even more attached to the dark-haired man standing beside me. I should be more upset about it than I am, because, really, I'm not upset at all by it. I blink against floating debris and focus on Blake's deviant expression.

Aside from the monstrous shed, there is another, smaller one a ways behind the house, and inside it, among tools and small machinery, is a red four-wheeler. It's dark in here, and smells like dust and oil. The air is like the inside of an oven set to *broil*, making it hard to breathe.

Each time I tell him something I've never done, he looks shocked, but also kind of sad for me, and I don't want that. I know my experiences are lacking—I don't want Blake to know I've never even been on a four-wheeler before. When Blake thinks of me in weeks, and years to come, I want him to only remember good things. Fun things. Happy things. Like I will when I think of him.

"Do we need helmets?" I ask, touching the dusty seat of the ATV.

Blake laughs and shakes his head. "No. Let me get it out and I'll take you for a ride. We can see more of the land that way."

The thought of traveling the countryside via four-wheeler spins my pulse with excitement. I trot from the shed and jump to the side of it, breathing in the fresh air, taking in the blue skies as I wait. I love where I am. I couldn't ask to be anywhere better. There isn't a single comparable place. I hear the engine pop, stutter, and chug to life, picking up strength as it warms up. The four-wheeler roars in reverse from the shed, bringing dust and Blake with it. I hop up and down, shaking with eagerness.

Blake looks up, the sun catching his grin, and my stomach shoots from side to side. His eyes glow with the promise of mayhem. "Ready for some fun?"

With a little squeal, I clamber up behind him. And then I hug his legs with mine, and Blake freezes, and things get awkward. Fast. "Um…so. Where do I put my feet?"

"Foot pegs," he says faintly. "Behind mine."

"Oh." I drop my feet to the narrow metal slabs below, feeling my skin heat up.

He glances over his shoulder. "Have you not—"

"I so have," I interrupt. "So many times I've forgotten how."

Facing forward, Blake nods. "Put your arms around my waist," he instructs, and I happily oblige.

He pushes on the throttle, and with me whooping, we speed along the terrain. Blake's laughter waves over the wind when I cry out and reflexively tighten my grip on him as we hit a small ditch. The ride is bumpy and noisy, and the wind rushes at my face, blowing hair in my eyes and mouth. A few times I think I'm going to fall off the back of it. But I hang on, my heart racing, and I have a grin so wide stamped to my face that it actually begins to hurt after a while. Up and up we go, passing trees and narrowly missing others. We're in a forest of sorts, and it's magical.

Blake navigates the ATV to flat land and kills the engine.

My legs feel unusually stretched and sore, and I sort of slide from the side of the four-wheeler, aware that Blake is silently amused by my actions. My knees buckle and I straighten them, wobbly on my feet. I turn toward the sound of water, slamming into something warm and good smelling. Blake. His hands scald my skin where they rest upon my hips, and as if he too is burned by the touch, he hastily drops them and takes a step back. I pretend not to notice. Maybe he's working on replacing the walls he took down, just like I should be.

Which one of us is smarter, I wonder. The one who decides to keep the walls down, or the one who thinks they need them back up?

"It's beautiful here," I state without looking at him. I pretend my hair isn't a snarled helmet on the top of my head, and that I'm not covered in a layer of sweat.

"It makes you want to stay, doesn't it?"

My gaze flies to his, seeing a flash of understanding in the darkness of his features. Blake leans one shoulder against a nearby tree, his arms crossed. His black hair is rumpled from the ride, and my body warms at the image of my fingers running through it. The *My Little Pony* T-shit shirt gives him an abnormally masculine vibe and the straight-legged jeans make his legs seem endless. He is the essence of what a man who belongs in the wild looks like. I stare at his hard mouth, imagining it softened with need in the throes of a passionate kiss. Remembering it as exactly that less than two hours ago.

"It's peaceful here, enough to make everything in life seem simple, conquerable," he continues, rubbing the side of his jaw. "It's an illusion, but it's a nice one."

"I like illusions. Reality is boring."

Blake's eyes lock on mine. "But isn't this reality too?"

My breaths come faster, and I look down from his probing gaze. He's asking about us, and what this is. What it will become, if anything. It's a reality that will soon become an illusion. A memory that will change over time, and fade, and become different from the truth.

Heaviness fills me, and I fight it. I straighten my spine, and put a smile on my face. "Reality, illusion, whatever. It's been fun, Blake. Nothing more, nothing less."

His gaze doesn't waver, and I know he's about to call my bluff. "That's odd, because I thought we had a moment that first night when we were outside—you know, when you decided to take a nap in my truck."

"Oh? Tell me about it," I encourage silkily. That night was twenty emotions ago. Fifty confessions ago.

"I'll tell you *all* about it, Opal." His promise is deep and low, sending shivers down my spine.

He's mocking me, but it's dipped in playfulness. I mimic his stance against the tree, satisfaction unfurling and weaving through me when his eyes narrow. The bark is rough and pricks the skin it touches. He angles his body toward me. I do the same, nothing but the smallest of spaces dividing us. Whispers scream in the silence surrounding us, shout that this is dangerous, that I shouldn't antagonize an unpredictable beast. I ignore them, ignore the sensible part of me that says to not give in to how Blake makes me feel.

I love how Blake makes me feel.

"The birds were chirping—"

"Those were bats," I cut in with a wink.

He gives me a look and continues. "The sunset was beautiful, the sky alive in colors of red and pink and purple."

"It was black out," I correct.

"A warm breeze—"

"We were both shivering. Anything else?"

The corners of Blake's mouth move up, and just as suddenly, go back to their flat line.

"Actually, you're right. We did have a moment," I state, tucking hair behind my ears. It sprouts back to where it wants to be.

"Enlighten me." Blake's voice is menace wrapped up in a purr.

"It was that instant when you were near the truck door, and you looked at me, and…I'll remember it always. It was…poetic." I smile, imitating the candor of his tone.

He blinks, his mouth turning down.

"You looked right at me, and…you said—and I can't explain the sheer beauty, the unparalleled poignancy, of your words—you said…*get out of my truck*." I close my eyes and inhale with a look of bliss on my face, opening them to watch emotion trickle away from the sharply cut features before me.

The mask falls away for the briefest of instances, like a window blind allowing light into a dark room only to close, leaving the blackness to grow in its absence. Blake's jaw shifts forward and the stillness encasing him in ice alludes to the havoc thrumming, unknown and unseen, through his taut body.

"You're going to miss me, aren't you?" I say. "Life will be so much duller with me gone. You'll have to talk to yourself and answer in my place, just to have any kind of joy." I bite back a smile at Blake's glare. I touch the roughness of his jaw, wanting to kiss the frown from his lips. He's going to miss me, and I'm going to miss him.

Shutters snap over his eyes, neither denying nor affirming it.

"It's okay. You'll tell me when you're ready. But I want you to know that you don't have to hide it." I lean closer, my head at level with his collarbone. I lift my eyes to his and say softly, "It doesn't have to be one of your secrets."

Somberness takes over his face. "There's a reason for the secrecy, for why I hide. I've done shitty things. I'm not exactly a good person."

"Well, you're not a bad person."

"Really?" Blake holds my gaze. "Did you not listen to anything I told you about my past?"

I shake my head and sigh. I've screwed up—a lot. I don't dwell on every mistake I've made. Instead, I try to not make them again. "Bad choices don't make you a bad person. As far as I've seen so far, you're a pretty decent person."

"Oh, yeah? And how did you come to that conclusion?"

"Feeling vain, are you? You need me to list every good deed you've done since I met you?"

Blake shifts his jaw and rolls his shoulders, turning his face from my view.

"Stop thinking about the crap you've done in the past and start focusing on what you can do in the future." I touch his bicep, feel the muscles bunch, and then I flick his ear, just because.

Blake turns to scowl at me, and I kiss the scowl from his face. He pulls away to tell me, "You're nuts, you know that?"

Grinning, I shrug. "Life is pretty mundane without a little chaos."

His throat bobs up and down as he swallows. And then with movements so fast I don't see them, I'm in Blake's arms, and he's kissing me as he walks. I kiss him back, hungrily—inconsolable with the knowledge that soon my lips will no longer know the feel of his. Before I can make a move or sound in protestation, I'm sitting in a creek with Blake beside me, and he's laughing at the look on my face as cold water hits me.

I splash water at his face.

Blinking, Blake shakes water droplets from his eyes. And then he smolders them at me, like he has been known to do. "You're asking for it, Opal."

"Oh?" I splash more water at him. "Asking for what, Blake?"

He puts his face inches from mine, and I get lost in the swirling gray depths of his eyes. "A little of my chaos."

"Just a little?" I ask, my voice like a whisper of air.

Blake turns his head the slightest amount and puts his mouth beside mine. "Or a lot."

And we're back to kissing, and other things.

* * *

Opal

We spend the day walking around the land, Blake telling me stories and memories as we traipse across the immediate countryside.

At one point, he holds my hand.

He tells me how his grandfather got the pond dug out with the intention of it being a swimming hole for the kids staying at the future shelter, but that was as far as he got before he passed.

I tell him about the time when I was thirteen that I was bet to eat a cup of honey mustard for ten dollars. I ate it, and got my ten dollars. I also got a stomachache.

Another time, he puts an arm around my shoulders and pulls me to his side.

Blake tells me he personally finished the pond a handful of years ago. He tells me of all the many dreams his grandfather had, and how a lot of them died with him.

I tell him that dreams don't die, even if the people who have them do. And then I go on to tell him about a dream of mine I used to have where Freddy Krueger was my dad.

He laughs. He laughs so much, and I realize as I listen to the deep roughness of it, that I want to hear him laugh all the time.

Blake tells me all kinds of things about his grandfather, and nothing about himself. Even so, I learn a lot about Blake, just by paying attention to the way he talks about his Grandpa John.

And when he gets quiet and sad, I hug him, and then I make him laugh again. I'm not sure what I say or do that is so funny. I don't even have to try to be funny, and he laughs. I like that.

He loved his grandfather fiercely. He loved him the way everyone should be loved.

I would like to be loved that fiercely.

By the time Blake puts away the four-wheeler and we go inside to eat and wash up, my skin is crispy, and I'm tired. My muscles ache, and there is a blister from my boots on the back of my left ankle. Once I'm stable enough in work and home, I'm going to need to invest in some tennis shoes. But that's an undistinguished plan with no immediate way to be established. And I can't really picture myself content anywhere, working some aimless job.

Drawing has always been my passion. I just don't know how to make a career out of it, or if I can. Or if I'd succeed. I tell myself not to let fear override my dream, and it helps. What is fear if you don't give in to it? Nothing. It has no power unless you feed it.

In the first floor bathroom, I watch Blake run fingers through hair damp from a recent shower, my eyes dropping to his bare back and the black boxer briefs covering some of my favorite parts to leer at.

"If you want me naked again, just tell me," he says as he faces me.

I strive for a casual pose as I roll my eyes and bang my elbow against the wall. Swallowing back a curse word, I tell him, "You wish."

Blake winks. "I don't have to wish."

"Get out. I'm taking a bath," I command, pointing to the doorway. I've been aching for a bath for days, and I'm determined to have one before I leave here.

His eyes rake over my frame. "Need me to wash your back?"

When I don't answer, Blake shrugs and leaves.

I quickly set about filling up the claw foot tub with steaming hot water. I pour a good amount of manly smelling shampoo into the tub and watch the suds grow. And then, with a happy sigh, I immerse myself in it, not even caring how the heat makes my skin sting. I'll gladly take it, to feel this content. Blowing at bubbles, I make a path between them with my breath before dunking myself and popping back up. I close my eyes and sink deeper down into the rub, the water gently lapping against my chin.

The relaxed atmosphere lasts all of three minutes.

A black, whiskered face and paws pop up over the tub ledge and I scream, unintentionally splashing water onto the animal. Teeth flash at me as the cat shows its discontent before ducking away from any further water attacks. Heart pounding, I look at the door I forgot to close and then peer at the floor near the sink where the cat is. It has to be the unfriendly cat from the other night—the one who sent me a death wish with its eyes while I swam in the pond.

"Blake?" I call, my eyes locked on the feline.

The cat glares up at me with yellow eyes. It meows, the sound deep and growly. So far, it appears to be an anti-social, possibly rabid, cat.

"It's not like I *invited* you in here," I grumble.

A growl is its response.

"Yeah?" Blake replies from somewhere in the house.

"Do you have a cat you forget to tell me about?"

The cat meows again, letting me know it is not okay with me talking.

"What?" he barks in a voice that sounds much closer than it did a second ago.

"A cat!" My voice is high and strangled. I like cats, but this one doesn't seem to like me. "There's a cat in here!"

"What the hell?"

Something flies through the air and plops into the water with me. I catapult upright with a shriek and fall over the tub ledge and onto the floor in my haste to get away from whatever it is. Wincing at the feeling of hipbone and elbow smacking into hard tile, I lie still in a puddle of bathwater as I catch my breath. Was it a mouse, a bat, what? I flip wet hair from my eyes and look into yellow ones. The cat looks bored, but it's clearly covering up its evil deed. I swear the lips around its teeth lift up in a nasty grin.

"What kind of a cat are you? You're satanic," I tell it.

The cat yawns and licks a paw.

Tiny bumps of cold raise my flesh as I slowly get to my feet, and I look around the room for a towel. There's one hanging over the door, all the way across the room. I have to pass the cat to get to it. I don't especially want to do that.

"Blake, where are you?" I demand loudly, frustration darkening my tone.

Arms wrapped around my upper half, I gingerly make my way to the tub and peer down. Floating on top of the water is a misshapen brown thing. I lean closer, toes inching forward in the pool of water I'm standing in. Taking a bottle of shampoo from a nearby shelf, I poke at it a few times. It sinks down and pops back up, causing me to jump.

"Don't be a baby," I tell myself.

The black cat agrees.

I glare at the cat sitting by my feet, its tail lazily flicking at my legs. "What did you throw in the bathtub, and why? Is Blake yours? Is that it? If it comes to a fight over him, you can have him."

When I get no response, I turn back to the tub.

"What is it?" I wonder. My calves get nudged by a furry head and I tense up, wondering if I'm about to get attacked. "Stop it."

A foamy layer of suds has blurred the object more. It can't be a living thing. There was no sound, no struggle. The trepidation I first felt has turned into exasperation—namely aimed at me. I square my shoulders. "Okay. This has gone on long enough. It's obvious Blake is not going to come to your rescue, so just take care of it already and find out what's in the tub."

Cringe in place, I lean down in slow motion. My hand is outstretched, toes solidly planted on a slippery floor. And then my feet begin to move apart. I look down, watching my legs get farther away from one another.

It gets to the point where I fear I may do the splits, or worse, move the wrong way and knock myself out on the tub ledge.

"Opal? What are you doing?"

Panic sets in, obliterating the knowledge that Blake is near. Arms pin wheeling, I fight to stay upright when it's clear I am meant to fall. The catalyst of the moment is when the devil cat rams its head into the backs of my legs, just hard enough to send me to my inevitable uncoordinated landing.

Hands grab me, fumble with the slipperiness of my skin, and eventually manage to halt my descent. Blake holds me like he just dipped me during some strange dance. Straightening us, he says, "If you really wanted your back washed, all you had to do was say so. You didn't have to call in a stray cat to get me in here."

My eyes dart around the now empty room. "Did you see that? Where did it come from? How did it get in here?"

"The front door wasn't shut all the way. It must have snuck in when we weren't looking. I don't know where it came from." His eyes twinkle. "Want a pet?"

"Not that one," I state. "It threw something in the tub and rammed me with its head like it *wanted* me to fall. You saw it; you know this time I'm *not* lying."

He narrows his eyes and looks toward the bathtub. Dropping his hands from me, he approaches the tub as he says over his shoulder, "By the way, those were some impressive dance moves."

"I call that one 'Trying Not to Die.' It's going to be a hit."

Blake smirks at me before turning his attention to whatever is floating in the bathwater. I hang back, not really wanting to come face to face with some rodent or whatever is in there. I grab a towel and wrap it around my body, forgetting to breathe as I watch Blake. When he puts his hand in the water, I wince, waiting for his arm to come away with a bloody nub where his hand is supposed to be. Instead, his hand comes out whole and intact, holding something. I expel a loud breath.

"It's a sock," he announces.

"A sock?" I sound dubious. I am dubious.

Blake stands and shows me the sodden garment. "Yeah. I don't know whose sock it is, but that's what it is."

"And the cat?" I nervously eye the doorway, waiting for the bringer of death to appear once more.

"I'll make sure it's gone."

"Okay. I'm just going to..." I move for the door and grip the doorknob in my hand. "Wait in here, until I know it's for sure gone."

Blake's eyebrows lower. "Sure." He pauses as he's about to pass me. "Are you okay?"

"Yes," I say in a super peppy voice, even adding a nod to authenticate it. And then I shut the door after him and keep my back to it, just in case.

It's close to ten minutes until I hear from Blake again. "The house is clear."

"Are you sure?"

"Yeah. It's on the porch right now eating bread and drinking milk."

I jerk away from the door and fling it open. "Blake!"

He's all innocent eyes. "What? It was hungry. And you should see it—it's got its arms around the sock like it's hugging it. Cutest thing ever."

Glaring at him, I follow him into the living room, and keeping a good distance between the window and me, look out and down. Dark has claimed the night, but the porch light shines bright and strong. Sure enough, the cat is lying on the porch with the sock between its arms as it drinks milk from an old sour cream container.

"I guess it just hates you," he says cheerfully.

As if sensing its nemesis, the cat looks up and stares at me, like it's waiting for me to remove myself from its presence before it will return to its meal.

Without a word, I turn to make my way up the stairs to get dressed.

I dress in panties and one of Blake's T-shirts—it's purple with a picture of Prince on it, and ends at my knees. I'm hit by the need to sleep and fight a yawn. There are different ways to be tired—some from pure exhaustion, and others with fullness. I am the latter. I'm not ignorant enough to think that my past won't eventually catch up with me, or that any of this is lasting beyond tomorrow, but for now, things are good. For tonight, I am exactly where I want to be—as long as that cat goes away.

I search the downstairs for Blake, and not finding him, I take the brown throw from the back of the couch and wrap it around my shoulders before heading out into the night. The temperature outside is nice—a little cooler when the wind blows, but not enough that I'm uncomfortable.

"Where's the cat?" I ask cautiously.

"Gone. Must have known you were coming."

"Ha ha."

A low chuckle reaches me.

Blake sits on the rickety porch swing with its peeling white paint. My eyes move to the shed, thinking of all the projects it would entail to get it up to snuff. It would keep me busy for months. My gaze travels over the land, seeing everything it could be. This place needs life. Laughter. This place needs people to make more memories.

I glance at Blake. He stares back. Or just two people. Two people could make lots of memories. I think of sledding in the winter, ice skating on the pond. Building snowmen. I could plant a garden in the spring. Swim in the pond on the warmer days. Draw Blake. Kiss Blake. Spend my nights with Blake.

I give myself an internal shake. *Stop it, Opal. You need to be free. No ties. And anyway, he's probably leaving the country. And you have someone in Montana you need to see, and others you hopefully don't see.* No point in thinking of possibilities with something that will never happen.

"What is it with you and my T-shirts?"

I glance down at Prince and grin. "You have great taste in T-shirts."

Blake scoots over to make room for me. I sit down before my tired legs give out, making sure the blanket blocks my bare skin from the cool wood. The sky is studded with white stars, and I watch the tree limbs move with the wind, the music of the leaves beautiful. Blake doesn't say anything, and I try not to. It lasts for about thirty seconds.

"Are you going to repaint this?" I touch the arm of the swing and my finger comes away flecked in white.

Blake shifts on the seat, his arm now resting against mine. His warmth seeps through the blanket, making a hot spot on my arm. "Maybe. If I stay."

I push with my legs, and the swing creaks as it slowly moves forward and back. "What's the deciding factor on whether or not you stay?"

Blake's arm shifts up and down as he shrugs. "I don't know. I guess I'm waiting for a sign." He glances at me, his eyebrows lifted as if to say he knows how silly his words sound.

I smile at him before turning my focus to the sky. Vast, dark, and endless—that's the night sky. Full of dreams and opportunities. Everything seems possible under a star-filled sky. "Maybe if you wish on a shooting star, you'll get your answer."

"And maybe I'll just feel lame."

"That too." I grin and push at the floor with my foot, causing the swing to move faster.

"Where are you going from here? Tomorrow, when we get to Bismarck, where will you go?" His eyes are serious.

"I don't know," I answer truthfully, unable to hold his stare for long. "I mean, I have one place I have to stop, but after that? Wherever sounds good, I guess. I'll just close my eyes, put my finger on a map, and pick my next destination."

"And you're okay with that? Just—jumping around from place to place. That's okay to you? That's how you want to live?" A hint of scorn darkens his voice.

I hop down from the swing, not liking his tone. Not liking the judgment, and definitely not liking how I care what he thinks. "What about you? It isn't like you have your whole life mapped out either. And you have more choices than me. You have *options*. I don't have anything."

I shake my head at how self-pitying that sounds, and hurry to alter my words. "I just want somewhere to belong. If you don't belong with someone, at least you belong here, right? You have a place to call yours, Blake, and you don't even know if you want it."

The injustice of it pricks my skin like the bites of hundreds of bugs. People take what they have for granted, all the time. I didn't have anything growing up, and I'm not complaining about that. But I see how wasteful people are with things that a lot of people don't ever have. This place—this place could be so much. I don't know the circumstances of Blake's childhood. I can tell it was bad. If nothing else, he had a grandfather who loved him. A man who loved him enough to leave him his legacy. The ungrateful shit can't be happy with that? Oh no, he has to go off to some other country to find out the true meaning of life.

My face burns; my hands fist.

Blake carefully stands. He doesn't try to come closer, wariness stitched to his posture. "You're right. I'm as clueless as they come."

"Why can't you be happy with what you have?" A crack sounds in the middle of the sentence. I really want to know. What is it about Blake that can never be satisfied? And maybe if I understand what drives him, I'll understand what drives me. But I'll never tell him that.

His jaw turns to stone, his eyes like lightning bolts in the dark. "I grew up with my dad telling me I was a waste of space and my mom pretending it didn't happen. My mom was into her prescription drugs, choosing not to notice when he hit me, or screamed at me, or locked me in my room for hours. There was a special closet, just for me. It was dark, and tiny, and smelled like mothballs. I used to have nightmares about it."

"Blake," I whisper.

He looks away, his stiff stance warning me to not talk. "My dad wanted to control me, and I became out of control. My mom has mental issues, and I inherited some of them. It wasn't all my parents' fault. I had problems on my own, but it got worse after my grandpa died. He was a stable rock, and then he was gone, and I was lost. I want to finish everything he started, but I'm worried I can't. I'm worried I'll screw it up. I don't want to let him down, not over this."

The ravaged expression on his face shreds my heart. I unconsciously step closer, and he purposely steps back.

His voice is thick when he asks, "Do you know what it's like to be suicidal, to have depression?"

I shake my head, my throat closing.

"I've tried to kill myself. I overdosed on drugs. Once on purpose, and the other time—the other time I don't know. It was years ago, but I did. And I'll never try it again, but the depression stays. That never goes away. Because of my addictive personality, I refuse all medication. The only one who can help me is me, and every day is a fight." His voice is bleak, broken.

My fingers curl, wanting to reach for him. Just as I'm about to give in, he turns from me. Like he has to hide, like he is ashamed.

"What's it like, having depression?" I ask quietly.

"It makes it hard to get out of bed some days. It makes it seem like giving up is the only thing that makes sense. There are some days when I feel so lost that I'm surprised I even know who I am. It makes me never satisfied, because I always feel like there's a hole in me. There is something missing that I can never find."

Blake shakes his head as he turns to face me, running a hand through his hair. "My grandpa saw that. He tried to help. And then he wasn't there, and I turned to drugs to fill the void."

He takes a step toward me, a hint of desperation in his next words. "I could have everything, and I would still feel incomplete. Something in me isn't right, something that can't be fixed. I don't try to replace what I'm missing anymore. I just try to live with it. But I'm always searching, even when I tell myself to stop. I'm always looking."

"I understand."

His eyebrows lower. "Do you? You lie, Opal." Blake laughs abruptly. "You lie about everything. You could be lying now." His eyes are dark and somber, begging for me to be telling the truth, to comprehend what it's like for him.

"I don't lie about important things, Blake. I'm not lying about understanding. I don't know how it feels to have depression, but I understand what you're telling me." I close the distance between us, my chest tight, and I touch his soft hair, brushing it back from his forehead. My eyes lift to his. "I don't lie about my feelings."

"What are your feelings?" he asks in a low voice, holding my gaze prisoner with his.

I can't tell him. I'm not even sure what they are. But I can tell him about me, and maybe he'll understand what I'm giving him. I reach for Blake's hand. It's cool and dry, and I squeeze his fingers.

"Less than three weeks ago, I was living in Illinois with my boyfriend Jonesy," I say.

"What the hell kind of a name is Jonesy?"

I smile faintly. "It's a nickname. He's over six-and-a-half feet tall, and he's a beast of a man. His first name is Jonathan, but no one calls him that."

"Do you love him?"

I look at Blake as I let go of his hand. If he's asking that, it means my answer matters to him. "No. Once, I think I did, but it was so long ago that I'm not sure. He was…exciting. I liked that." For a while.

"What happened?" A breeze fills the silence, playing with Blake's hair.

I scratch at the side of my nose, wondering how best to explain. I drop my hand and decide I might as well just say it. "Jonesy is a robber."

He blinks. "I'm sorry, what?"

Shifting my feet, I meet his gaze. "You know, like…as a job? Jonesy robs places. For money…and other stuff. Say he filled out an application; in the job spot, he would put 'robber.' I mean, not that he ever would do that, but if he did, that's what it would say."

"What does he rob?" Blake asks quietly.

"Mostly grocery stores."

His head jerks back. "Okay, now I know you're lying."

I chew on my lower lip, wishing this time I really was. "It's a tribute… to me. Because I like food a lot. He always takes my favorite snacks."

"He robs grocery stores for *food*?"

"Yeah. I mean, no one could ever accuse Jonesy of being a genius. And hey, if you're going to rob a place for food, you might as well make it a grocery store. They do have the best selections of fresh meat and produce." It's a poor joke, and my shoulders slump as I wait for a reaction.

Blake makes a sound and then walks to the other end of the porch. With the length of the porch between us, he turns back toward me. "Do you rob them with him?"

"No," I answer forcefully. "Of course not."

His eyes are hot on my face. "But you know about it, and you don't do anything."

"At first."

Guilt scorches my skin. It sounds terrible, but initially, it didn't bother me all that much. But then Jonesy got involved with a rougher crowd, and he evolved from grocery store food robberies to things that included stealing money and other valuables, from businesses and homes. His new friends insisted Jonesy carry a weapon—thankfully, he refused. And then, to highlight the wrongness of it all, there was a little girl to consider. Everything changed when I met that little girl.

"Is that why you left?"

"No," I whisper. My throat aches, burns with what I'm about to say. "I left because I turned in him and his accomplices. I made an anonymous call about a home robbery taking place."

My biggest truth. The reason I put states between me and Illinois. Some of the gang is in jail, but the rest haven't yet been caught. "I don't know if they're looking for me or not, but I didn't want to hang around in case they were."

Blake doesn't say anything, and I can't tell what he's thinking.

"Jonesy is harmless," I continue. Blake's expression blackens. "What he does is wrong," I retract, "but he's harmless—he never brought a gun to the robberies, or any other weapon—even when the gang got on his case about it. He wouldn't hurt anyone, not intentionally."

My tone begs Blake to understand. "He has a daughter. Her name is Paisley, and she's seven." Tears form in my eyes. "I set them up—I did it for her."

He blinks, a crack of emotion flittering across his face before disappearing.

The pain in my heart is debilitating. I can scarcely breathe around it. "The last time he robbed a store, someone got hurt, and I just…I just kept thinking about Paisley. Jonesy was getting in deep with these guys, and he wouldn't listen to me when I told him they were bad news. I pictured the life he was giving his daughter, and the life she might end up with, and I—I put in an anonymous phone call to the police, and he and three others were arrested. There are still two unaccounted for."

Blake says nothing.

I swallow thickly. "I did it for Paisley. She lost her mom, and all she had was Jonesy…and me."

Paisley Jordan's mom died when she was six, and she was put in her dad's care not soon after Jonesy and I started dating. I wasn't aware he had a daughter until he got the phone call saying her mother died. Jonesy never talked about Paisley, and I don't know if it was his decision, or Paisley's mom's, but he never saw her either. Not until she came to live with him.

"I love Paisley," I whisper.

Another crack forms in Blake's face, and this one stays. His eyes tell me what his mouth won't. I take an unsteady breath, wiping at my leaking eyes.

It isn't that Jonesy is unkind to her. He's not. Jonesy is more absentminded than anything, like he forgets she's around. He doesn't have any basic knowledge of kids, and although I know he cares for her, he can't give Paisley what she needs—not now anyway. Jonesy is a man who thinks he's invincible and above the law. I was about to call things off with him when he suddenly had a daughter to raise. I couldn't leave her, not right away. She'd just lost her mom, and she had a felon for a dad, and then her criminal dad got involved with worse ones.

And then I fell in love with her, and I didn't want to leave.

I tried to tell Jonesy that Paisley needed him to be her dad. I tried to get him to stop robbing places and get a legitimate job. And he wouldn't. He said he was providing for her in the only way he knew how. He said after a few more jobs, his cohorts assured him they would be making big money, and eventually, it would be enough to retire and live on. I'm not the best person, but even I could see what he was doing was wrong.

"She was sent to live with her uncle and aunt—her mom's sister—in another state. She was taken from everything she knew. I feel terrible about it, about all of it. That she has Jonesy for a dad, that she lost her mom." I shrug. "That I was what she was left with to try to decide what was best for her.

"I wonder if I helped her, or if I made things worse." In my heart, I think I did the right thing. But then, I'm not exactly the best at making decisions, if my dating record is anything to go by.

Paisley's aunt and uncle live in Montana, and that's my next stop. Her relatives have a child of their own around her age. I know she gets along with them all. This is good for her. She has a loving family, and a home, and stability. It's all I ever wanted as a kid, and my choices allowed Paisley to have something I couldn't. Still, I feel like I abandoned her, even though she was the one to go. I have to see them all together with my own eyes, just once, before I'll really believe Paisley is where she should be.

I left the state soon after Paisley, fearing Jonesy would get out of jail and hunt me down, or one of his slime ball friends would come after me.

Blake didn't make a sound as he moved, but somehow, he's directly before me, and then his arms are around me, and he's holding me. So tight, it hurts to breathe. Just right. Tremors course through me, and his arms lock harder around me. Blake rubs a slow circle in my back, and I relax against him, my head fitting perfectly beneath his chin.

"You did the best you could in a bad situation," he tells me, conviction strengthening his voice, turning it to whiskey.

I tip my head back, and meet his stormy eyes. The tears dry; the sorrow fades. All because I'm looking at a man who believes in me. I touch my index finger to the dimple in his chin. His unshaven skin is rough and welcome.

"Be reckless with me, Blake, just this once," I offer.

His eyebrows lower, two lightning bolts joining the thunder of his eyes. His mouth hitches on one end, causing my stomach to spin. "If it involves a second attempt at cooking, I'm going to have to pass."

"I can cook," I protest, stepping from his embrace.

"That's usually the first step to burning something, yes. You cook it, overcook it, burn it, cause a fire. There are steps."

I spin around, walking backward toward the edge of the porch. "I tell you what, if we ever see each other again after tomorrow, I'll cook tater tot casserole." I pretend my words don't cause a pinprick of pain to gather inside me. *If we ever see each other again after tomorrow...*

"Tater tot casserole," he repeats slowly, watching me closely.

I slide my feet back, nodding as I go. "Yes. Have you ever had it?"

Blake scratches the side of his head. "I don't know, but it sounds like it's probably a good thing if I haven't."

"Paisley loved it and wanted me to make it every week. And you know if a kid likes it, it has to be good. I'll prove it. If we ever see each other again," I add, hopping down from the porch step. Again with the sting, again with pretending it isn't there.

I pick up the blanket, wad it up, and throw it at Blake. It hits his stomach and falls to the porch. Leaning his shoulder against the framework of the porch, Blake crosses his arms. "What are you doing?"

"Being reckless."

"If standing in the dark and being cold is your idea of being reckless, then I might have to teach you a thing or two...more." He says that last word in a whisper that induces images of us, naked.

"Don't act like I didn't teach you a thing or two myself," I say haughtily. If anything, I taught him how to laugh during sex. That doesn't even sound right. In fact, that sounds really bad.

Blake's eyes smolder. "Oh, you did."

Curiosity piqued, I squint my eyes and demand, "Like what?"

He grins, and the flash of white teeth is darkly seductive. I imagine his teeth nipping at my skin, and I shiver, from the cold, from the way Blake makes me feel. "I don't kiss and tell," is his low reply.

I snort. "You just kiss, right?" And kiss. And kiss.

Blake pauses, and my heartbeat is caught in the grip of it. "Yes."

Exhaling slowly, I rub a shaking hand to the side of my neck. I'm not sure what I'm doing, but I need to move on from the sexuality presently throbbing in the air that separates us. I don't really have a plan. But it's our last night together, and I think it should be epic. I don't exactly know what qualifies as epic. Me plus Blake is a good start. I search my brain, trying to think of options. I mean, obviously there is sex. Sex would be an epic way to spend our last night together. But I don't want that—well, I do, but I want something else too.

Stop thinking about sex, I scold myself.

"What do you want to do with your life, Opal?"

The question comes out of nowhere, and surprises me. His eyes are like blades against my soul. Sharp. Glinting. Fatal.

I want to only have between us the simplicity of truth. So, in my own way, this is as reckless as I can get. Opening up to someone, being totally honest. I should be scared, but I'm not. I take a fresh inhalation of air into my lungs. And then I show Blake a piece of my heart.

"I don't know what I want to do with my life, but I know what I want to do with you, if we had more time."

"Tell me," he softly beckons.

"I want to watch cheesy movies with you, and I want you to tell me something funny, and I want you to tell me something sad. I want to—I want to tell you something unimportant, like how I make tater tot casserole, and I want you to humor me, even though you don't really want to know how I make tater tot casserole. I want to draw you—all of you. I want you to ask me something meaningful, and I want you to care about my answer. I want a hundred little things that seem silly, but are everything," I say in the darkness, my eyes locked on the glow of his.

Blake stares at me, a statue of unrealized wonder. He drops his arms and moves, his footsteps even and sure as he makes his way toward me, never once breaking his hold on my gaze. Blake stops when he is a touch away. The world of unspoken thoughts that make up people are paused between us, hovering on lips, waiting to be discovered.

"Tell me your tater tot casserole recipe."

It is the most perfect response. I smile, and it wobbles, but it's strong. I place my hand to his sharp cheek, and he briefly holds it there. I feel my heartbeat speed up and I move past him, toward the house. Leaning down to retrieve the blanket, I wrap it around my shoulders and shuffle back to the warmth of the house. Up the stairs, down the hall, and into Blake's bedroom.

8

Opal

I set the blanket on the bed and turn, knowing Blake followed.

"I thought you wanted to watch cheesy movies?" He stops in the doorway, a hand on either side of the doorframe. The light of the hallway silhouettes him, giving his brooding persona darkness it doesn't need. Blake is already intimidating. "I don't have cable or satellite, but there are some DVDs."

"If we do everything tonight, what will we do the next time we meet? Don't answer that," I hastily add as a lustful gleam appears in his eyes.

"You mean, besides make tater tot casserole?" His hands fall away from the doorframe. He turns on the light and enters the room. Blake looks down at me, the severity of his features softened by the emotion in his eyes. "Will there be a next time?"

"I guess we'll see. I have lots of places to see, people to draw. Money to make. Who knows where I'll end up?" I try to make my tone flippant and carefree, but it catches around the lump in my throat.

He doesn't say anything.

"Anyway, won't you be in Australia?"

Blake touches my hair, fingering the strands as his eyes delve into mine. He doesn't talk until he has my full attention. "I want to work with kids because I understand how helpless they can feel, and I want to let them know they don't have to feel that way. No matter how bad things can get, they can always get better too."

"You don't need a degree to help kids," I inform him.

"I know." He nods, confliction like cracks of discontent on his face. "And Australia…I have the ticket and the passport. I'm scheduled to leave in less than fourteen days. I should go."

"You should go," I agree, even though my inner voice screams that he shouldn't.

His gaze drops. "I've been dreading confronting my dad, but since I've been with you, I've barely thought of him. But…I know I need to talk to him. I also feel like I need to be here, and maybe work on my grandpa's dream. It feels like it's my dream just as much as it was his."

There they are—Blake's truths.

"Then you should," I tell him around a tight throat. "You should do all of those things."

"What if…" He smoothes down my hair, studies it to keep his eyes hidden from mine. "What if I can't do it?"

"You just have to believe in yourself."

His mouth goes thin; his hand moves away. Blake's gaze shifts to me and beyond. "I don't know if I can."

Another truth, although this one is harder to hear.

"Well, I do." I smile up at him. "When you doubt yourself, remind yourself that I don't."

Clouds sweep across his face, and I turn to the bed, wondering why I told him that. This whole potentially epic night is turning maudlin.

I plop down on the bed and fold my hands over my stomach. Closing my eyes, I wait for him to either come to bed, or go. The sound of the light switch turning off fills the quiet, and then the bed lowers with his weight.

He moves closer, and my breaths spasm. Blake slides an arm beneath my neck and pulls me to his side. I breathe deeply, turning to better fit against him. My head rests on his chest. I inhale his scent, feel his warmth, and I sink into his partial embrace. I never liked it when Jonesy held me. He breathed heavy, and he squished me more than hugged me. I like it when Blake holds me. A lot.

"So," he says.

I tense.

"Tell me how you make tater tot casserole."

I laugh and put an arm around him, anchoring myself to him. "You can make it with ground turkey, if you care about your health."

"Which is a nonissue for you."

My lips curve up. "Exactly. I use ground beef. One pound. I brown it in a frying pan."

"Mmm. Keep talking. You're making me…hungry." He sounds hungry, all right—hungry for me.

"You can use whatever vegetables you like—I prefer mixed, of the canned variety. Frozen is supposedly better for you, but I like to go all out. I have no shame when it comes to food."

Blake's fingers stroke my hair. "Sounds tantalizing."

"In a nine-by-thirteen pan, I mix together the vegetables, drained hamburger—"

"You drain it?" he interrupts. "Isn't that cheating? You know, kind of healthy?"

"You're overdoing the interest. I can't even take you seriously right now," I say wryly.

His chest shakes with stifled laughter. "I'll tone it down."

I smile sleepily, my hand flexing against his ribcage. "French onion soup mix is the secret ingredient. I like cream of celery soup with it, but you can use mushroom or chicken. Two cans. Super healthy."

"The healthiest," he murmurs.

"I mix it all together, add some cheddar cheese, dump a full bag of tater tots on top—a *full bag,* Blake. Anything else is not enough—and then I put it in the oven. When it's done, I add more cheese on top. It sounds awesome, right?"

When he doesn't respond, I go to my elbows and stare down at his face in the dark. His eyes are closed, his breathing even and relaxed. Leaning up, I press my lips to his left cheek, and then his right. I kiss his forehead and his chin. I kiss his hawkish nose. And when his lips quirk, I kiss them as well.

9

Blake

My eyes fly open to the sound of large machinery, nonstop pounding in my head, and Opal's hair suffocating me. She doesn't have a lot of it, but it's thick and cantankerous. I push it away from my face, and then I wrap my arms around her and mold my front to her backside.

Never one to commit to anything, before Opal there has not been another woman here. I haven't liked anyone enough to show them my home; to share with them what my grandfather left me. I don't do relationships. I don't do attachments. I don't do a lot of things I've done since meeting Opal. I brush the back of my hand down the side of her arm. I don't even know her last name.

In the hours between consciousness and slumber, we talked, and kissed, and held each other, and it was better than sex—or at least just as good. Not that I'll ever admit such a thing. She sighs in her sleep and scoots her bottom dangerously close to my man parts. With my eyes closed, I press my face against her shoulder and hug her for maybe the last time.

The pounding isn't only in my head, but also outside. I sit up, careful not to disrupt Opal, and I turn in the direction of the window. Walking over to it, the sun greets me, along with the excavating equipment owned by Dan Kline. I open the window and stick out my head, cool air brushing across my face.

There is a shiny black Dodge truck parked down the road, on the other side of the waterhole presently being filled. A blond duo moves into my line of vision. A chill slithers down my spine, and I flinch back from the window, staring at Opal's sleeping form as my pulse hitchhikes its way out of my body. Grennedy is here. *Why* are they here? What possible reason could they have for showing up? Then I remember the unanswered texts and phone calls, and I groan, thumping the back of my head against the wall. Shit. I forgot about them.

Hearing the noise, Opal sits up, sleepily blinking at me. Her hair sticks up around her head, and her eyes are swollen. The Prince T-shirt hangs off one shoulder, exposing sun-kissed skin. God, she looks hot. "What are you doing?"

Graham and Kennedy can't meet her, but it isn't like I can exactly hide her.

"Oh, you know, contemplating why I ever thought being sober was a good life choice."

Opal's eyebrows furrow.

"Blake! If you don't answer the door, we will be forced to…forcefully… force our way in!" The voice comes from directly beneath the open window, is screechy, high-pitched, and should not be in North Dakota. In a softer voice, she concludes with, "That sounded ridiculous. Why did you let me say that?"

"If only I'd known what you were about to say."

"Get with it, Graham. You should know who you're sleeping with."

"I know you pretty well."

"But not well enough to know the awesomeness I'm about to say before I say it."

"Even I have my limits."

We stare at one another, listening to my half-brother and his girlfriend have their form of normal conversation.

"I don't think he's here," Kennedy comments.

"Who is that?" Opal wonders, getting up and shuffling toward me. She shivers as the cool wind from the open window hits her, rubbing her arms.

"He's here. His truck is here."

"Maybe he went for a walk."

A pause, and then they both laugh.

Opal's eyes shoot to mine, a frown showing her unease. "Blake? What's going on?"

I don't move. I don't speak. All I can do is look into honey eyes and wish this wasn't happening. When Opal meets Graham and Kennedy, it's all over. It's time to go back to reality. I knew it was anyway, what with the ditch being filled in at this very moment. It's time to say goodbye. But this—Opal—I didn't want to have to share her with anyone, least of all Grennedy.

Giving me a look, Opal places her hands on the window ledge and peers down. "Who are those people?"

"Who are you?" is called back by Kennedy.

"Lori," Opal replies, glancing at me.

"Is Blake up there with you, Lori?" Graham asks.

"I'm not sure." She moves back from the window, looking at me. "Are you here?"

"Lori?" I ask.

Opal shrugs. "Habit. She owned a daycare. I stayed with her for almost a year, and helped her out with the kids after school. You have no idea how much babies poop."

"It's my half-brother and his girlfriend," I confess, running fingers through my hair as I walk to the opposite side of the room.

"I didn't know you had a brother. I mean, not that I should, but…" Opal trails off when I face her. "You're not happy about them being here."

"Not especially." Rolling my shoulders, I determine it's best to get this over with instead of drawing it out. I look at Opal. "Can you…" I hesitate, not sure how to word it in a way that isn't offensive. "Can you hang out up here for a bit, just until I can figure out how to handle this?"

Something happens to Opal. It's nothing really obvious, but it's like a little of her light fades. Her shoulders go limp; her eyes dim. Even her crazy hair loses some of its spunk. "Sure. I'll just hide out until the coast is clear."

"It's not like that," I insist, crossing the room to her. I take her face in my hands and gaze into thousands of untold stories, hopes, dreams, all kept locked up tight in the warm eyes watching me. I want to know them all. I want that more than anything, but if nothing else, I know this is my final day in her company. "I'm embarrassed of *them*, not you."

Her light comes back, blinding me with the brightness of her smile. "I can't wait to meet them then."

A groan is all I can manage.

I don't bother changing out of my T-shirt and shorts I slept in, quickly brushing my teeth before heading down to face Graham and Kennedy. My chest tightens and I breathe against it. I unlock the door and open it to two golden-haired beauties. Barbie and Ken, or as I like to call them, Grennedy. It fits. They're basically one strange entity.

"Blake!" Kennedy, dressed in a purple skirt and black top, propels herself at me. Slim arms wrap around my neck and squeeze. "Tell me you didn't miss me."

"I didn't miss you," I say into long, blond hair that smells like bubble gum. I awkwardly hug her back, her body lacking the curves I've come to expect when I hold a woman.

"Without lying." She pulls back, her brown eyes sparkling in spite of the fatigue surrounding them.

"Trust me, I'm not."

"It's okay," she whispers loudly. "Graham knows we're friends. He's okay with it. You don't have to pretend like you don't think I'm the coolest person ever."

I lift an eyebrow at my brother.

"You look good," Graham says, his hands in the pockets of his shorts. He sounds surprised, like he was expecting to find me in a drug-induced stupor.

Except for the hint of worry adding lines around his mouth and the glint of exhaustion in his eyes, Graham is a picture of composure with his unwrinkled sea-green shirt that amplifies the green of his eyes and khaki shorts, the flip of his bangs exactly as it should be. My brother and I don't look a thing alike, something that's never bothered me until now. Everything about him is physically perfect—the same cannot be said for me.

And I wonder, as I take in the flawlessness that is my older brother, what Opal will think when she looks at him and compares.

"He does look good," Kennedy agrees, her head tilted like she can't figure out how that happened. Her eyes look me up and down. "For a pasty-skinned hermit dressed in gym shorts and a Mr. T shirt."

"Your flowery words are touching."

She shrugs like it's no big deal.

"I always look good." I look at Graham. "Why are you here?"

"You were supposed to call me as soon as you got back," Graham states, moving past me into the house.

"You didn't call," Kennedy adds as she follows her boyfriend inside.

I close the door and lean against it. I rub my eyes, focusing on the two people I never envisioned standing where they are. "Yeah. I forgot. Sorry."

"You forgot," my brother repeats slowly, his tone full of doubt. With the calm and grace only Graham can effortlessly have, he crosses his arms and levels his eyes on me. "How does that happen, knowing your concerned b—"

"Obsessive, perfectionist, melodramatic," Kennedy happily interjects, beaming at her boyfriend.

"Concerned," he emphasizes, his eyes drilling into his girlfriend's. Graham looks at me. "How do you forget to return the many calls and texts from your *concerned* brother?"

"I was...distracted."

Kennedy whirls around, a smirk on her face as she focuses on me. "By…Lori?" She wiggles her eyebrows.

"Don't do that," I say in a tone halfway between a demand and a plea.

"Don't do what?" she demands, eyebrows half-raised.

I gesture to her face. "Your eyebrows. Stop."

Letting her face fall into an expression of resignation, Kennedy moves toward Graham, grumbling as she goes, "Wouldn't want to have any kind of fun around stone-faced, joy-hating, non-smiler Blake."

"That's right. We wouldn't." I move away from the door, turning to open it. "Well, now that you know I'm alive and well, you can be on your way."

Floorboards creak above and Kennedy and Graham direct their eyes overhead. The water pipes rumble as the shower is turned on. Graham looks from the ceiling to me, his mouth opening to pose a question he never gets to ask, because Kennedy is way ahead of him. "What room was Lori in when we had that monumental window conversation?"

My jaw tenses, already knowing where this is going. "The bedroom."

"Whose?" she asks like an owl.

I glare without answering.

"So…" She looks around and then offers a palm. "High five."

"No."

The thing with Kennedy is that she's basically like a kid, and I tend to quickly become impatient with her. Because she isn't a kid, no matter that she acts like one most of the time.

Dropping her hand, she shrugs and touches a bookcase full of knickknacks and books. "This is your grandpa's place? Graham explained it all on the way over. Are you keeping it? I would keep it, turn it into a winery. Or, well, my own personal winery." Kennedy smirks.

"Drinking wine isn't the same as making it," Graham tells her, smiling wryly.

"It's just as important. I could be a wine taste tester. I have the qualifications." Kennedy raises her eyebrows as she directs her attention to me. "So, what are your plans? Australia, college, or staying in North Dakota? All of the above?"

I shift my stance. There was an instant this past summer when I would have told Kennedy anything and everything about me and my history, but that fleeting moment was gone before it was ever really here. I only open up to a small percentage of people, and Kennedy is no longer an option. And that's okay.

She and Graham make sense in a way I don't understand but now respect.

"Speaking of plans, I brought wine. You know, necessities," Kennedy trills when I remain silent, speed-walking past me to the porch where two pieces of luggage and a brown paper bag are set against the side of the house.

"It's like she has total disregard for my addictive personality," I tell Graham, feeling my muscles constrict with irritation. Asshole-ish as it may seem, I hope they don't plan on staying here. I really, really, really hope they don't plan on staying here.

"You know Kennedy," my brother states with a wan smile.

Yes. Unfortunately, I do.

Graham steps outside, immediately returning with their luggage. Unsurprisingly, Kennedy has the wine. "We planned on staying for a day or two, if it's all right. We left yesterday after work and drove all night. We're both tired."

"Really tired," Kennedy adds, yawning into her arm. Then she looks at me. "But not so tired that I can't meet your upstairs friend."

My teeth grind against one another. "Best news ever," I say faintly, stiffly moving for the stairs.

Graham pauses, studying me. "This could have been avoided if you'd simply answered your phone, or called me back. Knowing your plan when you got here was to confront our father, I was worried. Dad is unpredictable, and I didn't know what to think."

"I haven't actually talked to him yet." There he is, the older brother every guy wants, whether they'll ever admit or not. I guiltily look down, away from my brother's striking eyes. "I had the volume turned off. I was..."

"Distracted. Right. I remember." His eyes move to the stairwell that leads upstairs as a thoughtful look claims his features. Turning back to me, he states, "It's amazing how much this place looks the same as it did the last time I was here."

"Yeah. Grandpa never liked change all that much."

Graham nods, taking in the time-preserved living room. "I always liked John. When I came during the summer, he didn't treat me like I was an outsider."

I swallow with difficulty. It's odd. I always felt like I didn't belong, but Graham was experiencing it right along with me. According to Benson Malone, nothing we ever did was good enough. Our dad was living a double life for a time, with Graham's mom, and with mine. Graham and I didn't know what was going on, but in a way, we got punished just the same. Before he stopped coming altogether, Graham would visit for a few weeks each summer, and most of that time we spent here, if we were allowed.

Wine in hand, Kennedy plops down on the couch, cuddling the bag to her like it is her most favorite stuffed animal. It crumples as she situates herself on the couch, one arm protectively hugging it to her side. Her eyelids droop, and within seconds she's out. Looking up, I find Graham's focus entirely on her.

"This would make a great memory for the future Grennedy kids. Picture-perfect," I say to my brother.

He smiles, his eyes locked on his sleeping girlfriend. He looks content, or delirious. If anyone asks, I'm going with delirious. "Always entertaining, that's Kennedy."

It's interesting that he doesn't even bat an eye at the implication that there will be future Grennedy kids. I knew it was serious between them, but I guess I didn't realize *how* serious. My attention moves to Kennedy. Her mouth is slack, a trickle of drool gathering there. I can't see her as a mother. I just can't. She'd probably put wine in the baby bottles and feed them pureed pizza.

"She's the one?" I ask, knowing it to be true.

Graham's eyes flicker to mine and back to his girlfriend. "She's the only one."

Something thuds upstairs and my brother gives me a curious look. "When do we get to meet your distraction? Or is she going to hide up there all day?"

"Uh…" Rubbing the back of my neck, I aim my eyes at the stairwell, wishing there was a way to make Opal and me disappear, because it's obvious my brother and his girlfriend aren't going anywhere.

"I can already tell it'll be interesting." Humor gleams in his eyes.

"I know I'm looking forward to it," I say with mock cheerfulness.

The thuds turn into pounding on the steps, but they're too fast and heavy to be footsteps. It's more like stumbling or falling. As I turn to face the stairs, I open my arms to flaying limbs, a rolling form, and enthusiastic curses.

* * *

Opal

I know I'm not beautiful. The best I've ever been called is cute. I am not the kind of woman men look at as I enter a room. I am not the one they fantasize about. And that's all okay. I can't change how I look. But when Blake looks at me, I feel like I am everything I never thought I was. I feel pretty, and desirable. It's like he thinks I'm amazing just as I am.

And when I fall down the last of the stairs and just about smack my face on the floor, he is there to catch me, looking down at me with an expression that tells me he is concerned—that's in the way his eyebrows lower; he is exasperated—that's evident in the dark shade of his eyes, and that he's fighting not to laugh—that is obviously apparent with the twitching of his lips. *There.* I see some form of adoration flitter across his face. That's the look I want to see in a man's eyes when they're on me. Blake laughs as he rights me.

Using a tender hand, he smoothes wet strands of hair from my eyes. "Your anxiousness to reconnect with me is worrisome."

"In your dreams," I mumble, but I'm smiling.

"Every one of them," he rejoins.

Blake's eyes deepen with promises better unrevealed, especially since we have a mute audience. I can literally feel the shock in the air, and as I turn to face his visitors, I can see it too. Their mirrored gaping looks would be funny, if I knew why they were looking at me like I have two heads. I feel as if I'm blasted by two brilliant suns as I take in their tanned skin, blond hair, and symmetrical features. They're too pretty to be real—the guy more so than the woman.

The woman gets up from the couch and slowly turns her head to meet the eyes of the man beside her. I find it odd that she's protectively holding to her chest a brown paper bag that appears to be covering up a bottle of wine, but who am I to judge?

"Did you hear that? It sounded like *laughter*. Like, Blake *laughed*?" she asks through lips that barely move. Her voice sounds young, like a child's was mismatched with an adult's.

"Yeah. I think so. It isn't like I've heard it all that often to be sure," the man responds. "I think it was laughter. Or choking. It could have been choking."

Blake sighs.

"True. He even smiled a little. I think." She tips her head to the side. "Maybe it was a grimace. I can't be sure, because, well, smiling for him so *rarely* happens."

"It definitely could have been a grimace. Maybe a frown?"

"No." Her blond hair sways around her shoulders as she shakes her head. "I think his frowns are supposed to be smiles. He just isn't aware that smiling is actually something you do when you're happy."

"Happy," the man repeats, as if he's never heard the word used in a sentence about Blake.

It's all very strange.

They both turn their gazes to Blake. His hands burn my waist where they rest, his eyes unflinching from mine when I focus on him. It's as if he's purposely avoiding looking at them. I study his features, not seeing any resemblance to his half-brother. Blake stares back, his jaw stiff. Waiting. I kiss the dent in his chin and his eyes soften.

They're about the same height and have a similar build, but his brother is taller, and Blake is more muscular. Plus, his brother is too perfect. Blake is beautifully flawed. I tell him so with my eyes. His fingers tighten on my sides, and shocks of heat sweep through me.

"Are you going to introduce us, or are we all going to awkwardly stand around?" the woman prompts.

"I was hoping if I stood still long enough, you'd forget I was here," is Blake's answer. "And hey, at least you got your wine prop. That's something—and by the way, not awkward at all."

She sniffs, looking down at her arms. "You know the kind of relationship wine and I have."

"An alcoholic one?" he guesses.

"Hiya," I greet with more enthusiasm than I'm feeling. "I'm—" Blake's grip tightens on my waist. I lift my eyebrows at the frown on his face. I'm not sure what he's trying to tell me, if anything. "—the housekeeper. Lori. I…clean…and stuff."

Blake snorts, dropping his hands and stepping back. His expression says he can't wait to see what story I come up with next. I'm flustered and confused. I don't know who I'm supposed to be right now. Opal doesn't seem right. Opal is private, for Blake alone to know. I look at his brother and his girlfriend. I'm not comfortable sharing the real me with them.

"Do housekeepers generally kiss their employers on the chin?" Blake's brother asks.

I look at Blake and he looks back.

"Sure. Affectionate ones," I reply, widening my eyes at him.

Blake winks.

"Affection and Blake don't really mesh," the woman states.

I narrow my eyes at her, wondering how she would know such a thing. And she's wrong—he has been affectionate, with me. "Who are you?" I demand.

"Who are *you*?" she shoots back, looking pleased by her comeback that wasn't really a comeback.

"Speaking of who is who," the blond-haired man quickly intervenes as he steps forward, bringing his beauty close, and the scent of freshly laundered clothes. He offers a hand. "I'm Graham, Blake's brother."

I shake his hand, feeling calluses. The roughness says he's a worker, and I respect that. He isn't just pretty looks.

"And you're Lori, the housekeeper." He watches me as he continues to move our gripped hands up and down. Even the stubble of facial hair lining his jaw glints like gold. He's too pretty—pretty people make me edgy. Graham's expression is splintered between doubt and interest.

"Yes. That's me. I know where the elbow grease is, and how to polish wood with spit—you know, all the tricks. I've been cleaning houses around the area since I was thirteen." My arm feels like it's going to eventually be pulled from its socket at this rate.

Blake clears his throat.

"Eighteen," I correct.

"Let go of her hand, Graham," Blake says, and Graham instantly drops it.

"I'm Kennedy, girlfriend of Graham, and all-around awesome individual. Just ask Blake. Or maybe not," the woman tells me, looking hesitant to release her wine in place of taking my hand.

The noise outside suddenly quits, and the ensuing quiet is potent.

A tall man with scraggly gray hair and a lined face opens the door and pops his head inside, finding Blake with his eyes. "Hey, there, Blake. We got you all filled in. You're good to go."

"Thanks, Dan. What do I owe you?" Blake moves for the kitchen, pausing at Dan's next words.

"Don't worry about it. I'll send a bill. Have a good day."

The door shuts before Blake can answer, and then he turns to me. His face reveals nothing, but it doesn't have to for me to know that he is not looking forward to sending me on my way. I will admit it to myself, and not another single soul—I don't want to go either.

"The road is fixed," he says unnecessarily.

I nod, my eyes locked so fiercely on him that they burn, and still I can't look away. I forget about Graham and Kennedy. All I see is Blake, because I know pretty soon, I'll never see him again. My throat is tight, and it is painful to breathe.

"I guess I should get my stuff," I say in a voice that doesn't sound like mine.

"Do you see that?" Kennedy whispers loudly.

"See what?" Graham warily replies.

"I'll, uh, take a quick shower while you get ready to go," Blake tells me, turning to the stairs. "Make myself decent."

I swallow thickly, only breaking eye contact when Blake is no longer facing me. I shift my attention to Graham and Kennedy, and quickly shift it to the stairwell I'd like to be on. They're looking at us much too intently. It's nerve-wracking.

"The way they're completely ignoring us, like they're more important than we are."

Graham chuckles. "To their way of thinking, they probably are."

"Nonsense," she scoffs.

I hurry after Blake, absurdly glad to no longer be in his visitors' company.

"You already look more than decent," I whisper as I follow him up the stairs, staring at a thin, pink scar on his left calf muscle.

Blake glances back at me, a faint smile lining his face. "You sound really sad about that."

"I'm going to miss you," I admit once we crest the stairs.

He faces me, the skin between his eyebrows pinched. Blake opens his mouth.

"Don't say anything back. I just wanted you to know. And..." I look down at my bare feet, remnants of pink nail polish lingering on a few of the toenails. "Thank you."

I watch as his throat works to swallow. "For?" he finally gets out.

"Everything," I say offhandedly, already wanting to take back my words and what they imply.

"If we ever have a housekeeper, and you're that friendly with her, I will get revenge in ways you don't want to know," Kennedy says from downstairs.

"I kind of want to know," Graham answers.

"Think of words like *The Golden Girls*, and *marathon*."

"Please, no." Graham groans. "Besides, it's a moot point. Why would we ever get a housekeeper? You know they wouldn't clean the way I like."

"I guess you're safe."

"So safe," is murmured back.

"They're really odd, you know that?" I say to Blake.

Blake's eyes lighten and he pats at a particularly stubborn chunk of hair that refuses to lie down on his head. "Trust me, I know."

Nervous in a way I don't understand, I fix my gaze on the bedroom beyond Blake. My backpack is in there, along with my clothes and other meager possessions. Lingering isn't going to do either of us any good. I step forward at the same time Blake moves for me, and then we're kissing. His hands are on my face, his mouth hot and demanding. I press against him, wanting every inch of me touching him, and Blake responds to me with passion so consuming I feel my heart drop to my stomach.

How will kissing another man ever feel right after this?

I tug my mouth from his and kiss his neck, my breathing uneven and fast. My heart beating strong. I wrap my arms around his back and squeeze, and Blake squeezes me back. He brushes his cheek along my temple, his facial hair gently scraping my skin. Blake's heart pounds next to my ear, and I close my eyes and try to memorize the sound of it and this moment. Out of all the places I've been, and all the people I've met, I found my favorite of each here.

Pulling away is the last thing I want to do, and when I finally do, Blake also briefly resists before releasing me.

"Clothes," I announce, pointing at the bedroom.

"Shower," he replies, pointing in the opposite direction.

I nod, and move for the bedroom, but he goes the same way and blocks me. I move the other way, and he unintentionally does the same. We pause, the seriousness of the moment lightened by our inability to get by one another. I look into his gray eyes flecked with paler streaks of light, like stars exploded in the irises. My stomach twists into a knot, and I pretend the uncomfortable tightness isn't there.

"I'll go right," I inform him.

"Got it. I'll go the other way." He pauses. "Left. I'll go left."

My mouth stretches into a smile as we successfully pass each other, and I go about collecting my things to the sound of Blake showering. It doesn't take long to gather up my stuff—along with a red Imagine Dragons T-shirt of Blake's—and I spend the rest of the time until Blake is ready sitting in the middle of his bed. Thinking. Already missing him. I shrug against my emotions, knowing there isn't another option.

I'm on my way to Paisley, and Blake's going to Australia.

I study the drawing of Blake as I take it from the backpack, looking over his unsmiling features. I smooth the perpetual wrinkle of his brow, the straight line of his mouth. Kennedy doesn't know him like I know him—not even his brother does. I just met him, and I see him better than them. He laughs. He smiles. He can be happy. He's more than affectionate. I gaze into lifeless eyes drawn with a charcoal pencil, and I see the light hidden from most, like the sun peeking from behind a cloud.

"Mr. Sunshine," I say out loud, a smile in my tone.

It has a sarcastic ring to it, when coupled with Blake's personality, but it also has a bit of truth. I twirl a lock of hair around my finger, gazing at the paper. I tug too hard and wince, dropping my hand. *Mr. Sunshine.* I go still, his face locked in my vision. My eyes narrow as thoughts collect, take form. Excitement prickles my skin as direction and purpose clamp their hold onto me.

I could do something with Mr. Sunshine.

Blake saunters into the room, disrupting my thoughts. With little attention paid to me, and efficient movements, he grabs clothes from his dresser drawers and gets dressed. I catch a glimpse of pale, toned butt cheeks before they are covered up. It's probably best that he dresses in a hurry and keeps his goods locked away, or I might never get out of here. He seems to realize that.

Turning to me, he pauses as he takes in my position on his bed and what I'm holding. His black hair falls over his forehead, obscuring one eye to give him a roguish look that only adds to his dark attractiveness. "Is that me?"

This belongs to Blake. It's him. He paid for it. I don't want to part with it, but I can easily draw him from memory. His image pulses there, large and bright. In my head, in my heart.

"Yes. It's yours." I hold up the circus drawing. "Bought and paid for, remember?"

Blake slowly crosses the room and takes it, staring down at the drawing. "Thanks."

I swallow thickly. "It was a good time, wasn't it?"

"Yeah. It was."

Blake sets the picture on the dresser and lifts his eyes to mine, a perfectly blank expression on his face. My frail smile falters. Even with the nothingness masking his thoughts, his gaze sears me, reaches right into me and turns my limbs weak, my brain useless. I've never been looked at before with such raw intensity. Blake looks at me like I shine. He moves away from the dresser, breaking the stare. I try to breathe, and it takes a few tries before I can manage it.

Vaulting from the bed, I sling my arms through the straps of my pink bag and meet Blake at the door, bouncing on the balls of my feet. The quicker I get away from him, and toward my next destination, the less it will sting. "Let's go, Joe."

Blake moves forward, hesitates, and then grabs me into a hard hug. I love his scent, his feel. The hardness and warmth of him. He presses his lips to my forehead, making my heart go upside down, and then he lets me go. It's over before it really began, but the feel of him echoes through me.

The descent to the first level of the house is quiet, and when we step into the living room, it's even quieter. His brother and girlfriend are asleep on the couch, one head on each end with Kennedy's feet in Graham's face. Even in slumber, she has the wine bottle tucked to her side. I look to Blake, wanting to ask what her deal is with wine, but the look on his face says to not bother.

"They look cute," I whisper.

"Yeah, cute like sleeping, rabid raccoons."

I give him a thumbs-up sign and make my way from the house with a tight chest. It clenches, harder and harder, the nearer I get to the truck. I breathe around the ache, telling myself it's nerves and hunger, but it isn't, not really.

Two days have passed since the last time we approached his grandfather's truck with the intent of heading into Bismarck. This time, it feels much different. We've lived years in days, and I hope I never forget the significance of them. With Blake, I was someone I like, and he seemed to accept who he was too.

Blake opens the truck door for me, finding me with his eyes and stamping their intensity into mine. I stop moving as a tendril of longing, and something more, pierces my heart.

One word. I get one word.

"Ready?"

Shifting my feet, I look down and back up. "I'm—just give me a minute, okay? To say goodbye." His mouth pulls down with confusion, and I gesture around us. "I'll never see this again. I want to appreciate it one last time." Except for the homeless demon cat.

The frown deepens, and shadows play across his features. Blake taps his fingers on the door, his arm braced against it. He doesn't look at me as he says, "If I asked you to stay, what would you say?"

My body turns to feathers; my heart soars. *Yes*, a thousand times, *yes*. And my body turns to lead, and my heart plummets as logic intervenes.

"I can't," I whisper, my voice thick with remorse. "I have something I need to—"

"What?" Blake demands, desperation in his voice. "What do you have to do that's so important? Where are you going, Opal? And with these criminals who may or may not be after you, how are you going to make sure you're *safe*?"

I shake my head, refusing to answer that. He is right. There might be corrupt men after me; I can't endanger Blake, or Paisley, with giving out details of my plans. I don't even know where I'll end up after Montana, but I know I have to go. I have to figure out myself before I can make any kind of commitment to anyone else. Be an adult on my own for a while. I owe Blake that. He deserves to be the only right choice, the only thing that makes sense.

"I'll be okay, don't worry. And…I couldn't stay anyway; you're leaving," I remind him.

Lines form around his already rigid mouth. Blake's eyes turn into what I imagine thunder would look like, if it was something that could be seen. The darkest gray and volatile—like spun pandemonium. "Yeah. Right. I'll be in the truck."

I open my mouth to protest; I even lift my hand to stop him, but I don't.

Instead, I turn my back to the truck, and sweep hair from my face when the wind blows it over my eyes. I take in the shed with the unfinished interior and unfulfilled dream, the old farmhouse with its character and peaceful ambience, the vast land, the pond, and I inhale slowly, breathing in the scents of grass, and dirt, and fresh air. It's all green, and alive with hope.

One day, I vow to myself, I'll return.

The driver's side door slams and a stiff-jawed Blake appears on the other side of the truck box. He rests his forearms on the side of the truck and scowls at the ground. His shoulders are taut, his head turned to the side.

"What is it?" I ask, tightening my grip on the straps of my backpack.

Blake shakes his head, and then he laughs, but it sounds twisted with disharmony. "The truck won't start."

"Wow." I shiver against an imaginary chill. "I almost think something doesn't want me to go. Not that I can blame it—whatever *it* is. You get nothing but quality time with me." I perk up. "Maybe it's your grandpa."

He looks up, a charge hitting me along with his eyes, and frowns.

"Kidding. Totally kidding."

Blake rubs the back of his dark head and squints at the newly graveled driveway. He doesn't say anything for a long time, and I take the silence to observe him. I have Blake's features, mannerisms, voice—everything—memorized. I swear if someone asked me his favorite color, even though he's never told me, I would somehow know. Blue. Not black. That's the color someone who doesn't know Blake would assume he likes, because it easily fits with his persona. But it's a lie.

Blue is vibrant, hopeful, strong.

Blue is the color to represent Blake Malone.

A gust of wind sweeps by, flattening grass and tugging at my shirt. It's like a warm hug, and I close my eyes to better enjoy it. And I somehow know the truck will start this time.

"Try it again," I tell Blake.

When I don't hear movement, I pop open my eyes. Blake studies me, something glinting in his eyes, turning them silver.

"I'm going to miss you too," he says roughly, turning away before I can reply.

The sound of the old engine starting breaks the stillness, and it's time.

10

Blake

Other than Opal singing along with the radio, the ride to Bismarck is quiet. She doesn't sing any better than the last time we were in a similar situation, and a smile is etched onto my face. She sits in the middle of the cab with her arm occasionally bumping into mine, her voice unusually loud and screechy with the close proximity. I'm sad about her going, but it's pushed to the back of my mind in her presence. I can't afford to be sad now; I have Opal for a little bit longer.

My smile grows when she hits a high note and her voice cracks. Opal clears her throat and continues on with the song. I glance at her, and she shrugs. Unapologetic. That's a good way to be. I knew from the moment I saw her, that she was different. It didn't even take a full day around her to know that she's special. And she is. There will never be another woman like Opal in my life. I know it.

The city is busy, vehicles getting the people within them to their destinations. Trees run rampant through Bismarck, splashing the area in greens, and in the distance, towering hills and mountains reign. They seem close, but they're really not. I pull into the parking lot of the first gas station I see, like Opal directed, and turn off the engine.

Facing her, I try to smile.

I fail.

"Tell me one secret, Blake, before I go," she encourages. "Just one."

"Why?"

"Tell me something no one else knows," Opal whispers, a silent plea in her eyes.

"I have none. I am an open book." What can I tell her that she doesn't already know? She knows all the things that matter. Anything else is inconsequential.

Opal's expression says she knows I'm lying. "We all have secrets. And you have more than most."

I reach over and touch a chunk of flipped up hair. "Tell me yours first."

"Okay, fine…sometimes I don't floss my teeth at night. And some days I go all day without changing out of my pajamas."

Opal slides closer to me. "I don't like fresh tomatoes, but I pretended I did once for a boyfriend who basically ate them with everything. I was actually relieved when we broke up, just because I was so sick of eating tomatoes. Like, literally sick.

"When I was eight, I stole a headband from a store, and then I felt bad and tried to return it, but when I did, they caught me and thought I was trying to steal it. Ironic, right? I haven't had my hair this short in a long time, and I'm not really sure why I had it cut so short."

As if unendingly inspired to declare all things, Opal continues. "I love cats—with exception to the scary one on your land. I fear, once I get settled somewhere, I will quite possibly one day be the neighborhood crazy cat lady. I also think the likelihood should bother me more than it does."

Laughter is pulled from me in a choked, unexpected burst, and I bite it back. Opal swallows, looking at me like I am some mystical being she can't quite place. I try to relax my stance and fail, wanting to shrink away from her knowing eyes. She's close enough to touch, and I find, the longer I'm near her, the thought of no longer being able to touch her twists my insides.

"Tell me, Blake Malone." She tilts her head and studies my tight-lipped face. "Tell me a secret."

Dipping my head forward, I stare into features masked by shadows and pale light. The gesture is to intimidate, but instead I feel thunderstruck as I gaze at Opal. Her face seems ordinary at first, but there is something sensual about the curve of her lips. And her eyes are pretty. I like the strength of her jaw. I like everything about her. *Everything.* Even her lies.

Who would have thought I'd find the truest of hearts locked inside a woman who routinely tells mistruths?

She stares back, silently challenging. Daring. I am intrigued by Opal. I am enthralled by her, I correct—only to myself. No one else needs to know the feelings I have for a woman I might never see again. Opal sways toward me, and I lower my head, tracing her lips with my eyes. My heart booms an unknown beat, and it's hard to draw air into my lungs. A few more inches and our mouths will touch. With our goodbyes a whisper away, kissing her is a bad idea.

Knowing this, I look into her fathomless eyes and ask, "Where did you meet Jane the dog?"

Opal blinks and pulls back, her eyes focusing on a spot above my left shoulder. A faint blush creeps up her neck. "What? Oh. Uh…um…wow." She lifts an unsteady hand to her forehead and pushes long bangs from her eyes. "I can't remember. This is really bad. A—a friend of mine has a dog named Jane."

"A friend?" I repeat dubiously.

"Yeah." She strains to produce a name, looking relieved when it finally comes to her. "Thor."

It takes me a moment to respond. "You have a friend named Thor? That's his real name?"

"Well, had. I haven't talked to him in years. I should look him up." Opal smiles, the act lifting the remaining fog from her expression. "His parents love all that mythological stuff, hence the name. What's really weird is that he kind of reminds me of the god with his long blond hair and tall frame—well, but he's not muscular. But, well, maybe he's changed, since that was a while ago."

She draws in a breath and continues. "We met at a comic book convention a few years ago, when I was thinking of—anyway, we hit it off, realized we lived near each other, and became friends. I walked his dog for him. Jane—like in the newish *Thor* movies? She was a little cocker spaniel with more personality than substance. She bit everyone but me, even Thor."

So this Thor, and his dog, meant something to her. And still do.

"I don't care," I interrupt, moving for the door. I'm being an ass, but jealousy is stronger than tact. I don't want to hear about her guy friend who looks like a god, or know that that bright smile on her face is for him.

I get out of the truck and take a painful breath, telling myself to knock it off. This is not the time to let emotion bypass logic. But she's leaving, and maybe she's going to see a blond-haired guy named Thor who has a dog named Jane. My mouth twists; my stomach churns. I literally feel sick, and I don't understand it. I want it to stop, but more than that, I want to know why it's happening.

Forget about the why right now. Stop being an ass. Give this to her. Tell her a secret truth.

I hear the door open and close, the sound of her approaching footsteps, and I say softly, "That day at the circus?" I swallow around the feel of razorblades in my throat, turning to face her. My brain is telling me to choke back the words; my heart won't allow it. "I didn't really believe it, but I told myself that day was going to be outstanding." I touch the side of her face, feel the completion with which she focuses on me in the way her gaze won't leave mine. I take a breath. "It was, Opal. It was outstanding."

It feels like a lackluster explanation of what Opal means to me, but I'm not good with talking about feelings. Running a hand over my face, I sigh. I open my mouth to try to say more, but I don't get the chance—Opal is suddenly glued to me, and her mouth is on mine, and I can feel her response to my words in the way she attacks me. I smile around the kiss, knowing she understands. She knows.

I want to keep kissing her, but instead I set her away from me. My hands rest on her hips and I stare into her eyes. "Your eyes make me think of honey, and they're always so sincere. So alive—even when you're talking out of your ass."

She exhales, laughs shakily.

"And I'm envious of your friend Thor, because he might get to see you again, and I probably won't."

Opal's voice shakes as she tells me, "I hope you and I get to see each other again."

"Me too," I say thickly.

Her hands touch my lower back, linger there. "I want to make comics. I mean…I think I do. I even have an idea for one. I wanted to when I was younger, but I didn't see it through. I didn't chase my dream. I'm ready to go after it now."

Pride blooms in my chest, floods through me. "Then you should do it. You can do anything, I know you can." I hesitate. "Even…even if it's with your friend Thor."

She smiles, joy and sorrow colliding. "What's next for you, Blake?"

I rub my eyes, suddenly tired in a way that doesn't make sense. Tired of feeling the way I do; of avoiding what I need to face. I shrug and look at the red and white building. "I don't know. Australia. And then…the shed, I guess. I'll work on completing the interior. After that, I don't know."

"And your dad?"

A frown captures my mouth. I look at Opal. Her eyes tell me everything will be okay. "Yeah. I can't keep putting that off."

She takes and squeezes my hand. "You can do anything you decide you can, just like you told me. Thanks again. So far, you've been the best part of this road trip. I mean that."

I swallow thickly, my hand tightening on hers. "How will I know you're okay? How will I be able to get ahold of you? That you aren't conning another unsuspecting person for a ride and food?"

Opal grins and tugs her hand from mine. "I'll be okay, Blake. Just know that."

She starts toward the gas station, and with fear propelling me, I race after her, cutting her off before she can leave. I could blink and she'd be gone. Move too slowly, and she'll disappear. That's how impulsive she is. Fear pumps through my veins, locks my throat. I try to talk, but nothing comes out. There is nothing I can say. And this is much more difficult than I thought it would be.

"What is it?" Opal asks, her head tilted.

"I just…" I fight to take a breath. Darkness flitters across her features, just enough to let me know this isn't as easy for her as she's acting. I exhale. "Just…" I shake my head. "Goodbye, Opal."

She turns to go, and my chest collapses. This is it. This is the last time I'll see her. My hands tremble and I ball them into fists. "Opal—"

Eyebrows lifted, Opal walks backward as she waits. Widening the distance, widening the gap from her life to mine. Her eyes are clear and mischievous, her hair a wild cloud about her head. I feel a pinch in my chest, knowing this is the last image I'll have of her. With her crazy hair and her shining eyes. Knowing when she goes, she'll take a part of me with her.

I take a step forward, my body moving without my command. I don't want her to go. She's fun and she's odd and she makes me laugh. She shows me the world through new eyes, better eyes. I look at her hands, wondering how they can make lines into pictures. I keep seeing myself drawn into a two-dimensional image that somehow captured my essence with nothing more than a pencil. She had the slope of my eyebrows, the shape of my eyes. She even perfected the sneer most times I am unaware I wear. But she also got the hint of sadness I try to hide, the glint of hope I sometimes wish I didn't have.

She knows me—the real me.

And she's as easy to tether as the wind. The freest damn spirit I've ever encountered.

I look around the parking lot, take in the empty vehicles, the people bustling to and from the store. Who knows what danger is nearby? What if someone from her past shows up? What if Jonesy is out of jail and looking for her? She can take care of herself, I know she can, but she shouldn't have to.

"What about food?" I hedge, panic sharpening my tone as I continue. "Your stomach is an endless pit, and I didn't feed you today, and how will you survive without food every five minutes?"

Opal gives me a knowing look. "I'll be fine, Blake."

I grip my head and squeeze, wanting to say a thousand things and my closed throat keeping them all unsaid.

"I'll be fine," she repeats, gently tugging my hands away from my head.

"This doesn't feel right," I tell her, speaking more frankly than I would with anyone else.

Opal pauses, her eyes tracing my features. "What doesn't feel right?"

You leaving. Me letting you.

With frustration sending a hand through my hair, I say roughly, "Just—be okay, all right?" I drop my hand and roll my shoulders. "Take care of yourself."

Her eyes darken a second before she sprints for me, jumping into my arms. I stumble back from the force of her body slamming into mine. Opal's arms lock around my neck, her legs hugging my hips, and she kisses me. She kisses me how I like to be kissed, how I taught her to kiss me. With passion, with hunger.

Possessiveness shoots through me. I think of her kissing other guys, and it makes me kiss her harder. I think of her sharing her light with someone else, and my arms barricade her to me. I'm a selfish man, and I want her all to myself. I want Opal's joy, and I want it to be for me. I want all her smiles; I want to be the reason she wants to smile.

But she needs her independence, and I have my responsibilities.

She unlocks her legs, sliding down the front of me and tearing a groan from my throat. Opal's fingers caress my hair, the back of my neck, cupping my jaw. She turns me inside out. I feel her pulling away, gradually. The kiss slows, becomes sweeter. It threads through my soul and sews it to hers.

I won't forget her.

This, whatever this is with Opal, this is real.

This is the stuff futures are built on, and we're letting it go.

We stand locked in each other's arms, her chest pushing against me with each breath, and mine doing the same. My heart pumps forcefully, recklessly. She asked me to be reckless. With Opal, I want to be.

I hold her head to my chest, resting my chin on it. I don't speak until my breathing evens. I hug her to me, wanting the feel of her imprinted to my arms so that it never fades. A goodbye has never felt more like an end to me.

"Find your home," I whisper against her hair.

Opal steps out of my embrace, sniffling as she looks up at me. Tears shimmer in her eyes, turning them to gleaming gold. She lightly punches my shoulder. "Forgive yourself."

I blink around the burning sensation in my eyes, and a lump blocks my windpipe. "Yeah. I'll work on that."

We stare at one another for a second that lasts a lifetime, and then with a sweet smile on her face, Opal waves and turns. I take a step forward, my body denying what is happening. Wanting to stop it. My heart beats out of control, with wrongness, with sorrow. My soul has been sliced in two. Opal walks out of my life, almost as much of a stranger as she was when she walked into it, and still the one person who's known me better than anyone else.

I turn back to the truck with a bitter taste in my mouth and heaviness in my heart.

11

Opal

I make it around the side of the building before the tears come. I let them fall, not trying to wipe them from my face. *Find your home*, he said. Well, I think I did, and it is him. I can clearly picture myself in the country, in his grandpa's home, with Blake. Anywhere with Blake. We'll plant a garden like his grandparents did, and I'll learn how to can and freeze vegetables and fruits. I can see his face, happy and free of the shadows. I can see him, dark against the light. Shining with his own beauty. Love, marriage, and children tickle my brain, and I push them away. Illusions, delusions; whatever they are, they aren't happening anytime soon.

I don't love him.

It's impossible to love someone only after knowing them a handful of days. Right?

What do you want to do with your life, Opal?

No one's ever asked me that before.

In a way I should have a long time ago, I really think about that question. I don't know why Blake asking had the power to make it sink into my brain, but it did. And now it's staying there, waiting to be answered. Tumultuous images pierce my eyes—scenes play out with no direction or order. I want peace. Laughter. I want a simple life, and I want it to have meaning. I see myself drawing. I see children, and they aren't mine, or maybe they are. I see a house in the country, and it looks distinctively like Blake's. But it's all far off in the distance, a life that I'm not yet ready to live. But someday, yes, I think I will be.

Blake wants to help children, but he doesn't know how. In my own unorthodox way, I want the same. He wants to reach their mind; I want to reach their heart. Blake wants them to know they aren't alone. I want to take away their loneliness. The strangest things have the power to do that—a book, a song, a drawing. Which brings me back to my 'Mr. Sunshine' idea, only I wouldn't even know where to start.

You start by drawing, a voice mocks.

I wrinkle up my nose and hitch my backpack higher on my shoulders, turning bleary eyes on my surroundings. The world can be overwhelming when I try to think of it as a whole, categorized future. It's better to separate, turn it into smaller sections that seem doable. I have an idea, I have the tools with which to make the idea a reality. I'll start there.

First, though, I have to figure out my physical placement. Blake's parting words resonate through me, alive with emotion. *Find your home.* Again and again, they sweep through my mind. I miss him already, and it hurts. I shake the ache away, knowing there will be plenty of time for that to later drive me mad.

Now what?

Looking up, I take in the cloud-ridden atmosphere and feel like I've been trying to outrun the sky. It's impossible. And I realize that the past is kind of like that. Might as well face it, right?

Therefore, now I go to Montana.

As if put before me by fate, I notice a derelict payphone near the gas station. I'm surprised to see one in existence. Shoving coins into it, I hold the greasy receiver to my ear and punch a series of numbers on the keypad. I've memorized them, seen the numbers over and over in my head. Thought of dialing them, decided not to, thought about it again. It could be a real bad idea. It could be pointless. It could take me nowhere but back to where I don't want to be. But I have to try, because if anything, that is something I want to say I did in life. I tried.

Ringing meets my ear, and I tighten my grip on the phone. I almost hope no one answers. Then I can say I tried with a slightly less amount of shame hovering over me. I'm scared she won't want to see me; I'm scared she's miserable. I'm scared about a lot of things. My heart pounds, trying to escape my body. She could hate me. She could never want to talk to me again. She could call me terrible things, and she might even get a few of them right.

She's seven, I remind myself, hoping her seven-year-old heart and brain are feeling generous toward me.

I told myself I was running from a life I no longer wanted, but I was equally running from guilt.

"Hello?" a strong, female voice greets.

I close my eyes and take a deep breath. I saw Tammy Royce each month throughout the year Paisley was with Jonesy. She wanted her niece to live with her as soon as her sister died, but Jonesy wouldn't allow it. She'd visit Paisley when she could, always with a sour look on her face and judging eyes. The funny thing is, though, that whenever she looked at Paisley, the bitterness instantly melted, and I could feel the love she felt for her niece. So I didn't care all that much what she thought of me. I knew she adored Paisley. Still, she's an intimidating woman.

"Hello? Who is this? I know someone is there; I hear you breathing," she adds waspishly.

"Um..." I clear my throat, and try again. "Hi. Hello. Is this..." I open my eyes. "That is, is this Tammy, Paisley Jordan's aunt? This is...Opal. Opal Allen. I—"

"I know who you are," Paisley's aunt interrupts.

"Oh. Okay." I let out a slow breath. "I just...how is she doing with—with everything?"

"Why has it taken you this long to contact Paisley? She's been asking about you every day."

I pull the receiver from my ear and give it a dubious look. I set it back to my ear. "She has?"

"Yes. You took care of her after—after Alison died. Did you think she would just forget about you within a few weeks?"

Pain explodes in my chest, and my eyes burn once more. "I thought she would be mad that I...that I had her taken away from her dad," I say softly, my voice strained and weak.

Tammy snorts. "Paisley barely knows Jonesy, and her time with him didn't help. The only one she would be mad about being taken from is you." Her voice softens when she says, "She thinks she did something wrong."

The pain grows, throbs, hurts so bad I can't breathe for a moment, or talk. "I'll..." I croak. I take a breath of air into my lungs and exhale. "I'd like to see her. Is that okay?"

"Where are you?" Tammy asks suspiciously.

"I'm in North Dakota." I blink as I wait for her to respond, wondering how she'll take that news. The last she knew, I was in Illinois.

"Why are you in North Dakota?"

"Um...just...traveling around the States, doing some sightseeing. I thought since I was only a state away, maybe I could stop by and see her." My carefree tone falls flat, and I cringe. *Please don't tell me I can't see her. Please.*

"Fine," she says after a pause. "Call when you reach Missoula, before you come over."

"Can I talk to her?"

Another beat of silence. "It's better if you don't. In case you don't make it. I don't want her to get her hopes up. She hasn't had much stability lately."

Meaning, if I decide to disappear on her. Again. I understand her aunt's reasoning, but it doesn't mean it doesn't sting just a bit. I kept my distance out of guilt, yes, but also because I didn't want someone following me to end up at Paisley's along with me.

In one way or another, Paisley's lost a lot of people. Her mom died, her dad was never really there for her, and then I abruptly left her as well. I thought she was better off without me.

I didn't know I mattered that much to Paisley, and I should have.

"Right. Okay." My hand trembles around the receiver, sweat breaking out across my forehead. "Uh…one more thing. Have you heard from—from Jonesy?" I ask, my throat closing around the words.

Tammy sighs. "Yes. He's written a couple letters to Paisley, saying he knows what he did was wrong, and that when he's out of jail, he'll be a better dad."

My shoulders droop with relief. "Well, that's promising."

"He turned in the last two guys, and because of that, his term was shortened, but he still won't be getting out of jail for a long while."

I freeze, my hand tight around the phone. "Oh?"

Another sigh. "He wrote to me as well, and wanted me to relay a message. He was hoping you'd write to him so that he can write back with an apology. He also said he doesn't blame you for turning them in, that he knows now how wrong he was, and that you tried to get him to stop."

"Uh…what? I didn't—that was an anonymous tip," I stammer, my face hot.

"He knows, Opal," she says gently. "I know too. I didn't thank you before for doing what was right for Paisley, but I am now. She needed you, and you were there."

"Yeah," I say faintly, too many facts jumbling up the inside of my brain. "I'll see you soon, probably in a day or so."

"I'll count on it."

I hang up the phone, thinking her parting words sounded a tad ominous, and stand without moving for a while. No one is after me. And Paisley—I did a good thing with Paisley. I blow out a loud, long breath of air, dizzy from all the news. I look behind me, almost like I think Blake will be there, ready and waiting to demand that he take me back to his home. Of course, he isn't.

I rub my hands on the fronts of my legs, searching the parking lot for a possible ride to get me to Missoula, Montana.

I think about Paisley. I told her goodbye, and I didn't try to contact her again. I thought it was best. I thought she would be okay with not seeing me again, even if I wasn't. I'm such a jerk sometimes. The problem with trying to be carefree is that, at times, it is more care*less* than free. When you want to conserve your emotions, sometimes you forget what they're meant for. It's good to care. It's good to need and want, and yes, there are times when it's good to hurt.

I hurt for Paisley, and I covered it up, tried to pretend it wasn't there. All that did was make it hurt more now.

And a part of my heart hurts for Blake too, for situations out of his control that morphed him into a man who is afraid to care, and have hope, and open up to others. It's a cluster of emotions that don't feel good, but puts things into startling clarity. I'm a lot like Blake, in some ways. I run. He runs. And now I have to stop, and I think he realizes the same for himself. It isn't enough anymore.

"Hey."

I jump, instinctively taking a step back from the man with missing teeth and body odor who stands really close to me. I study him, looking into his glassy brown eyes. I couldn't guess his age. There is a grocery bag over one of his bony arms, and from what I can tell, it holds a collection of clothes, books, and food. Comprehension hits me, hard and cold. He's homeless.

"You done? I need to make a phone call." He points a dirty, jagged nail at the payphone behind me.

"Um...yeah. I'm done." He continues to watch me, and after much longer than it should take, I figure out it's because I'm blocking the path to the phone. "Sorry!" I move to the side and let him pass, turning around to watch him shuffle toward the phone.

The man pats himself down, searching for change. I dig in my pocket for quarters, and with shallow breaths keeping the full force of his smell at bay, I set the money on the ledge beside the phone, quickly moving back when he looks over his shoulder.

On impulse, I sprint into the gas station and load up my arms with food and bottles of water. I noticed he doesn't have many teeth, so I opt for softer foods. Ignoring the cashier's bemused look as I open my arms to allow the food to fall onto the counter, I quickly pay, bouncing as I wait for him to bag it.

As if the world is temporarily on my side and agrees with my plans, I spot the man sitting on a bench just as a bus pulls up across the street from the gas station. A bus. Of course. I hightail it over to it, the bags hitting my legs as I go. It feels strange to leave this town that Blake grew up in, but at the same time, it feels nothing but right, because I know this isn't the end. A temporary one, for sure, but I will see Blake again. I'll make sure of it. I just hope he still wants to see me by then.

"This is for you," I tell the man, gesturing to the multiple plastic bags I set by his feet as I try to catch my breath.

He looks from the bags to me, suspicion turning his eyes a darker shade of brown. "Why?"

What do I say to that? And what does it say about humans that he has to ask?

"Just because," is all I say.

The man drops his gaze, clasps his hands together in his lap, and doesn't acknowledge me again. I turn away, listening as the bus puts on its brakes and comes to a shuddering stop. I get it. I don't like handouts either. Sometimes, though, it's about survival instead of pride. I don't know anything about him, or his circumstances. I just know I have a little bit, and he has less than that. I wonder if that way of thinking is what ultimately had Blake help me. He saw I needed help, and he helped me.

God, I love his heart—that he denies having.

It isn't until I'm walking to the bus that I hear softly from behind, "Thank you."

I smile and tighten my grip on my pink backpack. I nod without looking back, and climb up the first step. A road trip via bus isn't the strangest thing I've done. I think I can manage it.

12

Blake

It's too quiet when I get back to the house. And not because it's actually quiet, but because Opal isn't here.

After I left Opal at the gas station, I almost turned back. But I didn't. I kept driving. And driving. For hours. Aimlessly, and then with purpose. I drove past the house that I lived in as a child, knowing nothing will get better until I see my dad. I drove through the cemetery where Billie now resides.

I parked the truck on the road near the row of tombstones, walked to the simple gray stone that marks her resting place, and I apologized for the actions that took her life and gave me mine back, something I've never had the courage to do before. After Billie died, I finally woke up. I found I wanted to live. She couldn't, because of me. That guilt has kept me from a better life.

Opal told me to forgive myself. I always thought I needed it from everyone else, but maybe the one I need forgiveness from is me.

And lastly, I sat beside my grandfather's grave, and I told him about my life. Every regret, every hope. I confessed every sin, told every truth. I talked to my grandpa as if he was sitting beside me, listening with his head bent to the side, like he always did when he was in deep thought.

I told him about Opal, and how she makes me feel, and how I can't explain what it means, but that I already feel the loss of her.

Back on the porch at home, I drop my head forward and close my eyes. A gust of wind hits my back, tells me another storm is on the way. The sun is low in the sky, and its fiery heat is aimed right for me. Something falls inside the house and my shoulders jerk up and back. I can't deal with Grennedy right now.

I turn to leave once again, and the front door to the house swings open.

"Are you going to stay out here all day?"

I meet my brother's expectant gaze. "I was thinking about it."

Graham nods his golden head, a hand towel draped over a shoulder and a can of wood polisher in one hand. "Instead of moping, or whatever it is you're doing—"

"Brooding," Kennedy calls from inside.

He smiles faintly, showing a hint of unnaturally white teeth. "Do you want to talk about it?"

I shift my stance. "Why don't we talk about what you're doing with that towel and wood polisher? Are you and Kennedy into some kinky stuff I don't need to know about?"

His lips flatten. "Your house is appallingly dirty. I'm cleaning it."

I fight a smile. "Got a casserole in the oven too?"

"Chicken!" This, again, from Kennedy.

"I don't have chicken."

"You had next to nothing in your refrigerator and cupboards. We got some groceries while you were gone." Graham studies me, looking like he wants to ask questions about why I was gone so long, and where I went, and what I was doing, and why I am without Opal—who is Lori to him.

The sound of something heavy being moved across the floor reaches my ears, and I look around him through the open door, not wanting to answer the questions he wants to ask. I don't even know if I have answers.

"What is she doing in there anyway?" I spy a glimpse of the backs of Kennedy's legs before they lift to the air like she just threw herself face first on the couch.

"She's helping me clean." At my dubious look, he adds in a quieter voice, "She's mostly drinking wine and trying not to break things—and she thought we should talk alone."

"Great. I so love having heart to hearts with my big brother."

Graham lifts a finger, striding inside. He comes back minus the hand towel and can of wood polisher, but with his shirt twisted and his hair mussed. I swear there is a pink tint to his tan skin as he steps from the porch to the ground. I move to the ground as well. He hands me one of two beers he brought with him, and I catch the label of the NA brand.

"Must be serious if you brought out the non-alcoholic beer."

My brother fiddles with his cell phone, sliding it into the back pocket of his shorts. "I set the timer on the phone. We have twenty minutes until the chicken is ready."

"For?"

He starts walking toward the back of the house, and I follow. "Who is Lori, and what is she to you?"

"It's a long story." I uncap the non-alcoholic beer, and sip it.

"I've got all night," my brother tells me.

I glance at him.

He looks back, serious and attentive.

"Why are you really here?" I demand, turning my gaze to the swirling clouds above. They darken as I watch, fold in, and grow.

"Because you're my brother."

"Why are you drinking NA beer?"

Graham grins. "Because you're my brother."

I tap my bottle to his before I take another swig of the beer and reach down to pick up a stick, staring at the brittle brown bark in bemusement as images of Opal's smiling eyes and laughter kick me in the gut. "Her name isn't Lori."

From his expression, I can tell that he has to work to keep all the queries unspoken. Graham straightens his shirt, clears his throat. He's naturally high-strung, and I admire his present restraint.

He lets out a slow breath and levels his eyes on me. "Okay. What is her name?"

I look at the pond, and again, I see Opal. Shivering in the dark water, silhouetted by an approaching storm. "Opal," I say with a smile in my voice. I look at my brother. "Her name is Opal."

Graham goes still, his eyes locked on my face. I turn from his probing gaze. Some things—okay, most things—I like to keep private, but especially how I feel about Opal. I'm not ashamed by it. I just want it to be mine to know. No one else's.

"She more or less hijacked my truck in Illinois."

"She stole your truck?" Graham blinks in disbelief.

"I stopped at a gas station, and when I got back out to the truck, she was in it."

"But she didn't go anywhere?"

"Well, the keys weren't in it. But, I don't think she would have taken it anyway."

"You don't think?"

I look at Graham. "She was sleeping."

His eyebrows furrow. "And you didn't know her before this?"

"No."

"And then what?"

I shrug. "We got a motel room, went to a circus, came here."

"It all sounds really sensible," he comments.

I've thought of Opal nonstop since I met her. I tell myself the fascination with her will fade in time. I tell myself in a few days, maybe a week, I won't think of her near as often.

"Can you fall in love with someone in less than a week?" As soon as the words leave my mouth, I regret them. Instead of looking away, I focus on Graham's green eyes, and in them, I only see understanding. My shoulders loosen. It feels good to have someone who won't judge. I should have known I'd have that with Graham. After all, he is my brother.

"You can fall in love with someone in an instant," he replies, and I know he's thinking of Kennedy.

"How? It doesn't make sense that you can meet someone, and know, immediately, that they're the one."

Graham shrugs, staring straight ahead. "Love doesn't make sense, and I think that's how you know that's what it is. I saw Kennedy, and I just knew that she was supposed to be something to me. She was different from everyone else."

"Kennedy is definitely that."

My brother laughs, looking like a class act with his perfect looks and clothes, nonchalant pose, and beer. I can't even resent him for it; the guy has got the biggest heart. I'm glad he's here. Even though I am loath to concede it, I need him right now.

"A storm's coming," he states.

I look at the house with the lights on in every room. Graham doesn't like the dark, or enclosed spaces, courtesy of our dad's extraordinary disciplinary skills. Kennedy lit up the house for him. I love her for it.

"I'm going to see Dad tomorrow."

Graham stiffens immediately. His eyes lock on mine. "Do you want me to go with you?"

"No." I finish off the beer before I talk again. "I have to do it on my own. I have to say what I need to say, and then I have to let it all go."

"I'll be here when you get back," he promises.

I swallow against a tight throat and nod. "I know."

A minute passes before I speak again. "It's funny, you know? I always thought I needed someone else to protect me from him. I never realized I could do it on my own."

My brother studies the bottle in his hand. "I'm glad you realize it now."

"Me too."

He slings an arm around me as we walk back to the house. My inclination is to move out of his partial embrace, but I don't, and the longer I let Graham give me a semi-hug, the more it doesn't seem odd. I feel changed, like the past so many days have altered my perception.

It's okay to want things.

"Where did she go?" he asks, obviously still stuck on the Opal story.

"I don't know."

"Will you see her again?"

"I don't know that either." This country is vast, and overflowing with people. All I have is a first name. No address, no phone number. If we are to meet again, it isn't up to me.

A bird chirps on his phone just as we reach the porch steps. I'm not even surprised by the perfectly timed arrival. Things have a funny way of working out like that for Graham. He drops his arm from my shoulders and retrieves his phone, quickly silencing the alarm as he walks up the steps.

"We plan on leaving in the morning—after you're back from talking to Dad." Graham reaches the door and looks back at me.

"Stay. If you want," I add, vulnerability telling me I shouldn't have brought it up. I'm standing on the grass looking up at my brother, and the symbolism of the moment hits me. I've always looked up to him. Unfortunately, I let bitterness blanket my love for him. I'm not doing it anymore.

It's okay to need things too, but it's imperative to know to need them from the right people.

I used to think I hated my brother. I was jealous of how strong he appeared. He didn't put up with our dad's crap. He knew the kind of person he wanted to be. Graham made good decisions. All I did was continually screw up.

I never hated Graham. I hated that I wasn't like him.

Graham's eyes darken, and he fiddles with the doorknob as he shifts his attention to the floor. "If you're okay with it…we don't want to impose. I know you have—"

The door is wrenched open, and Kennedy stands inside its frame, a bag of chips tucked under her arm. She pops a potato chip in her mouth and says around it, "We will definitely stay another day or two. We would love that almost as much as you would love that. Won't we, *Barbie*?"

"Yes, *Ken*, we'd love that," Graham agrees, giving his girlfriend a slanted look.

"Love is a strong word," I tease.

Kennedy nods enthusiastically, shoving a handful of chips between her lips. "It so is. And I know you love us, and we love you, so…let's eat. I'm hungry."

I inhale and exhale before following the duo inside.

It's okay to love.

13

Blake

The sky is starless and sunless as I leave the house, like a black void on the world. It's fitting with my present destination. My dad has the ability to suck the joy out of anything. My shoulders reflexively bend forward to protect my body from the chilled air. A storm raged last night, and now it's crisp and cool. Funny how calm it is after a storm. I was living in the storm for years, and I feel it ebbing away. Finally.

It was a struggle to get myself out of the bed this morning. I could lie and say it was because it was cold and I wanted to stay warm, or that I was tired. I could even say it was because I knew I wouldn't see Opal today, and there is a little bit of truth to that. The hopelessness descended as it likes to do, told me to curl into a ball, and sink into myself. To forget about anything but the dark.

But mainly, it was knowing where I was going, and that I was about to see my dad.

I stop at a gas station, telling myself I need coffee, knowing I really need more time. I chug the bitter, burning brew as I stare at the house I grew up in. I get out of the truck, the sound of the door shutting unusually loud in the stillness. A few lights are on, as I figured they would be. This is the time to catch my dad, in the morning hours before he heads to the gym and then to work where he oversees the running of multiple computer software stores. I take a steadying breath and walk up to the door.

The last time I saw my dad was when I was visiting Graham in Wisconsin, and the police were involved. I'm not expecting an emotional, joyous reunion, and I wouldn't be surprised if I get a fist to the face. I knock on the door and wait.

My mom opens the door, blinking at me like she doesn't know who I am, or isn't fully awake. I have her eyes, her facial shape. Her mental instabilities.

"Hi, Mom."

"Blake?" My name is slurred as it leaves her mouth. "What—what are you doing here? It's so early. I didn't know you were coming. Is everything okay?"

She's aged since I last saw her; there are lines under her eyes and around her mouth I don't remember. The pink satin robe is untied, revealing her white and pink pajama shirt and bottoms. She lost her hair from doing chemo when the cancer was rampant through her body, and now she keeps the graying brown locks short for easy care.

"I'm good," I tell her. "Everything's fine."

"Are you back at Dad's? You should have told me. I would have visited." Faint accusation sharpens her words.

"Yeah. For a few days now. It's a mess there, Mom. You don't want to visit yet."

She rarely drives, and it makes her sad to go to her childhood home. I've offered to take her over in the past, but something always came up on her end. She was too tired, or she had errands to run. There were always excuses.

I angle my head down, hair falling into my eyes. "Is Dad around? I need to talk to him."

Vivian Malone swallows, her already dim light fading a little more. "Your father doesn't live here, Blake."

"What?" Ice shoots down my spine. "Why not? Since when?"

"Come in. Let me explain," she urges, opening the door wider and moving to the side to allow me by.

It smells like Benson Malone in the spacious entryway—rich and bitter. Even if he is no longer here, this is the home of a man who loves money and control more than his family. The walls are white, the ceilings tall, nothing but black tiles for flooring. It's a cold house, full of dark memories. The furnishings and accent colors are bold, unmistakable. They demand notice, much like my father.

The years I spent here, the days of anxiety, every second wondering what I would do or not do to anger him. Hating myself. Yearning to give up. Wanting to die. He told me I was weak; he told me I was worthless. A mistake. I heard those words every day, and I eventually believed them. My shoulders stiffen and a muscle jumps in my jaw. I turn in a slow loop, not trusting that he isn't here, that he won't show up and slam me down with his words, or worse, his hands.

To him, fear is respect.

My mom rubs a circle into her elbow, her eyebrows pinched together as she watches me. "Would you like me to make some coffee?"

I palm the back of my neck and shrug. "Sure. If you're having some, I'll take a cup."

She gestures for me to follow her into the kitchen. I oblige, blinking against the light as it streams through the room from the overhead canning lights. The stainless steel appliances and cupboards made out of dark hickory gleam with dollar signs. Only the best for my dad. I stay near the doorway, the patter of her bare feet on the tiles the only sound in the room. We've never been close, but it feels like there are miles between us.

I wait until my mom has the coffee brewing to talk. "Why isn't Dad here? What happened?"

"Please, sit." My mom pulls out a chair from the long table. "I'll get the coffee and explain."

I ate cereal at this table. I didn't do my homework right when I was thirteen, and with a cruel hand on the back of my neck had my face shoved against this table. I place my palms down on the smooth surface and study my fingers. Everyone has the power to hurt. These hands are as capable as anyone's. The thought of harming a child causes sweat to break out on my forehead, and I wonder, for the billionth time, how my dad could do it.

My mom sets two steaming mugs of coffee on the table and sits beside me. She smells the same as she always did—like coffee and chamomile. I used to long for that scent when my dad locked me in my bedroom. I'd fantasize about her rescuing me and whisking us away to a new home, a new life. The hope died as I got older, until it was like I never thought it. She never saved me. She couldn't even save herself.

It wasn't only about the depression and other mental instabilities. It wasn't only about the prescription medications. She lost her mom at a young age. She lost three babies before they were born—two before me and one after. She had a husband who never treated her right and slept around on her. I get that my mom needed help. I get that she's had a lot to deal with. I even get why she chose to numb it all. Didn't I do the same?

"How have you been? I haven't seen you in months," she says quietly, pushing hair from my brow. "This house is too big for only me. It makes me miss the time you were here. I should sell it, but it's been my home for over twenty years. It's not that easy to let go of something you've come to rely on."

Sliding one of the cups in front of me, I study the heated air as it wafts from the coffee. "I'm okay. What's going on, Mom?"

"When the doctors said the cancer was gone, I told him to go." She shrugs, her gray eyes downcast.

I go still, even as my heart rate picks up. "You told Dad to go?"

Her gaze flutters to me and away. My mom's jaw goes taut. "Yes. I'm trying to better myself, Blake, and I couldn't do that while continuing to live with him."

I take a slow breath, pride for my mom sweeping up my spine. "And how long ago was that?"

"I don't recall, specifically, but it was close to six months ago. You remember when I was sick, don't you?"

My head jerks in a semblance of a nod. How could I forget that? When my dad came to Wisconsin with his story of my mom being sick and needing me, he wasn't even with her. I'm not surprised, but I am disgusted. He made up an elaborate story, all to control me. I remind myself that he didn't win.

"Why didn't you tell me?" I ask.

Gray eyes pulsing with sudden life lock on me. "I wanted to be in a good place first. I'm…getting there, but it takes time."

I swallow. Blindsided as I am by it, this is a step in the right direction. "Is he in Bismarck?"

"Yes, but…why would you want to talk with your father, Blake? You've never gotten along." She says it like it was a choice I had, like I decided to be difficult and not make more of an effort.

Shoving the chair backward, I stand and look at my mom. I carefully right the chair as it teeters, trying to leash my volatile emotions. There's no point in being upset with her—she can't change the past. She can't fix what my dad's destroyed. All my mom can do is move forward, and finally, thank God, it looks like she is.

"Will you give me the address?"

"Yes. Of course. It's not that far from here." She gets to her feet and takes a pen and piece of paper from a drawer. With quick strokes of the pen, she produces an address.

"Thanks." I push the piece of paper in my back pocket.

"Are you going so soon? You didn't touch your coffee."

I encase my mom in a tight hug and press a kiss to her brow. She feels like loose skin and bones in my arms, undiscovered hopes and dreams. *It isn't too late, Mom.* I hug her harder before releasing her. "I have to talk to Dad, while I have the courage."

She nods with understanding, even as disappointment floods her expression.

My legs carry me to the exit, and the blood in my veins pumps with dread for where I'm going.

"Blake?"

I pause near the door, turning to face her.

"Will you…" She stops, smoothing a lock of brown hair on the crown of her head. "Be happy," she says, changing the direction of her words.

I incline my head, my hand heavy and unmoving on the doorknob. "Take care of yourself, Mom." It isn't enough—a lackluster request. She's making an effort; I have to do the same. I lift my gaze and look into her wide gray eyes. "Maybe…maybe we can hang out once in a while. After I get some things straightened out."

Joy spreads across her features, and I blink at the transformation. "I'd like that. I'll be here."

I nod, some of the tightness that lives inside my chest unraveling.

The sky is changing colors as I leave the house. Pinks and peaches adding life to the gray. For whatever reason, it makes me think of Opal. She's like that—a ray of color on a colorless day. I wonder where she is, if she's okay. I drive through the mostly empty streets, pulling the truck up to the address written on the paper. Two-storied and simple in appearance, the blue house is more modest than I would have pictured for my dad. I step down from the truck, going still as a light inside comes on. Being here is asking for trouble. My hands shake and the craving for a cigarette violently hits me.

There is no hello when he sees me on his doorstep. The same green eyes my brother has look back at me, but Benson Malone's are cruel whereas Graham's are kind. I have his dark hair, his jawline. Sometimes I think I have his darkness. I worry about that—that I would be cruel to my kids if I ever had any. My fingers curl in denial even as the possibility pumps through my veins with his blood.

"What do you want?" His voice is deep and cold. It brings back anger, and fear. Years of trying to understand a man I never could.

"I came here to tell you something." The muscles in my neck are tight, and my body is posed to react to whatever may come.

He crosses his burly arms. "I don't want to hear it."

I push past him and step into a living room that has his scent imbedded in the air. It makes my stomach clench. Other than dark furniture and a few decorative pieces, the room is mostly empty, like him. I face my dad. "It doesn't matter if you want to hear it or not. I have to say it, and then I'll go."

His eyes narrow. "Are you here for money? Because you'll get nothing from me, Blake."

"I don't want anything from you," I tell him in a clipped tone.

"You must. Otherwise you wouldn't be here." He opens his arms. "How may I be of service?"

"I forgive you."

His eyes darken and he drops his arms. "I never asked you to."

"I know that, and you most likely never will. But I'm forgiving you anyway—for my peace of mind."

"You forgive me?" He laughs. "For what? For trying to make you strong? For trying to show you how a real man acts? You're pathetic. Get the hell out of here, and don't come back." The look he gives me is dismissive, and he turns away.

"I won't come back," I promise, no longer angry. No longer blameful. I'm calm, and I'm okay. I head for the door.

"Murderer," he hisses from behind.

The muscles in my back jump and I flinch, coming to a stop.

"Drug addict."

I swallow, but there is a hard rock in my throat, making it impossible.

"Weak."

He's called me all of this before, enough times that I should be immune.

"Worthless."

"And what are you, Dad?" I ask, my eyes trained on the door. The rhythm of my heart is quick enough that there doesn't seem to be a pause. It's a single line of unending motion. "You're a man who has to control those around him because he really knows nothing is in his control."

Fingers dig into my bicep, hard with fury, and I'm jerked around. My dad's eyes shine with danger. "All those years of trying to make you into something with potential, and all you did was show me you're a mistake."

"I am not a mistake," I say slowly, thickly.

"Prove it. Be a man. Hit me." He thrusts his jaw forward and taps the cleft in his chin. "Come on, Blake, show me what those fists can do."

"I'm not hitting you." Sweat covers my body. I'm that kid again, that boy who could never do anything right.

He shoves me and I stumble back. "Because you're a wimp. You always were. You couldn't even stand up to me in Wisconsin. Had to have your big brother fight your battle for you. At least one of my sons has a backbone."

"Shut up," I mutter, my eyes burning.

"Don't like hearing that, do you? Graham's strong, and you're weak. Now why don't you get out of here and go find your drugs like you know you want to. Go cry about how unfair your life is."

I'm better than the drugs, better than the weak part of me that wants them, even now. He's right about me. I was all of those things, but I'm not anymore. I made bad decisions, but where was he? He was watching me fall, smug and righteous. He wanted me to fail, and I did.

I became exactly what he told me I was.

Not anymore.

My jaw tightens and I lock eyes with him. A smile of victory lines his face. He thinks he's won. But I'm done playing his games. My nostrils flare and I feel my face twist. Something snaps inside me, and with an animalistic roar, I push him back against the wall and slam my fist into the plaster beside his head. The wall crunches, and pain erupts in my knuckles.

Chest heaving, blood boiling with vehemence, I see the fear in his eyes. I see us in reverse. I see me looking at him, a scared boy facing the unpredictable beast. He is me, and I am him. I shake my head, trying to dislodge the thought.

"I…am not…you," I grind out, our faces close enough that my nose touches his. I close my eyes, and thump my forehead to his, pressing hard against his head like I can destroy him, and love him. Forehead painfully smashed to forehead. It's the only hug he's ever allowed, and it's the last I'll give him. He never gave me anything, and I gave him too much.

"You don't have power over me anymore," I tell my dad. "I'm taking it back."

Straightening, I move away and stare at the blank wall. I can be that. Blank. Unwritten. Clear. I can start over. I feel freer, better. I take a deep breath. I turn and look at my dad where he remains near the wall. He looks small, defeated.

"Cowards hit kids, not men, I say."

There is no triumph in this, only relief. It isn't about breaking someone like he thinks. It isn't about control. I see my worth, finally, as I look at my sham of a father and decide I'll never be like him.

We decide how we're going to be, right? My father decided the kind of man he wanted to be. I have the power to decide how I want to be. I can't let fear and regret dictate how I live my life. My head drops forward. I've been letting myself down, not to mention everyone around me. I told myself I was worthless, just like my dad, and just like my dad, I believed it. I'm not worthless. People around me can see it, why can't I? Opal saw it.

Opal.

I shouldn't have let her walk away, but I also know she is not the kind to chase. That would only make her run farther. She'll deny needing me or anyone else until she can no longer produce the words, but everyone needs someone. Even if it's just a friend. I want to be her friend, and if she'll let me, I want to be her hero. First, though, I have to be my own. Right here, this moment, this is me facing the past, and beating it. This is me finally being the hero I've always needed.

"I forgive myself, and I forgive you," I tell him for the final time, and I leave.

14

Opal

Due to the bus breaking down, I make it to Montana a day and a half past when I thought I would. It's been three days since my last Blake-fessional, and it feels like three thousand. I arrive in Missoula, Montana tired, dirty, and with an extra hundred dollars Blake snuck into my bag at some point. The cad—that I miss like I can't believe. Shrugging off the ache that won't leave, I look around the busy streets lined with factories and businesses. I have the address written down on a crumpled piece of paper, but in keeping with Tammy's request, I need to find a phone to call ahead before showing up at their house.

As if fate is seriously on my side lately, a kid with long blond hair skateboards toward me, his eyes down on the cell phone in his hands.

"Hello," I call out as I step in his path, wincing when he jerks in surprise and falls forward. I maybe should have thought that out more. His skateboard rolls past me, minus its conductor. I fetch his stickered board, offering it to his sprawled form. I keep my tone airy and pleasant when I say, "Sorry about that."

He carefully reaches out for his skateboard with one hand, his eyes never leaving mine. "What do you want?"

I nod toward the cell phone clutched in his other hand. "Can I borrow your phone?"

Hopping to his feet, the boy swipes bangs from his eyes and drops the board to the pavement. He jumps on it, one supersized tennis shoe on the ground posed to send him on his way, and he pushes off. "No."

"I'll give you twenty bucks!"

It's amazing how fast he gets off his skateboard and hands me his phone—after I procure a twenty-dollar bill.

"Thanks," I mutter, chewing my fingernail as I wait for someone to pick up. Goose bumps form mazes on my skin as the temperature further drops. Tammy answers, and her reply to my greeting is less than warm. "I'm in Missoula," I add after a prolonged silence in which I envision her glaring at the phone.

"And?"

I sigh, rubbing my chin on my shoulder. "And I'd like to see Paisley, if that's okay."

"Paisley overheard us talking. She got excited, thinking you would be here by now, and when that didn't happen, she got upset. Really upset. This will not turn into a routine," she states. "You can't just call whenever you like and expect to be able to see her—and not show up when you're expected. There have to rules, schedules—"

"I would have been here sooner, but the bus I rode over on broke down," I interrupt. "I just want to see her this once, all right? I'm not staying in the area."

Pain follows the knowledge that this will be the final time I see Paisley Jordan for a long while. I knew her all of one year—not even a year, in actuality—but it felt like she was a part of my heart for much longer. And I know that, for as long as it beats, she will stay in it.

"Well." She sighs, her voice softer when she speaks again. "Okay. We're having homemade pizza for supper. You can join us if you like. It will be ready within the hour."

"I'll be there," I vow, ending the call. I hand the cell phone back to the teenager. "Thanks again."

He gives me a single nod before rolling down the hill, his hair fluttering in the wind.

Instead of finding a taxi, I take the city bus to the Royce residence, ending up in one of the newer subdivisions of the city. I look around, finding the house number on the nearest house. I start walking, searching for the home that is now Paisley's.

The lots are spacious and tree-ridden, flowers and bushes lining fences and houses. Everything has a new, crisp, expensive feel to it. I bypass laughing, playing children. The sound of a lawnmower hits the air, sharp and powerful. I search my brain for what Tammy's husband does for a job, and I come up blank. I know Tammy doesn't work outside of the home. Whatever it is, her husband either makes a lot of money, or they have a lot of debt.

I look at the white house with black trim and a burgundy door. The lawn, as if recently maintained, is clear of leaves and sticks. A wrought iron bench rests in the yard beneath a flourishing tree with yellow and orange flowers surrounding it. Along one half of the house, there are rocks engraved with four names: Tammy, Donald, Eileen, and Paisley. I tilt my head as I take it all in. Sometimes you just get a feeling about a place—or, I do, at any rate. I have a good feeling about this one.

Before I can take a step toward the paved path that leads to the house, the front door swings open and out bursts Paisley, who is a flash of gangly limbs, a blue dress, and strawberry blond hair, and then I'm tackled by a seven-year-old who smells like apples and every good thing in the world. We land on the ground, her arms so tight around my neck I can't breathe, her face pressed hard to my chest. My backpack digs into my spine, but I don't move.

"Did you miss me?" I breathlessly joke, smoothing down her tousled hair.

Her grip tautens, the crown of her head banging against my chin as she nods.

"I said I'd see you again," I quietly remind her, feeling warm wetness seep through my shirt to mark my skin with the tears of a child.

"You didn't…say…when." Paisley loosens her grasp on my neck just enough to meet my eyes with her tear-filled blue ones. She has Jonesy's eyes, Jonesy's heart. Luckily, she has her mother's common sense and intelligence.

I sit us up and situate her to my side, careful to keep an arm around her. Paisley locks her arms around my waist, burrowing her face in my shoulder. I am aware we have witnesses, but I don't bother to acknowledge Paisley's family standing on the porch. Right now, it's just her and me. I owe her a proper hello. So I hold her, and I don't say much for a while.

After enough time to get some of my courage in check, I open my mouth, and pause. I blow out a noisy breath of air. "I'm sorry for my crappy goodbye. I'm sorry…" I blink my eyes as my throat tightens. "I'm sorry I couldn't be with you, kid."

"It's okay," comes out meekly from the girl beside me. "I know you can't be my mom."

My breath catches as I exhale, and I pull her closer. My knees are bent, and there is a cramp forming in my left side. I keep holding her.

"That's right, because you already have an amazing mom." I think of Blake's words, of his belief that people never really leave us, and I tell Paisley, "She's still with you. You know that, right?"

A broken sound leaves her, a sniffle, and then she nods again. "I know."

I look to her aunt, uncle, and cousin. They're all tall and thin, brown-haired, and have hawk eyes on us. "Are they treating you right?"

Paisley nods. "Yeah. Eileen, my cousin, lets me wear her favorite pink shirt sometimes."

I smile. "That's nice of her. You're liking it here then? Everything's going good?"

She nods again, and some of the worry unfurls from my being.

"Good. I heard you have pizza, and that's a good thing, because let me tell you, I am hungry."

Paisley laughs and finally releases me. "You're always hungry."

"You got that right."

Once Paisley is standing, she offers her hands to me. I pretend I'm stuck to the ground, producing giggles from her, before finally allowing her to pull me up.

Bouncing along beside me as I walk to the house, she asks, "Will you make me tater tot casserole again sometime?"

"You bet." I don't know when, but I'll make it happen. "And why am I not surprised that that is one of your first questions?"

Paisley grins, showing a place where a tooth was the last time I saw her.

"Where'd your tooth go?"

She shrugs. "I don't know, but I got five dollars for it."

"Wow. That's one rich tooth fairy."

"Where did you go after you left?" she asks as we approach her awaiting family.

"I went to North Dakota."

Wide eyes focus on me. "Really? Why? What did you do?"

"I'll tell you all about it later," I whisper, stopping before the trio.

Something weird happens. They all break out in smiles and hugs, and Tammy hugs me the hardest. "Thank you for coming," she murmurs, and I can only nod, emotion blocking my vocal chords.

"Is it true you can draw *anyone*?" her cousin Eileen asks, leading the way inside the house.

"She can even draw animals," Paisley brags, holding my hand.

"I'll draw you both after supper, how's that sound?" I wink at the girls.

The meal goes by without a hitch, both Tammy and Donald being polite about the whole thing. Donald, who I am told has a career in advertising, asks me about my drawings. I tell him about my comic series idea, and he offers suggestions on how to promote my work, should I ever decide to seriously pursue a career with them. All in all, it's a decent time. I help Tammy with the dishes afterward, and she tells me I am welcome to come back at any time, even without calling ahead. I can tell that's a big deal to her, and I thank her for trusting me with Paisley.

"Do you have to go already?" Paisley asks from her bed. She bathed and dressed in yellow pajamas while I helped Tammy with cleanup. She looks small and sad, her damp hair as weighted down as her shoulders.

A lamp offers muted light to the lavender walls and cream curtains and bedding. It's a beautiful room, exactly the kind I would have liked to have as a child.

"I do." I finish up the drawing of her and Eileen, setting the paper on the desk I used to draw it. I shift and the small chair creaks against my weight. "But I'll call, and I'll visit when I can, and I'll even send mail. And, hey, I don't want you to be sad about me, okay?"

Eyes lowered, she nods and picks at the pink fur of the cat I gave her when she came to live with me and Jonesy. "Are you going back to North Dakota?"

"I don't know," I answer honestly.

"Will you tell me about it now?"

"Yep." I stand and move to the white-framed daybed, kicking off my boots before clambering up beside Paisley. She scoots over to give me more room, and then she rests her head in the crook of my shoulder. I stroke her fine hair and smile. "I got to be in a circus."

"Really?" Paisley's voice squeaks and she catapults up, staring at me in wonder.

"Really." My smile grows. "And I got to swim in a pond at night and ride on a four-wheeler. Have you ever been on one of those before?"

Eyes wide, she shakes her head.

"But best of all, I met someone really special. His name is Blake," I say softly.

Settling back against me, Paisley asks, "Is he a prince?"

My fingers pause on her cheek, moving again as I talk. "Kind of. Like a dark, misunderstood, beautiful prince. And he has his own castle, but at first, he didn't know how to rule it."

"Why not?" she mumbles, sleep thickening her voice.

"He was scared to have hope." I press a kiss to her warm forehead.

"Did he stop being scared?"

"I think so, in the end." I hug Paisley and close my eyes, gently rubbing my cheek to the softness of her hair. "Don't ever give up hope, okay, kid?"

"Okay," she slurs.

"Promise." I sit back, opening my eyes.

"I promise."

"All right." Tammy appears in the doorway, a faint smile on her face. I smile back. "I have to go now, but you know it isn't forever. I'll see you around."

Paisley sighs and nestles down into her bed. "I love you, Opal."

"I love you too, kid." I give her a final kiss on the cheek before I go.

"What will you do now?" Tammy asks as I sling on my backpack and head for the front door.

I shrug and grip the doorknob. "I'll figure it out. Take care of her."

"I will. She's as much a part of my family as my husband and daughter."

Opening the door, I smile as I turn to leave.

"Opal, wait."

Eyebrows lifted, I turn back and meet Tammy's direct gaze.

She doesn't move for so long I wonder if she's able, but then, with a sigh, she shakes her head and removes something from the pocket of her jeans. It's a piece of folded paper. "This is for you. Jonesy asked me to give it to you, should I happen to see you."

I take a step toward outside and freedom. I don't want to know what Jonesy has to say. "I don't—no, I don't want it."

"I read it," Tammy confesses, not looking the least bit guilty. "You should too."

She walks briskly toward me and I turn to eye the darkened night, wondering if I can make it outside before she reaches me. Seeming to know my thoughts, Tammy hurries her pace, grabbing my wrist as I am about to walk through the doorway. I look at her fingers, surprised by the strength in them.

"Take it." Opening my hand, she sets the paper in my palm, and closes my hand into a fist over it. She meets my eyes, hers uncompromising. "Read it."

"Can't you just tell me what it says?" I try one last time.

Her dark eyes narrow.

I swallow and slowly nod. "Okay. I'll read it."

Tammy releases me only when I put the paper in my pocket, and rubbing my sore wrist, I leave the Royce house with a sense of rightness. Paisley will have the family, the permanence, I never did. It was good that I was with Jonesy when I was, or Paisley might still be with him, or worse. I guess at that instant in time, I had a purpose, and I made the most of it. In the twisted way of life, good things came out of bad.

With a sigh, and a feeling of dread whirling around in my stomach, I unfold the paper.

Opal, I know it was you who called the cops on me, but that's okay. I needed to be shown I was wrong, and being in jail has shown me that. I won't come after you, and no one else will. Don't worry about Paisley. I'm going to be a great dad when I get out.

-Jonathan

Well. That's that, I guess.

I give the house a final wave, knowing there is a motel less than two miles away. I'll get a room for the night, and as an added bonus, I'll have a phone for the night. There is someone I need to call if I want to get started on my future.

15

Blake

There was one piece of advice I was given during the summer—a singular, clear moment in the nonsense that usually comes out of Kennedy's mouth—that has stuck with me over the weeks since I said goodbye to Opal. I didn't believe the words at the time, and yet, I memorized them. Thought of them often. Saw them brought to life as I got to know Opal.

"One day you'll find someone you don't have to feel the need to hide from. She won't be something you think you want or need. She won't be your redemption. You'll know when you find her, because you'll want to change for you, not for her."

I'm still baffled by how accurate her words were. I wipe sweat from my forehead, roll my shoulders against a kink in my back, and take one last swipe with the paintbrush across the last spot of unpainted wall in the shed. In a spontaneous moment of Opal taking over my brain, I chose baby blue for the wall color, because, like a total mush head, I thought she'd like it. But even if she never sees it, it's calming to me. Makes me think of clear, blue skies.

I miss her. I miss her in the pause between each heartbeat. The sunless days. I miss her during the night when I reach out to the ghost of a memory. Whatever happens, or doesn't, I'm glad I got to know her. I'm glad for the ache, because it lets me know how deeply I let myself care for someone, and that gives me hope. I'm redeemable, and for a long time, I feared I wasn't. The wounds are still there, but they're scabbed over now. They don't hurt so much.

My hands are sore and my back is killing me; I have paint lodged under my nails that all the scrubbing in the world can't seem to get rid of, and a crick in my neck that doesn't seem to want to go away, but I feel good. Of value. I've painted every day since I last saw Opal. Fortunately, Graham stayed an extra few days to help me. Unfortunately, so did Kennedy.

I named the stray cat Baxter, and he presently sits near my boots. I lean back on my heels to lazily scratch at his chin. I think even the cat misses Opal, if only because she isn't around for him to antagonize. He closes his eyes and leans into my touch. This black cat has become my sidekick. He showed up again a week after Opal left, and as if knowing I needed a friend, has hung around since. He goes off for days at a time, but he always come back, carrying that damn brown sock in his mouth.

"What do you say, Bax? Should we call it a day?"

I don't have any long-term goals for the shed, and there's so much more to do with it. Maybe, one day, it can be turned into the vision my grandpa saw for it. Or maybe it will be used for something else. I don't know. But I know the incompletion of it can't continue. It's like looking at a lost dream every time I glance at it. I couldn't take it anymore, and with nothing else going on, I had no excuse to not work on it.

The black cat meows again and trots toward the door, looking back as if to tell me to hurry up.

I clean up the paint and supplies and step out of the shed, instantly chilled by the October air. The sun is out, but there are clouds swirling around, and it won't be long before it's snowing.

Hunching my shoulders against the icy wind, I turn in the direction of the pond. It can't be warmer than forty-something, but it doesn't deter me from removing everything but my boxers, and jumping into the frigid water. A curse is ripped from my throat as I shoot upright, wondering how Opal could do this, even if it was in August. The water wasn't *that* much warmer then.

From the edge of the pond, the cat watches me, his head cocked like he doesn't understand humans and their capacity for foolishness.

I tread water and laugh around chattering teeth, whipping my head to the side to remove hair from my eyes. More times than I like to admit, I thought about leaving here and escaping to Australia. I was at the airport, ready to go, and I couldn't do it. I told myself I had no idea how to successfully fulfill my grandfather's dream, that I was in no way close to the kind of man my grandfather was, and that I might as well leave the country like I initially planned. I envisioned what Opal would say to me, and it would be to stop being an ass and get to work. Anyone would contemplate the level of my sanity if they knew that I have conversations with Opal every day—in my head.

When I can no longer feel my toes, my fingertips are numb, and I fear I may have permanently frozen a place I'd rather not, I heft myself out of the water. Shaking with tremors, I grab my clothes and boots and hurry to the warmth of the house. I used to be lonely, but that isn't the case anymore. I've learned to enjoy solitude. My problem before was that I hated myself, and being alone with me, well, that wasn't exactly a good time. Now, though, it isn't so bad. I'm okay with me.

I take a quick, blistering hot shower, dress in black lounge pants and a brown T-shirt, and shove my feet into a pair of worn tennis shoes. Used to the routine, Baxter walks with me to the truck and meows a goodbye. Keys in hand, I hop into the truck and navigate it toward the city. I pull up in front of the community center and shut off the engine, jingling the keys in my hand as I view my surroundings. *You can do this*, a voice tells me, and it sounds like Grandpa John. I grin and wink at nothing in particular.

I hear a gasp and look up.

Josie Nelson, a volunteer at the community center, looks back at me, wide-eyed and open-mouthed. She's kind of shy, but seems nice enough. I noticed her face turns red a lot when I'm around, like now. I squint my eyes, wondering at her reaction, and then I turn my head to hide a wince. She thinks I winked at her. It isn't like I can tell her, no, I was actually winking at my dead grandpa.

"Hey, Josie," I say evenly, nodding as I step around her.

But she turns with me, rapidly brushing brown hair from the side of her face. "Hey, um, hi…Blake."

"Hey," I greet again, my footsteps quickening.

"So, um, are you…uh…" She jogs to catch up to me.

I'm almost to the door. Three more steps and I'm there, and whatever she is about to say won't be said.

"That is…would you maybe want to get a drink or something…sometime?" Josie asks in a rush just as I swing open the door.

I twist my head to the side to look at her. "I don't drink."

Color streaks across her face and she shifts her feet. "Right. I knew that. I just…it could be anything. Lemonade. Water. Or nothing—we don't have to drink." She nervously laughs.

Holding open the door with my shoulder, I partially turn to face her. Our eyes meet, and before I can say anything, her face drops, and she takes a step in reverse. I used to be good at hiding what I'm thinking, so good I did it without effort, but at some point recently, I dropped the façade.

"Oh," she breathes like a sad whisper.

"I can't do that, Josie," I tell her kindly.

Nodding, she widens the space even more between us, her eyes darting behind her like she is hoping a rescue car will magically appear and take her away. "Right. Okay. I see that. I thought…never mind."

"There's someone," I blurt, the words choking me as they come up. Not because of their meaning—but because the someone isn't with me. "I care about someone."

Relief chases shadows from her face and Josie straightens. "Oh, thank God. I thought it was me."

"It's not you." I wink again, directly at her this time, and she laughs shakily.

"Good to know." Her smile is small, but genuine.

I nod as I move away from the door, and it shuts, leaving Josie outside with me inside. Looking around the spacious room with white walls and an overabundance of plants, I nod to volunteers and kids alike as I stride down the hall toward the gymnasium. It smells like Italian herbs and cheese in the sandstone building, a lingering reminder of the pizza party the staff had for the kids last night.

Inside the gym where a handful of kids play basketball, hip-hop music controls the scene, and I think of Opal in the truck, rapping along to a song I'll never understand. A smile overtakes my face. Air caresses the top of my hair as I duck just in time to miss getting a basketball to the head. I look behind me to the basketball as it slams into the wall before returning my gaze forward.

"Heads up!"

I give Lavender a look. "Little late with the warning there, weren't you?"

The twelve-year-old shrugs and gets another basketball, dribbling it between her hands. "Could be your reflexes are just really slow, being old like you are."

"I suppose my hearing is off too?"

Lavender passes the ball to me. "That's what I'm guessing."

I aim and shoot, missing like I occasionally do.

The dark-skinned girl shakes her head of black springy curls and darts after the ball. She's tall and thin, seemingly more legs and arms than anything else. "How long have we been shooting hoops now? You're as bad as you were the first day. Maybe even worse."

I've been volunteering my time at the community center for weeks now. It doesn't pay anything, but I have enough saved to be okay while I figure out what I ultimately want to do, career-wise. During the morning hours, I work in the shed, and in the afternoon, I come here. I saw a flyer at the grocery store asking for volunteers, and I impulsively showed up the next day. This place helps me as much as it does the kids.

Recently, I was asked by one of the coordinators to talk about the issues I had as a teen and young adult, and so far, I've spoken two times to a group about it. Oddly enough, it was cathartic. There's a therapist who comes to talk with the kids, and I set up an appointment with him—for me. I realized I don't have to fight my demons alone. Instead of holding them in, drawing them out is the way to go. Like my mom, I'm getting my shit together. The idea of being a substance abuse counselor has been flittering through my mind, and eventually, I'll further consider it. But right now, I'm good where I'm at.

"Oh, come on, we both know it's not possible for me to get any worse than I already am."

Lavender giggles. "That's true."

I know that Lavender comes from a broken home with a mother who cares more about dating than spending time with her daughter, and that she's never met her father. I know that her best friend, Clarence, a boy with shaggy blond hair and glasses, is as much her family as her mom. Maybe more so, in the ways that really count.

I know that every kid here makes me think of Opal, in some way.

"Where's Clarence?" I make a shot and pump a fist in the air.

Lavender makes a face. "His mom said he couldn't come today. Chores."

I wasn't assigned to Lavender. It's more like she assigned herself to me, and I'm glad she did. We don't say words of any real value during our time together, but I don't think we have to. I'm here for Lavender, and we play ball. It's simple, and it works. Words aren't always the way to reach people. Sometimes just spending time with someone is enough to let them know they matter.

I twist my features into exaggerated horror. "What a cruel, cruel mother."

In true Lavender fashion, she snorts and makes ten baskets in a row within the span of seconds. Her purple shirt has a small tear near the shoulder and there is a hole in her left tennis shoe, but she's smiling, and that's all that matters right now. As we spend the next hour shooting baskets and talking nonsense, I lose count of how many times she laughs and smiles, and I consider that a win.

It's dark by the time I make it back to my house.

Exhausted but somehow too wired to sleep, with two peanut butter and jelly sandwiches on a plate, I sit before the desktop computer I stationed in the empty office space of an upstairs room. I've been trying to locate Opal for the past month. I'm not sure why. She knows where I am, and she hasn't tried to contact me. The logical conclusion to draw would be that she doesn't care to be reacquainted with me. But I don't believe that. She kissed me like it meant something. I don't know what she's doing, but it isn't avoiding me. For the first time since my grandfather, I have unwavering faith in another human being.

I'm waiting for Opal to realize it.

About a month ago, I read online about Jonathan "Jonesy" Laxton and his association with the Morgenstern gang—a family of delinquents who made their living off robbing others. It turns out Jonesy turned in the last two to help lessen his own sentence. Opal's safe. I didn't know how coiled up my body was until I heard that, and some of the tension evaporated.

As I polish off one sandwich, I type a dozen different combinations of words into the online search engine, hoping something pops up. It isn't until I'm seven pages in that something catches my eye. *The Mr. Sunshine Chronicles*: Issue #1 by Opal Allen.

"Allen," I say out loud. Assuming it's my Opal, I finally know her last name. I blink at the "my Opal" thought. And then my chest loosens at the rightness of it.

Clicking on the link, I see a collage of black and white drawings set up like comic strips. The first square shows a guy standing with his hands on his hips, his profile set in a scowl as he glares at a truck. A truck that looks a lot like my truck. I lean forward, bringing my eyes inches from the screen. The guy looks a lot like me too.

In the next square, it shows a short woman with flyaway hair sleeping inside the truck, looking unnaturally innocent—too innocent to be Opal. In the comic, her name is Piper. Half of my mouth slides up at the name. The third has her looking worriedly out at the man as he jabs a finger at her and shouts at her to get out of his truck.

Snorting, I sit back in the chair and stare at the drawings. Well, Opal's been busy, and it's clear she's thinking of me. Drawing me, even. Something slides through me, and I realize what it is as it thrums inside my chest. Pride. She's doing it—Opal's making her comics. My eyes shoot to the last available drawing, and it's of me shoving pancakes into my mouth while offering Piper a diminutive-looking egg. The slant of my eyebrows suggests wickedness, like I'm offering poisoned food to poor, starving Piper.

"Really?" I mutter.

I thoughtfully chew the second sandwich as I study the images, not even tasting the peanut butter or jelly. I pause with the last mouthful of food in my mouth.

"Mr. Sunshine," I say slowly.

I'm Mr. Sunshine? I choke on the food as I try to swallow around a burst of laughter.

I scroll down and find another name under how to contact the creator: Thor Landers. My eyes sink into the name as I imagine all kinds of things I don't want to visualize. I picture muscles and flowing blond hair and perfect teeth and Opal looking lovingly at her friend with her hands clasped beneath her chin as she sighs with longing. The veins in my neck tighten.

It doesn't matter that Opal said he wasn't exactly muscular, and that there was no hint of adoration in her tone as she spoke of him. It only matters that she's in contact with him, and not me. Below his name is an email address. I tap my fingertips on the desk as I think. Contacting him wouldn't be the same as contacting Opal. It wouldn't be chasing after her—it would be a concerned friend asking another friend how she's doing, and making sure she knows her ex-boyfriend is no longer a threat. That's all. Completely harmless, and without ulterior motives.

Right.

* * *

Opal

For the third week in a row, I ask Thor, "That's all he said in the email? You're sure?"

His sigh from the other end of the phone line is long and unreasonably melodramatic. "Yes. He asked if you were doing okay, and he said to let you know that you're safe, and to not tell you he'd contacted me."

"Well, I see how well you listen." I grin and pop the pan of tater tot casserole in the oven.

Hot air whooshes over my face and I quickly shut the oven door with my hip. My mouth is already watering at the thought of devouring the casserole, but this pan is not for me. I have another premade one ready in the refrigerator, and if things play out today how I'm hoping, I'll be popping that baby in the oven later for me plus one. And if he doesn't like it, I'll just eat it all myself.

"How long are you going to do this?" my friend asks.

"Do what?" Using a wet washcloth, I wipe off the counter with my free hand and sit down at the small white table I got at a garage sale for twenty bucks. I found two chairs at another one and painted them red. I furnished my home in secondhand items, but to me, each one was new. I love them all, blemished and worn like they are. They're perfect. Everything in this place is perfect.

And it's all mine.

"Pretend like he isn't every single thought in your head."

"He isn't," I insist, turning my attention to the living room of the apartment. It's tiny, and there isn't much in it, but the windows are fantastic, letting in an abundant supply of sunshine whenever the sun is out. "He's only every other thought," I add, rolling my eyes at myself.

"Opal."

"Thor."

"Just go over there and talk to him. What's the worst that can happen?"

My hand tightens around the cell phone I purchased a month ago. It's basic and cheap—exactly what I like. Keeping my tone deceptively light, I tell Thor, "Oh, I don't know. Maybe he decided whatever happened between us was entertaining but wasn't all that meaningful to him. Maybe he's dating someone."

That thought likes to stab my heart about thirty times a day, and at the most inopportune moments, like when I'm working at the art supply store and there are people around and all I want to do is find a gallon of chocolate and stick my head into it. Stupid heart. At least I can now say I have officially fallen in love, although if I'd known how bad it could hurt, I think I might have tried better to avoid it.

"Maybe he isn't. Maybe," Thor begins cautiously. "He's waiting for you."

I straighten my posture, my pulse tripping at the possibility. "Maybe he's waiting for me to show up so he can sue me." I don't believe that for a second.

I've kept tabs on Blake. I know he didn't go to Australia. I know he volunteers at a youth center one block from my apartment building—not stalker-ish at all—but I don't know how he feels about *us*.

"Yeah. That's another thing. You really need him to sign something giving you permission to use his image. The comics are getting noticed, and you don't want this all to come back and bite you in the butt later on in your career."

If I ever needed a father figure, I got it in my good friend Thor Landers. And sensible. He's so sensible—for a guy who won't eat red M&Ms because he was once told they're injected with blood to give them their red color. When I asked him what the others were injected with then to get their colors, he got pale and wouldn't talk to me for a week.

"Career," I repeat. "It's weird to think of my drawings that way—as a way to make money. And I have, like, a total of fifty Twitter followers. I'm not exactly famous. I think I've made twenty dollars so far."

When I left Paisley's house, knowing he would help me get my comic series started, the person I called was Thor. He is like my mentor, in charge of emails and getting the comics up on websites and other platforms, and even most of the promoting, since I have no computer or internet. Thor teaches me, and it works out great for me, since I don't know much about any of that stuff anyway.

"It takes time to build a fan base. Your comics are unique; they aren't about your normal superheroes. They're more like a satire with everyday heroes. They're different, and different is good. These are a good thing, Opal."

I smile at the conviction in my friend's voice. "Thank you. I'm glad you think so." The scent of seasoned meat and potatoes enters my senses, and I happily breathe it in. "I have to go. We'll talk soon?"

"Yeah. Of course. But what are you going to do about Blake?"

"I'm going to see him."

The air pauses with Thor, and he heaves a relieved breath. "Oh. Good. *Finally.* When?"

I squint my eyes at the pink clock in the shape of an airplane above the stove. "As soon as the tater tot casserole is ready, which is in about forty minutes. Bye!"

I turn off the phone and set it on the table, hopping to my feet to nervously pace around the one-bedroomed place. The bedroom walls are decorated with drawings of all the people I've met over the years. They are my own personal photo album, all drawn by me. I have a lot of drawings of Blake. With so many facets to his personality and expressions, he's my favorite to draw. And, yeah, he's just my favorite. Period.

I've been in Bismarck, North Dakota for several weeks. As soon as I saw the sign for the city on my return, I knew I was where I needed to be. I got myself a job that pays enough to house and feed me, and I've been working on my comics in my free time. I had to do this before I could see Blake again. I hope he can understand that I had to take care of myself before I could one hundred percent care for him. I had to be whole, because you can't fit two halved pieces together and hope for the best.

It's been madness keeping my distance, but now I can approach him as a choice, and not an option. I have a home; I have money. I am stable. I'm choosing him for me, and no other reason.

I look out the living room window as snow flurries coast to the ground, immediately lost between traffic. The apartment building is located in a busier section of Bismarck; the streets always have vehicles on them, and the noise is constant enough that I don't hear it anymore. It isn't the country, and maybe I'll never again be at that white house with peeling paint and endless potentials, but it's one of my many dreams that I am.

I realize I might want something from Blake that he doesn't want to give me, and I'll have to deal with it, because this is now my home. The city is big enough that we can both live in the area without probably ever seeing one another, if that's the way it has to be. I shift my gaze to the building across the street, watching as an old blue and white truck parks in the parking lot of the community center. My breaths come faster, and my hands grip the windowsill as I stare. It's bliss, and torture, and a hundred declarations I want to shout through the window. I blink and step back, taking a steadying breath.

Although, with Blake directly on the other side of the street from me most days of the week, the chances of us never bumping into one another are pretty unlikely.

Longing pierces my chest as he steps from the truck, and I have to remind myself that it's not time yet. Almost, but not quite. I mean, I can't show up at the community center with half-cooked tater tot casserole and expect anyone there to ever want to eat it again after that. I slowly take in the scuffed black boots, black straight-legged jeans, and a black bomber jacket with a black T-shirt peeking out from the top. He reaches into the truck and comes away with a stack of papers, the whiteness of them striking against his clothes. I swallow and feel a faint smile claim my mouth.

Dressed all in black, like he doesn't want the world to know he secretly lives in color.

When Blake steps toward the door of the building and a semi blows by, effectively blocking my view of him, I move away from the window. I check the casserole, anxious and eager that it's almost ready. I can smell the meat, potato, and crispy onion scent, and again my mouth salivates. Two questions rotate in my head, both quite important. What if he doesn't like it? What if he doesn't want to see me? Over the weeks I've been here, I came up with various scenarios on the best way to let my presence be known, and when I told Thor the one I'd settled on, he groaned and asked me to reconsider, which is an obvious sign that I should *not* reconsider.

As I wait in the final moments until the tater tot casserole perfection is ready, I pull on Blake's shirt I generally sleep in most nights, a pair of brown leggings, and newish boots that don't make my feet hurt. There isn't any way to make my hair better, so I don't bother. Jacket on, and the piece of paper I wrote on carefully tucked inside my coat, I take the hot pan cocooned by a layer of cushiony fabric to protect my hands, and head out of the apartment and across the street.

My heartbeat works in triple time, and the sounds leaving my lips are somewhat worrisome, like I can't quite catch my breath. The air is icy, and even though the flurries have stopped, I know more are on the forecast. Businesses and retail stores are dotted along the streets, people continuously going in and out of them. I focus on the stone structure ahead and force my feet forward.

"Everything is going to be okay," I whisper to myself, really hoping I'm not lying.

Stepping into the warmth and flowery scent of the community center, as I walk down the hall to the kitchen area, I greet the workers and kids I know, and even the ones I don't. I've stopped in a couple times during the day when I wasn't working and knew Blake wouldn't be here, offering to draw the kids. More than I thought would took me up on the offer, and a volunteer asked me if I was interested in doing more with it.

When I asked what he had in mind, he said the children's sections in hospitals love that kind of stuff. I spent the next Saturday drawing sick and injured kids at one of the city's hospitals. But I drew them how they asked to be drawn, which was rarely how they really looked. And then I realized that that *was* how they looked—to themselves. It was the most humbling, fulfilling experience of my life. I wanted to be sad for the kids, but seeing their faces lit up told me I didn't have that right. If they're positive, I can be no less. The next weekend I have off from work, I plan to do the same.

I understand why Blake comes here. Maybe we don't make a difference, but if we do? You can't imitate that kind of feeling.

"Tater tot casserole?" Lavender asks hopefully as she turns the corner and sees me, her big brown eyes fixated on the pan in my hands.

I laugh. "You liked it, huh?" I brought some in last week, and it was gone within minutes. I guess if I only know how to make one thing, I can at least be good at it.

The girl turns and walks with me, closing her eyes and rubbing her stomach. Her blue shirt is a size too small and her jeans have holes in both knees. "Looooved it."

She opens her eyes as we reach the kitchen. "With the hours my mom works, and her boyfriend taking her out for meals, I do most of the cooking at home for me and my younger brother. Do you think you can teach me how to make it sometime? I think Christopher will really like it."

Even without having a mother, growing up I rarely was responsible for meals. The people I stayed with made sure I had food, and they were around when I was home. I always thought things were better for kids who lived with their real parents. I now see I was lucky, even if I never had a place to call home. Sometimes real parents aren't always the best ones.

"Of course. You tell me when you want to make it and I'll be here."

The kitchen is white and spacious with long card tables and foldup chairs taking up the middle of it. A row of cupboards line a wall, and there is a sink, refrigerator, oven, and microwave. It smells like coffee in here. I set down the pan and grab paper plates and plastic forks.

"*Yes*." Lavender's fist shoots up and she grabs a plate and fork, her eyes on the food.

"Have you see—" I begin.

She starts talking before I stop. "He's in the conference room, or whatever it's called, talking to a group of kids about depression and stuff. I didn't tell him," she adds, mischief sparkling in her eyes.

I exhale. "Okay. Remember what to do?"

Lavender digs her fork into the casserole and hefts a heaping forkful of it into her mouth, talking around it in a way that is oddly similar to me. "Yeah. Give him a plate of tater tot casserole, and the note."

"Yes." I wipe hair from my eyes and look around the room, my stomach dipping and spinning with the thought of seeing Blake up close after going without talking to him for so long.

I produce the paper from the inside of my coat and put in on the nearest table. "Okay." I meet Lavender's eyes. "I'm going now."

"Good luck," she says, laughing as she shovels another round of food into her mouth.

16

Blake

"As you've figured out by now, I'm not the greatest speaker," I tell the small group at the end of the twenty-minute session where they each told me something about themselves, and I told them something about me. A few laugh, but most remain silent. I tightly grip the papers between my hands. "To make this easier on all of us, I typed up what I wanted to say. What I wanted you to know. Read it; don't read it. Throw it away if you must. Whatever."

I hand out the words it took me three days to produce, my hands shaking with the need to crumple them up and throw them in the trash. I bared my soul on these pages, and I didn't do it lightly. "Just know that if you want, it's here for you to read."

The walls of this compact room could use a fresh coat of paint and brighter light bulbs, and it smells faintly of cigarettes, courtesy of Jacob Neeman's leather trench coat he never takes off, even when he's playing sports. In the past, I would have been craving a cigarette right along with him, as I can tell he is. He's fidgeting, and constantly looking at the clock above the door.

"All right," I say once the papers are all handed out, surprised that each of the seven teenagers took one. "How about we go grab a snack now?" They're gone before I've finished talking, and I grin to myself as I follow them out. Food is always an acceptable offering.

Lavender stands in wait, a plate of something that smells like onions, hamburger, fried potatoes, and cheese in her hands. It's like war on the senses. "This is for you."

"Good afternoon. It's great to see you here too. And hey, did you know we're supposed to get some more snow tonight?"

She shrugs her bony shoulders. "Whatever." Lavender offers the plate. "Take it."

I gingerly eye the mound of food as I take the plate. "What is it?"

"Tater tot casserole," Lavender says with exuberance.

My eyes fly to hers and I freeze. "What did you say?"

Rolling her eyes, Lavender takes a folded piece of paper from her pocket. "Better get those ears checked out soon." And she shoves the paper at me before skipping down the hall toward the kitchen.

Plate in one hand and paper in the other, I stare at my hands. The pounding of my heart tells me it can't be a coincidence. The dampness of my palms tells me if it is, I might cry. Setting down the plate on a chair near a water fountain, I unfold the paper. The paper reads in large block letters:

IF YOU EVER WANT TO SEE YOUR SHIRT AGAIN, COME OUTSIDE.

The confusion turns to hope, and then fear, and then I look toward the door. I've been missing an Imagine Dragons shirt since Opal left. I knew she probably took it, but honestly, I liked the idea of her wearing it. It can't be her, but damn, I want it to be. The paper falls from my hand as I jog toward the exit, not seeing anyone around me, not hearing anything.

It's cold out, and dreary, but I don't notice it. I just see her. Her back is to me, but I'd know that form anywhere. Deceptively petite and slim, hiding curves and delectableness. And the hair—the crazy hair I've missed choking on as I wake up. Her honey eyes; I need to see her honey eyes. My footsteps quicken, all of me paused with altering forms of dread and elation, even though I'm moving fast, and yet I'm not fast enough.

She turns, and my footsteps falter. I study her dancing eyes and mischievous grin, and damn if it doesn't feel like happiness explodes in my chest. My eyes are reacquainted with that which they covet. Opal's outfit is strange—a hot pink winter coat with a red shirt peeking out the bottom and brown leggings with purple snow boots, and her hair is wild about her face. She looks like Opal should. She looks amazing. I want to grab her, and profess all kinds of things I never thought I'd say out loud, let alone feel.

"It's about time you decided to show up," I say roughly. What a dumb ass first thing to say after being apart for months. *Too late now*, a voice tells me. Opal doesn't seem to mind.

Her head tilts. "Were you waiting for me?"

Always. "Yes."

"I borrowed your shirt," she says, fingering the hem of the red shirt visible around her jacket.

I take an uneven breath, willing my nerves to act natural. "You stole my shirt."

"I didn't *steal* it; I *borrowed* it," she scoffs, and in the next instant, she propels herself at me.

"How did you—" I get out before Opal's lips claim mine.

It's like instant, painful arousal at the feel of her, and the scent of coconuts invades my senses, just as Opal invades me. Her mouth is hot, demanding. She tastes like desire and cinnamon. I squeeze her butt cheeks and she jerks, her fingers tightening around my hair. I can't breathe, and I don't care. I want to never stop kissing her, until breathing is irrelevant. She bites my lower lip and I nip at her neck with my teeth, pushing against her until her back is flush with the truck. Throbbing with longing for her. Her scent, her body, her warmth, her smiles.

She pulls back to purr, "I want to cover you in syrup and eat you up."

I start to laugh, but Opal cuts me off once more with her mouth.

Grabbing my hair, she yanks my head back and I grunt, staring at her through half-lidded eyes. What I see in hers breaks me, but in the best of ways. I open my mouth, but words fail me. Too much—it's all too much. *I love her*, I think with absolute clarity. I take a shuddering breath, and as if she knows, her eyes shatter with emotion, and it's all for me. Opal bites the side of my neck, and I wince at the sting. It's savage, and volatile, and it makes my head swim.

I want to be inside her, and lost, and found, all within the lies and truths of Opal Allen.

"Wait." She shoves me away like she wasn't just attacking me. "Is there…I mean, are you…" Fear puckers her mouth, and she pushes trembling fingers through her hair, training her eyes down.

"No," I answer, knowing what she's asking. "There's no one."

Her shoulders drop with relief.

"Well," I backtrack. "There *is* someone, I guess."

Opal's eyes narrow and she crosses her arms, anger bleaching her skin of color. "Really? Who?"

"Baxter," I tell her, trying not to smile.

Her eyebrows shoot up. "Baxter? As in a guy Baxter?"

"As in a cat."

Confusion slides across her face, and then comprehension. "You made that devil cat a pet?"

"I really think you both need to give each other another chance. I feel like your first encounter was a simple misunderstanding."

She rolls her eyes. "Psssh. Or a simple failed murder attempt."

"He's mostly outside, and it's more like he made me a pet instead of the other way around."

Opal's eyes suddenly darken, and her features go slack. "Oh. I get it." She nods, smiling crookedly. "He adopted you, like Piper adopted me."

I shove my hands in my coat pockets. "Yeah. I guess." I take a deep breath and finally let the building questions leave my lips. "Where have you been? How did you know I would be here? Is everything okay? With Paisley, and you? What…what does this mean?"

Chest compressing and expanding with each ragged breath I take, I go still and stare into Opal's molasses eyes, waiting. My pulse shouts at her to say everything I want to hear. I press my lips together, keeping my thoughts unspoken.

"Funniest thing," Opal says quietly. "I live right there." She points to a brick apartment building across the street.

Frowning, I look from the building to her, not understanding.

She lifts her hands. "I swear I'm not stalking you. Much."

I blink.

"Paisley is more than okay. I know you know that Jonesy and all that mess is taken care of. And me—I'm finally okay," Opal says in a rush, clasping her fingers together and releasing them. "I've been here for weeks. I work at an art supply store two blocks away, and…I wanted to make sure I could take care of myself before—before I tried to contact you," she says. Her eyes shine like they stole all the stars from the sky and are holding them hostage in the honey-colored irises. "And I am."

"You live here," I state slowly. "In Bismarck."

Opal nods.

"Why?" I ask faintly.

She turns her head to the side. "Because this is the closest place to a home I've ever had, and being near you makes it even more so." Opal looks at me. "You're my home, Blake."

Blood flows to my head and I blink against a wave of dizziness. I hang my head as unnamed emotions fill me, swim through my veins, and destroy every last bit of shield I've ever built around myself. She just told me I'm her home, and hell yes, I'm going to be her home. But I have to ask—I have to be sure…

I look up and lock eyes with Opal. "You're not leaving?"

Smiling faintly, she shakes her head.

"Like, ever?"

"Never ever," Opal says softly.

Elation charges through me, turning my insides into spiraling, wonderful mayhem. I don't know how to explain what I feel, so I take a more accessible path. I tell her what I want, like she did with me her last night at my house.

"I want to be with you. I want to take you out on dates." I shift my eyes down and back to Opal. She doesn't appear to be breathing. I swallow, my palms damp. "I want to dance with you to slow songs, but more than that, I want to dance with you to fast ones, and cook beside you, and do absolutely nothing at all, but with you. I want you to read a book out loud to me in your sexy voice—a nonfiction book about, I don't know, the history of mushrooms."

Using the backside of my hand, I caress her soft cheek. Her eyes turn to liquid gold, and I drop my hand when it begins to shake. I cover up the tremble by shoving my hands in the pockets of my jacket. "What do you think?"

"I want to be with you too," she tells me without hesitation. "And all of that other stuff you mentioned, but…slowly. I'm finally being responsible, and weirdly enough, I like it. But yes, yes to all of it."

She smiles.

And I believe her.

"The mushroom book reading is a priority," I say, my insides smashed with love, and hope, and the promise of a future. I take her hand and squeeze, and she squeezes back.

"Definitely." She looks at the community center. "Let's go inside. I told Lavender I'd shoot hoops with her if she delivered the food and note to you."

I start to walk, and then pause. "You know Lavender?" My forehead crumples. "You shoot hoops?"

Opal shrugs and drops my hand, swinging her arms as she moves away from me. Not liking that, I hurry to close the space between us. "I'll tell you all about it inside."

Lavender waits for us in the gym, grinning broadly when we appear. She bumps her shoulder to Opal's, and Opal laughs. I look between her and Opal, seeing a duo of mayhem, and also an unlikely friendship. And I think it's awesome. Lavender's taller than Opal, but when she hands off the ball to Opal, it doesn't matter. Opal is fast and efficient, and all I can do is watch in shock as she rules the court.

"She's good, isn't she?" Lavender calls as she steals the ball from Opal. She makes a shot and throws the ball back to Opal. "Better than you, for sure."

Opal laughs and swipes sweaty hair from her forehead as she jogs over to me.

"Don't be mean," I say with mock sternness.

"What about you? How is everything? Did you talk to your dad?" Opal wonders as she dribbles the basketball from hand to hand, purposely keeping her tone light and her gaze on Lavender as she greets her friend Clarence.

Fixated on her hand movements, I reply absently, "Yeah." I look up. "How'd you learn to handle a ball like that?"

Opal presses her lips together, and I know she's fighting to not ask more about what happened with my dad.

"It's over," I say with finality, drawing her gaze to mine. "I've moved on. Whatever he is or isn't has to do with him, not me. And whatever I choose to be is entirely on me."

Dropping the basketball, Opal cups my face with her rough hands. With shining eyes and a sweet smile upturning her lips, she goes on her tiptoes to kiss my forehead, my nose, and finally, my lips. I'm surprised at first, and then I'm flooded with rawness, like my chest has been ripped open and my heart is on display, pumping away for Opal Allen.

"At one of the homes I was at, there was a kid who played basketball whenever he could. He showed me some things," Opal says in that way of hers that doesn't call attention to the things that hurt.

I feel my expression darken. "What kinds of things?"

She laughs and passes the ball to me. "Basketball things. He plays professionally now."

Truth.

"I saw the first issue of your comic series," I say an hour later as we leave the community center. The temperature has dropped more, and I can see the air as it leaves my mouth when I talk.

Opal freezes. "Oh. Yeah. I know. If you're not against it, I'd like your permission to keep producing them, since, well, we're kind of the stars of the show."

"I'm not against it, and yeah, whatever you need me to do, I'll do it. I enjoyed it, even though you made me out to look like the bad guy."

"You like to be perceived as the bad guy," she says knowingly.

"It's all about image, right?" I toss my truck keys in the air and catch them. "How do you know I saw it?"

"Thor told me you emailed him."

I grin. "Good. I was hoping he would."

Opal's mouth drops open. "You told him to *not* tell me you'd emailed him."

"I was confident he'd do the opposite."

She stops beside my truck. "What was the point of that?"

I look down at the keys in my hand. "I just wanted you to know I was thinking of you, that I hadn't forgotten. I wanted you to know that Jonesy and his friends were no longer a threat, and that you didn't have to keep running."

"I was done running by then, Blake." Opal leans up to kiss my cheek, purposely making a smacking noise.

My skin tingles in response.

She pulls away with a grin, and as her eyes sink into mine, her expression sobers. "I should…go." She nods her head toward the apartment building. "I have to work tomorrow."

"Right." I nod, looking down at the pavement. "I have to get up early too." Even though I can see her again tomorrow, it doesn't seem right to let her go already. I want to sleep beside her, and hold her all night. I want to do other things too, but even if we don't, I at least want to hold her as she dreams.

She steps toward the street, and I take a step toward her, everything inside me telling me not to let her go this time, not yet.

"Maybe we could hang out for a while at my place, if you want," Opal says hesitantly.

"Yes," I answer immediately, relief cooling my overheated skin. "Let's do that."

Grinning broadly, Opal clasps my hand with hers and pulls me across the street. There are so many things to say, and do, but we have time, and we have each other. The streetlights and stoplights blink above us, leading a path to Opal's. She's doing good, and I'm doing good. I'm proud of both of us. It's a new feeling, especially toward myself, but I like it.

She shows me around her apartment. The appliances are outdated and the rooms are microscopic, but she glows as she tells me the story behind each of the items inside it—a few of the tales I know aren't true, and the sparkle in her eyes tells me she knows I know.

Once again, I see our surroundings in her eyes. It's the best way to see the world, I decide. Opal sees the good in everything; she saw the good in me.

"I'm glad you're going after your dreams," she murmurs into my ear as we sway back and forth before the window in the living room. There's no music, but so what? The beat of our hearts makes its own.

"Out of all of my dreams, the dream of you is the best one," I tell her with sincerity, tightening my hold on her body.

"Wow." She swallows, her fingers trailing down the sides of my face. "That was Hallmark greeting card material."

"What can I say? I'm a romantic." I wink at her.

Opal winks back, jumbling up my brainwaves, and proceeds to shoot my heart through with an arrow clearly marked as hers. "Well, just so you know, I'm pretty sure you're my happy ending."

"You win," I gladly concede.

Her laughter wraps around me as I spin her around in the big finale of our soundless dance. The tater tot casserole she had stashed in the refrigerator is presently cooking away in the oven and turning the apartment into a bold-smelling hotbox of untasted food substances that may or may not be edible. I won't know until I try it, I guess.

"I think there are zombies hiding here," she whispers with wide eyes.

"Um…" I look around the apartment. "Where?"

A devilish gleam takes over Opal's face as she drops her hands from my neck and hops back, gyrating her hips in a slow circle that is oddly erotic. "In my pants," she finishes in a choked voice, and then she bursts out laughing along with me.

"You say the craziest things," I tell her.

Shrugging, Opal tugs off my shirt, and I stop thinking about what she does or does not say.

Bonus Chapter

Blake's letter to the class:

To anyone like me:

Having depression is like falling through a never-ending abyss of blackness, and all the while you're plummeting, it attacks you. It enters your heart, your soul. Everything that makes you, you, is affected. It's everywhere, and it feeds on hopelessness.

You don't understand why you feel the way you do. You don't know what's wrong. You try to fix it, and you can't. You think you should be happy, but you aren't. It's suffocating, and bleak, and overwhelming. You can stand in a room full of people and feel completely alone. You don't know how to ask for help. You think you'll be judged, and ridiculed, and be seen as weak.

It takes away your sense of belonging. You're lost. You don't know what you're doing. You don't know where you want to be. You don't even know yourself. It steals away every bit of goodness until you're empty. And you're numb. And the thing that makes the most sense, the thing you see with clarity so stunning it's white light in the dark, is the solution—and it is to give up.

Don't give up.

Find something, anything, which can pull you from the darkness. It can be a hobby, or as simple as going for a walk. It can be getting out of bed instead of staying in it, like you really want. It can be one person who doesn't understand depression but understands you. Get into motion when your mind tells you to sit. Distract yourself with activities to the point that there is no space for the blackness. Be around those who care about you, and make you smile.

Tell yourself positives, repeat them. Repeat them again. And again. Until it isn't so black in your world, until you find a flicker of yourself. The real you, not the shadow. You can do this. You're stronger than the depression. Don't forget. And trust me when I say: you don't have to do it alone. Talking about it with someone helps. There are medications that help; there are people who can help. Here are some numbers you can call.

US Suicide Hotline: 800-784-2433

NDMDA Depression Hotline – Support Group: 800-826-3632

Suicide Prevention Services Crisis Hotline: 800-784-2433
Suicide Prevention Services Depression Hotline: 630-482-9696
National Child Abuse Hotline: 800-422-4453
National Domestic Violence Hotline: 800-799-SAFE
National Domestic Violence Hotline: (TDD) 800-787-3224
National Youth Crisis Hotline: 800-448-4663

~ Blake

Look for the next Least Likely Romance by
USA Today Bestselling Author, Lindy Zart.

Coming in June 2018!

About the Author

Lindy Zart is the *USA Today* bestselling author of Roomies. She has been writing since she was a child. Luckily for readers, her writing has improved since then. She lives in Wisconsin with her family. Lindy loves hearing from people who enjoy her work. She also has a completely healthy obsession with the following: coffee, wine, bloody marys, peanut butter, and pizza.

Visit her at www.lindyzart.com

Printed in the United States
by Baker & Taylor Publisher Services